Praise for CRYSTAL VISION

"There is in [*Crystal Vision*] enough b p
several novels. . . . It is a remarkable ac. ......aay Review*

"[Sorrentino] is one of the great literary confectioners of our time."
—*Times Literary Supplement*

"A defiant paean to the human spirit . . . a book crammed with antic
invention, a marvelous mix of slapstick and the sublime."
—*San Francisco Chronicle*

"Sorrentino's rapidly alternating narrative current has a full charge of
mean, often obscene comedy and dazzling demolition of language and
story—but also an elusive, obliquely moving perception of 'real life'
coursing within. . . . Readers will relish such omnivorous imagining."
—*Library Journal*

"This is a conversation that is highly readable, funny, heart-breaking, and
delicious in its leaps, its landings, its gorgeous vocabulary mixups, and
ultimately in its imprisoned struggle to surmount itself and to understand
its magic tools (metaphors, memories, dreams, and repeated visions of
beautiful young women in beautiful young gardens)."
—*Best Sellers*

"With *Aberration of Starlight* and now *Crystal Vision,* Sorrentino
establishes himself as a major novelist, a cross between Studs Terkel
and John Barth, whose work deserves our attention."
—*Virginia Quarterly Review*

CRYSTAL VISION

GILBERT SORRENTINO

Dalkey Archive Press

Library of Congress Cataloging-in-Publication Data:

Sorrentino, Gilbert.
        Crystal vision / Gilbert Sorrentino. — 1st Dalkey Archive ed.
                p.   cm.
        ISBN 1-56478-159-3 (alk. paper)
        1. City and town life—New York (State)—New York—Fiction. 2. Neighborhood—
New York (State)—New York—Fiction. 3. Brooklyn (New York, N.Y.)—Fiction. 4. Tarot—
Fiction. I. Title.
    PS3569.07C7   1999
    813'.54—dc21
                                                                    98-54958
                                                                    CIP

This publication is partially supported by grants from the National Endowment for the Arts,
a federal agency, and the Illinois Arts Council, a state agency, and the Lannan Foundation.

Dalkey Archive Press
Illinois State University
Campus Box 4241
Normal, IL 61790-4241

Visit our website: www.dalkeyarchive.com

Printed on permanent/durable acid-free paper and bound in the United States of America.

Gran duol mi prese al cor quando lo 'ntesi
però che gente di molto valore
conobbi che 'n quel limbo eran sospesi.
—*Inferno, IV*

Chapters

Crystal Vision

1 The Flowers of Summer

I will call this drink the Flowers of Summer, the Magician says.

He is disguised this breathless August afternoon as Gene Phillips. He stands in the shade of the apartment building in which Mr. Phillips lives with Dorothy, his wife, and Marjorie, his daughter.

God only knows what flowers he's thinking of, Richie says.

Four roses! Fat Frankie laughs.

Red roses and lilies, Richie says. Red and white. Colors dear to the hearts of lovers, sonneteers, and softball teams.

Although I harbor profoundly in my heart, the Arab says, the opinion that Gene Phillips is a bumbling oaf, the very matrix of the core of this same organ goes out to him because of his courageous locus in this teary vale of sadness. And besides, despite the blows and ravishment attacks of life, he holds down a position as a salesman for the famed Angostura-Wupperman Corporation, as you are aware, manufacturers of the renownable bitters.

You can't make a decent Manhattan without Angostura, the Magician drawls, much the same as Mr. Phillips does. He stands in the shade, coatless, in a short-sleeved shirt. His round flushed face is at peace. He looks remarkably like Gene Phillips.

Remarkably like a goddam fool, Pepper says.

Dorothy Phillips is framed in the window just behind the Magician, her elbows on the sill. She arranges herself carefully so as not to spill her glass of gin and water.

Big Duck smiles, thinking of Dolores.

Big Duck may smile, the Magician says, but it's a cinch he's not going to marry Dolores. If he marries anyone, it's going to be somebody named Susan. And speaking of marriage, Marjorie Phillips will flee, or fly, into the arms of Joe the iceman's son, what's his name.

Thus comes about the sour fruits of misery, the Arab says. Without even the scantest profits for anyone.

Susan doesn't know this yet, the Magician says. Whoever she may be.

Mr. Phillips approaches Doc Friday at the bar in Pat's Tavern. How about a drink, Doc? A Manhattan? How about a Perfect Manhattan?

Angostura all the way! Doc Friday laughs.

I was just thinking about that time Willie Wepner fell on the picket fence, Mr. Phillips says.

The recipe, by the way, for a Flowers of Summer, the Magician says, is as follows: one-half ounce grenadine, one and one-half ounces milk, one and one-half ounces London dry gin, dash of bitters. Shake well with cracked ice and strain into cocktail glass. Garnish with a fresh strawberry. He looks up and down the street but apparently no one has been paying any attention to him. Apparently.

Dorothy Phillips is lying on the couch with a fresh gin and water, listening to the "Make-Believe Ballroom."

The Magician has changed, for some obscure reason—

A magical reason! the Magician says.

The Magician has changed, for some magical yet obscure reason, into a loose red shirt. He holds a glass high above his head, gestures, and changes the block into an enormous flower garden.

I am the Magician, he drones. If I will it, this block shall forever blossom in just this way.

Roses, lilies, pertunias, the Arab says.

And pinks and marigolds and zinnias and Christ knows what all else, Pepper says.

But I *don't* will it, the Magician says.

Dorothy Phillips sings: Shrimpers and rice! They're very nice!

An Army officer in Pat's Tavern orders a Flowers of Summer.

The guy's ordering a Flowers of Summer, Doc! Richie says.

So?

A Flowers of Summer! But it's made out of gin and cherry syrup. And white crème de menthe. And it's over ice. And in an Old-Fashioned glass!

An Old-Fashioned glass? Mr. Phillips says. Jesus Christ!

What the hell do I care what you think? Major Gentry says. And who the hell do you think you are, soldier?

Soldier? Richie says.

He's looking at me, Sergeant Nick Carruthers says. *I* didn't say anything.

This must be Master Sergeant Jim Gentry's older brother, Mr. Phillips says. The sarge is the world's leading authority on the *Culex* mosquito. They come from Texas—that's how I know.

Since *he* comes from Texas, Fat Frankie says. We know, we know, Gene!

The oddly arcanic thing about this, the Arab says, is that I have the strangely eerie suspicion in my cortex that it's Mr. Phillips who has disguised himself as the Magician.

You're goddam *right* he's the world's leading authority, Major Gentry says.

2 Headlines

Riffling through the morning newspapers on Vogler's stand, Professor Kooba sniffs with contempt at the headlines. He reads none of the stories that follow these headlines, certain that he has read them all before and will read them all again. Perhaps he is wrong.

A.R.T.O. CHIEF FACES PANEL QUIZ
MORE WOMEN READ, STUDY REVEALS
"SOLAR CROSS" VISIBLE THIS MONTH IN NORTHERN SKY
P. P. VAIL HIDES TRUTH, MISS CRUZ CHARGES
"RAT, O RAT!" OPENS AT LOEW'S THEATERS
MOTHER SUPERIOR ADMITS WRITING REVEALING BOOK
BRUNETTES FAVOR BLUE DESPITE FASHION DECREE
GOLDEN CRESCENT FOUND UNDER "EL" PILLARS
BONNIE JUNE ROAT VOTED "PRIESTESS" AT CHINESE
    APPLE FETE
J. B. CROSS WILL BUILD TEMPLE FOR PALMISTS
MISS BAJ TO EDIT "ORTA"
POMEGRANATES FINE IN SUMMER COOLERS
BIG HATS ARE IN FOR FALL
BURNE-JONES EXHIBIT AT MET

One of them strikes him as being a cut above total imbecility. Which one? the Arab asks.

3 The Test of Purity

When I was a kid once out in Staten Island on an overnight with the Boy Scouts, Pepper says, my whole life was made clear to me—I mean, I was given a chance to change and become someone else. Or *something* else, anyway.

That happened to *me!* Big Mickey says. And I was only hanging around with the Boy Scouts. I never joined the damn Boy Scouts.

O.K. But let's say it happened to me. I feel like talking.

O.K. But you don't *know* what happened to me.

I'll make it up to fit me. Who can it hurt? Who's listening anyway except you?

You never know. I got a reputation, you know.

When I was a kid once out in Staten Island on an overnight with the Boy Scouts, I got separated from the group and wandered along through the woods following a little stream. Suddenly I saw a terrific kind of light—a kind of glowing light—right in front of me.

That didn't happen to me. The whole thing was different with me.

All right! Are you going to interrupt me all the time? Or not?

No, go ahead. It's just that I remember what happened to me like it was yesterday.

A great big light, glowing in a little clearing right next to the stream. I looked into the clearing and there on a kind of big red plush chair was this gorgeous blonde. She was dressed in a kind of white gown with funny red designs all over it and on her head

7

she had a hat, a sort of hat with stars on it. It was the stars that gave out the light I saw.

A crown?

Yeah, sure. Call it a crown. She's got some kind of thing like a shield with another funny design on it next to the chair on the ground and she's holding a scepter, I guess, in her hand. But imagine my surprise when I looked close at her and saw that she was the leader of the Girl Scout troop that meets in the basement of the Lutheran church right up here on Fourth Avenue!

Oh, come on. That broad? A gorgeous blonde?

I'm telling you it was the same woman and she was gorgeous when I saw her there in the woods. I started to back out from this little clearing but she waves her scepter at me and I stop short. What is it, my son? she says. Your eyes are popping out of your head. You never saw the Empress of the Woods before?

My son?

This is the way she talked, don't blame me. I stand there. I don't know what to say. She says, You look as if maybe you think you know me, like from the neighborhood? I assure you, she says, I don't come from your neighborhood—I come from the elfin woods and babbling rills of laughing cataracts.

Oh, Jesus Christ! You're laying it on thick, Pepper!

But! she goes on. But! Because you have accidentally stumbled into my private lair, and lucky you came when you did, because a little earlier you would have caught me in the act of changing my clothes and I would have had to turn you into a tree, but! since you're here, I'm going to allow you to worship me. And all those goddam stars in her hat started to twinkle away.

Pepper. Pepper, nothing like this happened—I didn't meet *anybody* in the woods the day I knew I could have changed my life.

Ah, I say, thank you, thank you, O Empress Girl Scout Leader and Queen of the Woods! And believe it or not I fall down on my knees and begin to worship her. Poor deformed sprite, she says, or some damn thing like that, crawl and hobble up here to my knees and while you approach I'll dim the light of these glowing stars in my bonnet so your eyes won't get burned out of your handsome head.

I'll see you, Pepper, Big Mickey says, and starts off down the street toward the Royal Coffee Shop.

So I approach, Pepper continues. Pluck up all the golden corn that you see growing in front of me, she says. Take it back to your campsite or take it home, whatever you like—only don't be greedy. Also, you may drink of the crystal water of the laughing stream that flows here and also wash the sweat and grime from your face and tired brow. Then, and only then, you may touch the hem of my garment and softly caress it with your parched and cracked lips, taking care, mind you, that you don't touch in any way my *person* that lies concealed modestly beneath. So I do all this, and her garment smells like flowers and perfume and tastes sweet as sugar. Believe it or not, Mickey, whether or not she was that woman who you see going to the Lutheran church on Wednesday night, *here* she really was an empress.

Since Big Mickey has gone, he does not answer.

I'll answer for Mickey, Red Miller says. Wow! An empress! Wow!

Wow is right. Then she says, If you will be pure in heart and cut out the booze and be nicer to your wife, I guarantee you that your life will change and I'll turn you into a scientist. Look at me, poor trembling slob that you are! Look up at me and let me see if you are pure! So I look up at her and there she is, I mean gorgeous and beautiful and with a build to drive you crazy and all of a sudden, I swear to Christ, I'm looking at her and it's like she's got nothing on but her shoes and her hat! I mean she's sitting there on that chair absolutely naked. Your eyes, you dirty bastard, she says, tell me that you are about a zillion miles away from being pure in heart. And if you cannot gaze upon the Empress of the Woods with a clean heart, you can forget about any vows you may have considered having to do with laying off the sauce and being a decent husband. And I considered allowing *you* to be a scientist! Ha!

Wow! Red Miller says. Wow! You looked right through her clothes, hah? Her underwear and everything? Wow!

She waves her scepter and I fall over like I'm dead. I come to, there she is in her green uniform and her glasses and her hair pulled back in a bun and her big clunky hiking shoes on and she's directing a bunch of Girl Scouts who are rubbing my wrists and opening my collar and elevating my feet. You had a nasty fainting spell, she says. Lucky we happened upon you.

She talked like that? And what do you mean, in her green uniform? Who?

Shh. I look right into her eyes but I don't see any sign that she recognizes me. She's just the goddam Girl Scout leader, concerned about me. I think I can make it back to my camp, Miss, I say to her. Aren't you a little old for camp? she says. Old? I say. I'm just a kid.

What? What do you mean, kid? Red Miller asks.

But she insists on walking me back with two Scouts. I keep wondering what she'd say if she knew I saw her in the raw.

Saw *who* in the raw? The Girl Scout leader? I thought you said you saw through this other girl's clothes. What's going on here? And what did you mean saying you were a kid?

And I still wonder what she'd say if she knew I saw her sitting there naked.

Who? What?

I could have been a scientist, she said. But it was her fault. She's the one who fixed it so I could see through her clothes.

You were tested and failed, the Empress says from her clearing.

Goddam dumb story, Red Miller says. Dumb!

None of it ever happened, Big Mickey says, returning. Don't believe him. He took *my* story and turned it all around.

It was her fault, Pepper says. You should have seen her though.

4 The Emperor Idiotes

The Magician, immeasurably bored, decides that he will spend the day doing something. But what will he do?

One sees that despite that exterterrestrial and nonsublunarious powers that are the guerdon of their arcanic and shady birthrights, magicians too have their problems, like any ordinary slobs of mere mortals, the Arab says. But.

But what? Henny the bartender says.

What's Henny doing off? Richie asks. He should be behind the bar.

Drunk behind the bar, Irish Billy says.

Drunk or sober, Sergeant Nick Carruthers says, if we'd had a saloon like the Melody Room back in Selma, I would never have joined the Army.

This is called a *non sequr*, the Arab says.

The Magician causes to appear in front of Lambui's Limousine Rental Service what might pass for a throne. It's wooden, carved with sheep's heads here and there, and painted rather carelessly to resemble grey stone.

They look like rams' heads, Henny says.

I would have just stayed right there in good old, little old Selma, Alabama, Sergeant Nick says. Just breathing in that good old hot Southern air and thinking of marrying my childhood sweetheart far, far away in Athens at the university. Instead, I became a tank commander. He sighs.

Non. Se. Qur! the Arab says again.

Into this throne the Magician lowers his body.

Note it well, Richie says.

A white beard, Irish Billy says. Straight out of a chivalry

movie with James Mason. A scepter looks like a T-square with a doughnut on top.

Appellated as a *crux ansata*, the Arab says, that is, a cross with a handle, or, a handled cross.

Also, a gold spaldeen in his other hand, Irish Billy says.

Known as a globe, the Arab says. Symbological of power or something akin.

It's the "akin" that worries me, Henny says.

Drinking that icy cold Jax beer and working hard down to the body shop out near the highway, fishing for them big old bullheads Saturday mornings. Boy! Sergeant Nick sighs again.

A heartrending sigh, Richie says. If truth be told.

A sigh repletious with regrets and remorses and ruths, the Arab says.

Misplaced nostalgia, Henny says. Or something.

An invisible observer might conclude that Henny, despite the fact that he is not behind the Melody Room bar, is three sheets to the wind anyway.

A what observer? Irish Billy asks. Anyway—the Magician also has a kind of crown on his head with a little propeller on top like kids used to wear except they had beanies. *This* hat is a goddam production.

Like kids used to wear? Henny asks. You mean like kids are *going* to wear!

This is called a statement of obscure intents, of odd motivations, and of crepsular meanings, the Arab says.

Also, robes and things, Irish Billy says. The usual—the usual—I can't think of the word.

Appointments? Henny says.

Appurtenances? the Arab says.

Good, Irish Billy says. Right.

And sweet Billie Mae out behind the Grange Hall with me in the overpowering and overwhelming smell of the sweet magnolia blossoms and honeysuckle and persimmons and pecan pies with a big gleaming Alabama moon lighting up her purty face, Sergeant Nick says.

Billie Mae? Purty face? Jesus Christ! Lighten up, soldier, Henny says.

So, anyway, there he sits, the Magician, Irish Billy says.

And yet . . . and yet . . . go ahead . . . and yet . . . Richie says.

And yet, the Arab says, the puissance the Magician feels he obtains as this stern and splendid emperor, or king, probably an emperor seeing that he has this *crux ansata* in one mitt and a gold globe in the other, is dispelled, dissipated, and swept away by cruel gusts of noiseless laughter, because. *Because!*

Allow me to suggest here a blaze of trumpets, Richie says.

A blaze of trumpets indeed! the Arab says. *Because*—as I was saying before the musical interlusion—the Magician has unaccountedly and very very mistakenly given himself the face of the neighborhood's ranking idiot, Jo-Jo Cordell!

Slurper of ice cream, pisser in trousers, drooler of mouth, puncher of lips, Henny says.

A raw stain on the ecutcheon of the environs, the Arab says.

There he sits, the poor bastard, oblivious to the snickers of all who pass who think that he's Jo-Jo, dressed up for Halloween by his old grey mother, Irish Billy says. Thus the errors of empire. A glaring error in the glaring sun.

And just laying in the sun on Sundays, Sergeant Nick says, down to the old reservoir with a lunch of cold chicken and Dr. Pepper in the pickup. Whooo-eee!

This is called "in his own little dream world," the Arab says.

The Magician sits stolidly, sweat streaming from under his crown and down his face, alienated from the people and their opinions.

Thus is it ever, Henny says. *Sic semper.*

What? Irish Billy asks.

He was an altar boy, Richie says.

As a *sotto voce* aside, the Arab says, if I may be permitted, this startling resembalance of the Magician as Emperor to the misfortunate Jo-Jo, supreme idiot boy of the neighborhood—though rumor grasps it that he is at least thirty-five—is strengthened and girded by the fact that the Magician as Emperor uncountably keeps sputtering "my stickie, my ballie," a phrase made renowned by the aforementioned Jo-Jo.

And so the late afternoon shadows lengthen. Or they soon will.

5 Macy's San Francisco

When I go to San Francisco again, I hope I see the Pope there like last time, Little Mickey says.

What Pope? Big Mickey says. What San Francisco? You never been out of New York!

Brooklyn, Red Miller says. He never been out of Brooklyn.

Don't tell *me!* Little Mickey says. I don't tell everybody every place I go. I saw the Pope in San Francisco!

The kid is crazy, Santo Tuccio says. He gets crazier every day for Christ sake.

I saw the Pope right *there*—right in Macy's window in San Francisco. He had one of those funny crosses with three crosses across it, you know, and a big gold crown and a red robe like kings wear.

Yeah, Santo Tuccio says, like they wear in the *movies.* Kings! There ain't any more goddam *kings.*

There's a Pope! Little Mickey says.

Mickey, Red Miller says, where is San Francisco? Do you even know where it is?

Sure, Little Mickey says. It's out there near Idaho someplace out west.

Yeah, Santo Tuccio says. Sure. Spencer Tracy lives there with the Pope and Clark Gable. The kid is crazy.

You never been anywhere near San Francisco, Big Mickey says. Come on, Mick.

Fuckin crazy, Santo says.

Oh shut your mouth, Santo, Big Mickey says. Who the hell cares what you think? And there are goddam kings left in the world. You ever hear of England you goddam fool?

16

O.K., Santo says. O.K. The kid is still crazy. The other day his mother told me—

You shut your ass about my mother! You greasy slimy bastard!

Hey! Santo says. Hey! Nobody says that to me.

Sit down, Santo, Big Mickey says, or I'll bust you in the teeth.

Well, I'm going back anyway, Little Mickey says. And my mother is coming *with* me. Yeah, goddam right, Santo. My mother said she'll come *with* me.

Oh for Christ sake, Santo says. Why the hell don't you grow up?

The Pope said to me to take her back there, Little Mickey says. Get her away from *you.*

Little Mickey's mother is sitting on a rumpled day bed, drinking a ginger ale highball. She fishes under the yellowish sheets and pulls out one of Santo's socks, then throws it across the room. Filthy pig! she says, and adds some more whiskey to the glass.

I swear to God! Little Mickey says. I swear to God! He was blessing people in the street who were in front of the window right there at Macy's. I remember it really good, Mick, because there was these two bald guys he was blessing when I was there. That's how I remember it. And we're going there, The Pope said.

The Pope is holding an audience for some schoolboys from Melbourne. From what can be seen of him, he doesn't appear to be the sort of Pope who ever appeared in any Macy's window anywhere.

Besides, who says there's a Macy's in San Francisco anyway? Santo says. Do you know there's probably no Macy's in San Francisco? Hah? Hah? Goddam little liar.

Santo, take a walk, Red Miller says. I'll knock you from here to Macy's right here in New York.

Kid is full of—O.K., I'm going. Say hello to Clark Gable, will you? When you get to Macy's I mean.

I hate that bastard, Big Mickey says.

Little Mickey's mother answers the doorbell and lets Santo in. He frowns at the half-empty bottle of Wilson's on the end table.

The schoolboys from Melbourne are staring at the floor as the Pope gives them his blessing.

A number of addled and thoroughly confused people wander through San Francisco. They may be searching for Macy's.

I remember these bald guys, Little Mickey says. I really *was* there, Mick.

Maybe you were. Jesus, how I hate that son of a bitch.

Little Mickey suddenly begins to cry and Big Mickey takes him for a walk down to the pier. Hey, we'll take a ferry ride to Staten Island, O.K.?

The Pope is suffering from heartburn.

There's probably a Macy's in San Francisco, right Mick? Little Mickey asks.

Sure. There's a Macy's every place. It's like Broadway. Every place has got a Broadway. They even got a Broadway somewhere to hell and gone out in the sticks somewhere.

This guy really looked like the Pope, Little Mickey says.

You know what your goddam fool of a kid told me? Santo says.

Don't know and I don't give a goddam, Little Mickey's mother says. And for God's sake don't leave your dirty socks all over the goddam place. My mother comes here once in a while you know.

Oh yeah? I thought maybe she moved out to San Francisco. What?

6 A Problem of Memory

The trouble with remembering the past, Doc Friday says, is that you can only remember what happened. You remember what happened up to that point at which nothing more happened. And it's exactly at that point that you *want* to remember. You want to remember what might have happened—and you can't. Why? Because it didn't happen! Take romance, first love. Fugitive images of ecstasy or joy. I insist that this curious phenomenon is the cause of all the misery in the world although I admit that on the surface the whole thing may seem absurd.

Credo quia absurdum, Curtin says. St. Anselm said that. Who's to say he was wrong?

The son of a bitch is chucking in some Catholic-school Latin again, Irish Billy grumbles. So we got a half-assed philosopher and a Latin mumbler here.

St. Anselm's used to have some pretty good dances on Saturday night, Cheech says. Do they still give them?

They got a nice class of girls at those dances, Red Miller says.

A nice class of girls he says, the Sailor laughs. Lizzie Mulvaney is a nice class of girls?

Well, Red says. An exception.

Aha! Doc Friday says. The exception proves the rule as in my theory of the remembrance of what didn't happen making us all crazy.

I whiff the rankish odor of the effluvia of phoniness here, the Arab says. Phoniness and—and—what do I mean to say?

Sophistry! the Drummer says.

Exactly! Wondrous friend!

Look, Doc Friday says. Take instances of the bittersweet.

19

Take instances of lost opportunities. Take ruing the day, remorse, the heart melting with ruth. Imagine two young people,
a man and a woman. They stand under God's mellow and brilliant sun, an angel from heaven above looks down on them, his
arms spread in friendly blessing and benediction.

A blessing, a benediction, would, of necessity, Curtin says,
have to be friendly. Otherwise, it would be a malediction. "To
Carthage then I came, where a cauldron of unholy loves sang
about my ears." That's Augustine.

That's irrelevant, Irish Billy says.

At least he didn't talk Latin, Cheech says.

Thank you, Curtin, the Doc says. One angel, his arms spread
in benediction and etcetera, looks down on the two young
people. Say there's a couple of trees, green grass, a mountain in
the distance.

There always looms up a mountain in the distance, the Arab
says. You'll note that in the Doc's stories humankinds are never
in roachy furnished rooms or freezing apartments. Always in
the bucolical spots with mountains in the distance. Or oceans.

Thalassa! Thalassa! Curtin shouts. Xenophon.

Jesus Christ, Curtin, Irish Billy says. Let the man get his goddam mountains in.

These lovely and wonderful young people are innocently
naked with beautiful bodies of exquisite form, Doc Friday says.
They are stunned silly by each other's beauty. Absolutely natural. They fear nothing. They are like Adam and Eve in the garden except that if there's a snake around, he's a harmless old
codger. They are reaching out their hands to each other, ah, ah,
ahh, so shy.

Completely naked? the Drummer asks.

Completely naked, Doc Friday says.

Oh, the Drummer says, disappointed.

All right, Doc Friday says. You got this picture?

Everyone nods, some wearily.

Cut! Doc Friday says. Cut! Now—years and years and years

and years pass. These two young people have drifted apart, they've put on clothes, they've married other people also with clothes. Jobs, children, their hair is thin, teeth missing. The usual flatulence, fallen arches, myopia, indigestion, sagging breasts, grey hairs, paunches, and on and on.

One thing you have to say for the Doc, Irish Billy says. He's a real romantic guy.

Push ahead, Doc, the Arab says. Push on. Your exemplary tale is so fraughtful of interest that I am aflutter.

Now, listen carefully, the Doc says. These two once-young and lovely and naked people who are not now so young and not naked anymore and certainly not lovely, often think back on that magical day and are filled with ruthful regrets. And why?

They caught a cold? Red Miller says.

Pinched for indecent exposure? Irish Billy says. Or can you get pinched in romantic land?

Doc Friday looks up at the ceiling, searching there for succor. They are filled with regrets, he says, because, because—they are remembering, through their eyes swimming with tears, *what might have happened.* Their young and strong hands reached tremblingly and shyly toward each other, their blood raced hotly—yet purely—through their nude frames, their innocent and chaste veins.

Hotly yet purely? Curtin says. I don't know about that. It seems a contradiction in terms that Aquinas might have characterized as—

Aquinas was not there! Doc Friday says. What I mean to get across is that at the moment they reach for each other, that's it! I mean, that's it! Period. They did nothing else but reach. Not for them the honeyed words of sweet amour, not for them the blending of their two souls as one, not for them the dizzying gaze into the love-filled eyes of each other. Fini! Kaput! All over! So when they think of this glorious day it is not so goddam glorious anymore because whatever could have really been glorious about it never happened. Don't you get it?

It still redolates of—what was it, Drummer? the Arab says.

Sophistry, the Drummer replies.

Sophistry. Exactly. And I might add: cant. Sophistry and cant.

I feel that while your point is nicely made, Curtin says, that is, the curious remorse one feels for missed opportunities, your emphasis is too heavily sexual. There are other things to life.

It sounds like a *slice* of life to me, Irish Billy says. A gooey slice.

You're sure they're completely naked? the Drummer asks. I mean, all bare?

7 *La Vida es Sueño*

Let me tell you about this dream, Irish Billy says. One of the goddamndest things.

I dislike dreams, the Arab says. My own included. Not only are they wonted to bore you to pieces and filled chock to the brim with *non sequrs,* they are the cause of ennui psychoatrically speaking also. Besides, why should I desire to listen to your dream? I can bore myself by repeating to myself my own dreams.

Not *my* dream, Billy says. This is a dream Richie had and he told me about it. It's really a hell of a dream.

If you insist, the Arab says, looking over at the Drummer. It's either that or a tramping trek through the snow.

O.K. Richie, you know, hasn't seen his father in years, ten or fifteen or maybe even more years. So in the dream he decides to go down to Florida where the old man lives in the dream for a visit. In the dream he's married. His wife don't look like her but his wife is Cookie. You know how those things happen in a dream?

Frood has explained it all with grave candidness, the Arab says. But Cookie? My oh my.

Anyway, Richie and Cookie drive down in a pink Nash. They get there in like a second and the dream Florida is just a big flat plain all brown with a few dead trees here and there with Spanish moss draped off them even though Richie told me he knows that this stuff only grows on trees in Louisiana.

Spanish moss? A nice touch. An excellent touch. I didn't think Richie possessed this genre of subtleness in his brain.

Once in a while they see an orange tree or a lemon tree but mostly the goddam place looks like a big vacant lot. Just then, cutting across the plain toward them, comes a maroon Caddy and the guy driving it turns out to be Richie's brother and of course he hasn't *got* a brother.

Richie hasn't got any brothers, the Drummer says.

I just said that. But in the dream he's got at least this one guy who's his brother and he's in this maroon Caddy. Richie follows the guy to a big white house with flowers and palm trees and a big fountain. And on the front lawn there's a marble gnomon.

A marble *what?* the Arab says, taking a step toward Billy.

A gnomon. A sundial. Right on the lawn all marble.

Gnomon! Gnomon! Delicious! Richie, by God, is beginning to glow, even, may I impute, to glitter in my book. Gnomon. Gno-mon. Wonderful!

They go around in the back of the house and pass a woman with two kids who is definitely Richie's brother's wife, Richie's sister-in-law. She smiles at Richie and pushes the two kids kind of like toward him but he's rushing after his brother to get to the back. Then he sees his father in the middle of a patio made out of different colored flagstones sitting in a little open house—what do they call those little houses, Arab?

The Arab shuffles and looks at the Drummer, embarrassed. I'm afraid, he says, the word has exited from my mind. To use an old cliché, it's on the top of my tongue, but I can't—

Gazebo! Billy says. Right. His old man is sitting in a little like gazebo.

Of course, the Arab says. Of course! A gazebo. How dullardly of me to forget such a common household term. Gorgeous word.

The gazebo has a blue cloth draped on four corner poles instead of a roof to keep off the sun. Bright blue like the sky and spangled with stars.

Spangled with stars. My goodness, Drummer, this young man cannot only mosaically use such words as gazebo, he can also turn a handsome phrase. Excellent.

There's his father in the gazebo wearing a blue robe the same color as the cloth. In front of the gazebo are two stone sphinxes, one black and one white. As Richie comes up to him behind his brother, his father stands up. He don't even see Richie. He says, I'm leaving. I'm going to New York to see my son. Make reservations for me while I get started right now. Richie yells, Wait! I'm your son! I'm right here, I'm not in New York! But his father is gone. He looks around and his wife is gone and so is the Nash. He sees his brother driving away in the Caddy. Just then his sister-in-law comes up, only now she's his wife, who is Cookie, right? And she says she'd like the kids to meet their nice Uncle Richie, O.K.? Richie says no, he wants to go catch his father and his sister-in-law says how come he's in Florida because his father don't live in Florida. Who the hell would live in Florida? she says. And that's the dream.

This is the dream? the Arab says. This? Where's the irony? Where's the drama? Where's the denowment? Where's the morality?

That's the dream.

I have a rotten and putrid feeling that Richie made up this dream so that he could say gnomon and gazebo and spangled. That's the stinky and ingenerous feeling that is cascading through me. Drummer?

My feeling is equally rotten and putrid about this dream.

That's baloney, Irish Billy says. *I* used the words, not Richie.

You parroted and aped and mimicryed the words you mean, the Arab says.

No, they're my words. I thought I'd try them out for real, talking, like now.

And this is also *your* dream, the Arab says. Your phony dream.

No, it's Richie's dream. And Richie really actually went down to Florida anyway, I mean he *actually* went down to Florida to visit his father and he found out that he's got a brother who hasn't got a Caddy but he has got a Nash, only it's brown not pink. And the morning that he got there his father just left to go on a business trip to New York. Now. Is that a fantastic thing or is that a fantastic thing? A fantastic dream? The whole damn thing?

This trip Richie made, the Arab says. I must crudely and grossly enunciate that it is a pile of bullshit. That it did not happen.

It might have happened, Billy says.

And the dream didn't happen either. Spangled! Gnomon! For shame! Gazebo. Shame, shame!

It might have happened too.

How about the Spanish moss? the Drummer says. Arab, how about the Spanish moss? Arab, the Spanish—

Spanish moss! Shame, shame. Crushing provarications!

8 The Surrealist Fallacy

I know it's hard to impress upon you gentlemen the idea of a perfect pastoral scene, Professor Kooba says.

I call that snobbery, Professor, the Drummer says. *Some* of us are sensitive enough to understand the finer things—nature, trees, lakes in the misty mountains, cows—you name it.

Peace, Professor Kooba says. Permit me to apologize. I amend my statement to read, *some* of you gentlemen.

We don't need any perfect pastoral scenes, Irish Billy says. Perfect pastoral scenes! And what do you mean, "read"?

The country, as you think of it, Kooba, Doc Friday says, is no more than a clerk's idea. It has no relation to reality. Billy is correct. As a matter of fact, I feel that the very word "pastoral" has no basis in what is actually out there.

Nevertheless! Professor Kooba says. Assume that there may be a perfect pastoral scene. Within this scene, allow me to place one of our old acquaintances, Cookie LaNord, *née* Cookie . . . Cookie . . . what's her name?

We know the Cookie you mean, Irish Billy says. And, perfect pastoral scene or not, there's no possibility of Cookie ever being in it, or part of it, in any way, shape, or manner whatsoever.

So help me God! the Sailor says.

This must be Kooba's annual flirtation with surrealism, Doc Friday says. No wonder he's currently broke.

No wonder we're *all* currently broke, Cheech says. Instead of working, here we are on the goddam corner talking about Cookie out in the country. Jesus.

Pay no mind to Cheech, Kooba says. He's the guy was afraid to go home from the Royal one night after somebody told him a spooky story about the gypsy's hand.

Baloney! Cheech says. But he blushes.

I remember the evening well, the Drummer says. He even forgot to eat his bow tie and his coffee got cold.

It was a Mae West, you dumb bastard!

Gentlemen, gentlemen, Kooba says.

Go on, Kooba, the Sailor says. We got nothing to do. And if you don't talk, the Drummer will tell us about his dog act in vaudeville—when vaudeville *was* vaudeville!

Professor Kooba leans against a car and crosses his arms. I had no idea, he says, that the smallest whisper of a hint about the pastoral would cause such a scene. Such a hubbub.

Start again, Professor, Irish Billy says. The Sailor's right.

A damp, soft wind touched with a delicate aroma of salt and fish blows up from the Narrows.

A pastoral scene, Kooba says. Mountains in the background. Trees, black specks in a faraway pasture that we might as well call cows. The usual claptrap. But! In the foreground, in a long white flowing dress, there is a young woman whose face, as they say, is familiar. She looks like, and she probably is, Cookie LaNord. Cookie of the carnival! Cookie of the G-string and pasties, of the black net stockings and high heels. Cookie LaNord, whose fame in being frozen—ALIVE!—in a gigantic block of ice has spread her name far and wide among all the rural types in Christendom, and even in places so far flung as Indiana, regardless of their race, creed, or previous jobs. Observe her. In her long white dress she looks like a virgin, but we all know she lost her cherry right down the street in the park when she was just a slip of a lass of thirteen. Her face is serene. Around her waist is a chain of flowers, God only knows what kind, and at the other end of the chain there is a gigantic and ferocious lion! Cookie is slowly but surely closing up his slobbering maw. The sun beams down on old Montana. Around her head busy bees hum buzzing in a figure eight.

And? Doc Friday asks.

And? Kooba replies. And? Gentlemen, what, I ask you, do

you make of this scene? That is the pressing question. Why is the notorious Cookie, once in a while referred to as Cookie La-Gash, engaged in this oddball and thoroughly goofy act? Yet—one that is bursting with overtones of the peaceful, the pastoral, the all-around countryish.

Can she maybe be out at the carny owner's place in the country for a weekend of fun and meanwhile breaking in a new act—with animal? the Drummer says.

Precisely! Professor Kooba says. Exactly and precisely and bravo.

9 The Mysterious Ticineti

When I dwell upon Ticineti, the famed, the mysterious, the fixer, I am filled up to my eyeball teeth with an emulsion of awe and perplexitness, the Arab says.

Many of us feel the same way, Doc Friday says. He is eating a Mrs. Wagner's lemon pie and drinking a Pepsi. He calls this his beauty lunch.

Is he a fake and a phony? the Drummer asks. He gets things done, but . . .

For a stipend, the Arab says. For men, it variates. For women, of a certain type, rather maturesome, the fee is fixed, if you comprehend.

Aha! the Drummer says, his eyes gleaming behind his gold-rimmed glasses.

Your eyes, as usual, are gleaming, Drummer, Doc Friday says. With a moistened fingertip he is picking up pie crumbs from the counter.

People are forever and e'er picking up crumbs from tables and such objects with moistened fingertips, the Arab says. It is what can be called an ennui.

I do what I do, Doc Friday says, draining the last of his Pepsi.

What about Ticineti? the Drummer says. And certain of his female clients?

Ah, but yes, the Arab says. Imagine a maturesome house-wife, say of about thirty-five or forty years of age. A little teensy fragment or such of overweight, perhaps. Musky. Ripe is the word that Ticineti likes, so rumor stands. Such females of this overall description may easily negotiate with Ticineti for his assistance, which is always forthwith and post haste granted thus.

But how come he's in Sheepshead Bay? Doc Friday asks.

Is he truly there? the Arab says. There's an old codgery duffer there who anyway looks old who walks around in a long grey cloak with a hood and carries a staff-like shard of wood, and a lantern inside same of which burns a furious star . . .

Hold it, the Drummer says. I think I heard this luscious phrase you said just now—furious star—before. Not that it matters a damn.

You are correct to one thousand per cent that it doesn't matter a haul of beans, the Arab replies. If you live long enough and keep your ears ajar you are wont to hear everything twice. At least. A lantern then, within which a furious star burns. He has a grizzlied beard and busted-down and tattydemalion old sandals. He keeps his eyes fixed strongly on the ground with the lantern held up high like a man searching for two bits he dropped. It is bruited around that this old geezer is Ticineti in one of the costumes he likes, called the wise-man look.

But where does he come from? Doc Friday asks. He is sucking at a tooth.

Sucking at a tooth, Doc? the Arab asks. First you pick up crumbs with a moist finger, now you suck a tooth. In a trice you'll push your hat back on your head.

Do what I do, Doc Friday says. Now, where does he come from?

Who knows? the Arab says. They say he attended Fort Hamilton High School, where he spent an inordinant amount of studious time staring at the legs of one Mrs. Greenberg, an English teacher who was not too shy to sit on the desk and permit her skirts to ride up a jot or two. And if pictures do not fib, she was some dish of honeyed flesh! He sucks at a tooth.

Go on, the Drummer says. His eyes gleam.

It is whispered heather and yonder, the Arab continues, that he sold produce from a decrepitous horse-drawn wagon on the streets and invented—or teased into perfection—the following cries:

FA-REESSHH CAWN!
WAWDEE MEELOWNN!
DELL-WAYYHH PEETYEZ!
STRRAWW BREEEZ!

They also say, and to boots, that he owned a tire-repair shop like our amicus, good old Eddy, and each rosy dawn or even before in the gloaming dimness of four A.M., sprinkled the intersection near his shop with shards and chunks of busted glass and twisty nails. He has nine children. He often sported a golden earring in his left ear and sometimes wore a long drooping mustachios. Red bandanna. Straw hat. Your usual ginzola starotype.

He sang "Sorrento" and "Ciel la Lun'"? "Mama"? the Drummer asks, and begins to hum "Lola."

Without the most picayune doubts, dear comrade. He chomped upon nickels, put his thumb in the scale, gave apples to the local boys in blue. Often he would let fall a lemon or maybe a cucumber and spend a heavenly moment or two on hands and knees to gaze at close range at a knockout housewife's gams. Stockings with dark seams and high heels with thin straps across the top of the instep made him crunch and crush and crumble plums peaches and pears to a pulp in his perspirant and palpitating paws.

What? Doc Friday says. You mean nerves?

But exactly, the Arab says.

Dementia erotica, the Drummer says, the skin beneath his eyes gleaming with a film of sweat. I myself, if the truth be told, am not a man to turn away from a well-turned leg in sheer hose and a small foot in dainty slippers. It's said that Honest Abe Lincoln, our most beloved President, also suffered from this weakness.

Abraham Lincoln? What the hell does Abraham Lincoln have to do with this? Irish Billy says.

Get the hell *out* of here, Billy! the Arab yells. Meddlesome wretch!

He's gone, the Drummer says. Yes, Abraham Lincoln. Hmm. With such a failing I am absolutely amazed that he steered the ship of state with such a steady hand on the rudder, through the perilous seas as those in which he lived. I, with my own leg-mania, can just about get my ass to the unemployment office once a week to sign for my cheap little check that they grudge giving me anyway, the bastards.

To continue, the Arab says, if I may, with these fabulous tales of Ticineti.

Who? Irish Billy says.

Ticineti! Ticineti! the Arab says. In God's name, Billy, impose silence upon your mouth. You are not *in* this colloquium. Get out. Take a stroll. Or sit down and have a peaceful quiet egg cream. Here—here's the new *Modern Screen* with a sexual bombshell on the cover. Read!

Sexual bombshell, Billy says. Jesus! He leaves again.

To continue, as I said. Somehow, Ticineti began an association with the Magician, who the same intercedes for him in assisting to solve the problematical enigmas brought to him by hapless men—and of course hapless women with good pins. The phantasmal item called success is well-nigh assured when the Magician devolves on the scene.

Do they have a financial arrangement? Doc Friday asks, pushing his hat back on his head.

Who dare whisper same? They have something. Meantime, as I have enounced, Ticineti amuses himself by perambulating the streets of Sheepshead Bay in his uniform, looking at the ground and rising high his lantern in which there burns—with this, the Arab raises his hands in the manner of an orchestra leader.

A furious star! Irish Billy yells in the door and runs down the street.

Ughh! I loathe and despise a wisenheimer, the Arab says.

The Drummer's eyes gleam. He pushes his hat back on his head.

Doc Friday gazes at a bag of Spero potato chips. I like a nicely turned leg myself, he says.

10 Chance, Fortune

Hey Cookie! Ha ha! Hey Cookie! Burly laughs. If your skirt was any shorter you'd have two more cheeks to powder! Ha! Right, Santo?

She'd have some more hair to comb too, Santo says, if that goddam whorehouse skirt was maybe say an inch shorter.

And if you guys had one fuckin brain between you you'd be in a goddam museum, Cookie says.

Stamping the floor and guffawing, Burly and Santo walk out.

If your skirts were not so—daring, Cookie, the Arab says, you'd have no need to tolerate the vulgaristic sallies of those oafish varlets.

Mind your own business, Cookie says. Then she either leaves or retires to a phone booth in the rear of the store to call her agent, if she has an agent at this point in her show-business career.

At this point in her show-business career, Miss LaNord does *not* have an agent, Irish Billy says. But if she were to hire me as her agent, she might in the future be a star like Tempest Fury or Lily St. Cyr or Blaze Starr or Chestie Bustte.

Chestie Bustte? the Drummer says. There's a Chestie Bustte?

If there exists a woman by name of Chestie Bustte then bulls can read, the Arab says.

Read what? Curtin says. Books? Newspapers? Magazines? *A particular book? What if a bull reads Gulliver's Travels?*

How about the whale? Irish Billy says. I mean, suppose he had a thumb?

Suppose, the Arab says. I am intently supposing.

Oh, you know the old saying, Billy says. A whale with a thumb could rule the whole world.

Not according to *The Baltimore Catechism* he can't rule any goddam world, Curtin says.

Suppose the whale read that? the Drummer says. *The Baltimore Catechism?*

You mean the bull, Curtin says.

You'll note what Cookie starts with her rather daring and revealing modus of apparel, the Arab says. Her skirts are of a shortness that smacks, that even smashes of the quintessence of rut. When she leans with both elbows on the soda cooler so that her nether parts of her body protrude out into the air, back or front . . .

Thank God I'm too old to care, Professor Kooba says. If I were a younger man however . . .

You'd what? the Drummer asks. And if bulls could read *Gulliver's Travels* they'd do something. They'd do *something*, right Curtin?

They'd turn into whales, Irish Billy says.

If Cookie wasn't of the coreness of the vulgaristic, the Arab says, one could almost imagine . . . one could almost.

Almost, my ass, Curtin says. One look at her and your eyes start to smoke. She's what they call an occasion of sin, in my book.

What book is this? the Arab says. *The Baltimore Catechism?* The same tome that our friend, the bull, peruses?

When Georgie Huckle sees Cookie, Irish Billy says, if he didn't wear that enormous goddam hat all the time, night and day and even when he sleeps, his head would fly off like it exploded. As it is, his eyes roll around in his head like marbles. I wonder where he got that weird hat?

It is slyly mouthed about, the Arab says, that the renowned headgear is his father's, but I do not know of the veridicalness of this opinion. Perhaps we will discover the core of truth in it by in by. In events, anyway, the chapeau is supposed to cause his dame Lady Luck to smile and grin upon him and the neglect of wearing the sombrero would cause her to cease forever this activity. Then he would be in misfortune at the moments of contact with his doughty bookmaker when he comes up with a cheapskate deuce on a nag to show. Such goes the story but who is to know?

The hell with Georgie's hat, the Drummer says. But about reading animals . . . I remember a vaudeville act years ago in I think some burg outside Canton, Ohio, where a guy had an old broken-down lion could read.

Read what? Curtin says. Don't tell me *Gulliver's Travels!*

How would I know? The *Canton Gazette* maybe.

That was perchance no lion, dear bosom heart of an amigo, the Arab says. That may well have been what they terminologized in ancient Latin mythology a griffin, since griffins could read. Still can.

They don't exist, Arab, Curtin says. That's only a story.

How about those goddam angels of yours? the Drummer says. That are all over that *Baltimore Catechism!* Can they read?

Of course, Curtin says. What the hell would God make an illiterate angel for? An illiterate angel might as well hang out with all the jerks on the corner here. With Burly and the Sailor, for God's sake!

There goes Eddy Ellsworth, Irish Billy says. Jesus Christ. Will you look at those torn-up goddam disgusting and nauscating sneakers on the son of a bitch!

If Eddy Ellsworth were a human being, could *he* read? Professor Kooba says.

I am shocked, the Arab says. Shocked and hurtled succinctly into a deep amaze, Professor, by your words. You? A tolerant and wise scribe, a scholar of the old persuasiveness?

What happens if you take Kooba's Wings loosie away from him? Curtin asks.

Very funny, Professor Kooba says.

His ass falls off? Irish Billy answers.

Very, oh very *very* funny, Kooba says.

No, Curtin, says. "The Curse" disintegrates.

Oh! Ha. Ha. Ha. Ho. Ho. Hee. Really hilariously funny, Kooba says, holding his manuscript to his chest. If *any* of you people could read, you'd all have violent migraines with the strain of it all. I exclude you, Arab, and maybe the Drummer too. As for the rest of you—moronic idiots!

There fucking goes Eddy Ellsworth the other way now, Irish Billy says. If he had any goddam pride he'd buy himself a pair of shoes instead of those garbage pails he wears.

If he had any pride, Richie says, entering, what would we have to bitch about?

Ah, Richie, Curtin says. Good. Now listen, Richie, what do you think? Can angels read?

Sure, just like ducks can read. And geese.

Big Duck can read, can't he? Irish Billy asks.

He can certainly read his ravagements of acne in his countenance every morning in the mirror, the Arab says.

What the hell does Dolores *see* in that goddam greasemonkey? Irish Billy says. She's really kind of a nice girl.

I'm saying that angels can read! Curtin says. Come on, Richie. Be serious.

Hey, was Cookie in here? Richie asks. I can smell her perfume.

That ain't perfume, kid, Billy says.

I'm *saying* that *angels* can *read*, Curtin says. Come on! Richie?

Sure, yeah, yes. Sure they can. Just like cows and bulls.

That's what *I* said, the Arab says.

11 Electric Miracle

That *was* Bony Ruth, the Drummer says. She didn't even say hello. What's the matter with her lately, I wonder?

I have myself personally noticed lately a mild, not to say a temperate air of frigidness about Ruth of late, the Arab says.

Maybe her Uncle Pat died and left her all his empty Carstairs bottles, the Sailor says.

I know what it is, Johnny News says. Right from the horse's mouth. Only I knew about it—I mean about the method of it long ago, a method that they used in Russia during the war. Maybe still do, the Communist bastards, for all I know.

Ruth walks around with her fucking nose up in the air all the time and you're talking Communists? the Sailor says.

Indeed, Johnny, the Arab says. Enlighten us with your shafts and javelins of wisdom. What horse's mouth spoke to you?

O.K., Johnny says. He takes a position by the newsstand and folds his arms.

Oh Jesus, the Sailor says. When he stands over there! Maybe Ruth found out how to navigate that ferry in the fog you got lost on, Johnny?

Laugh if you want, Johnny News says. I'm telling you I know why she's acting so stuck-up lately. You want to hear or not?

Speak! the Arab says. We are each and every ear.

O.K. It's just that Ruthie talked to Ticineti about how could she make her chest bigger, you know, her bosoms?

We know her bosoms, the Sailor says. When we can find the fucking things we know them.

Sailor, the Arab says, this lighthearted raillerism and levity will offend our good and excellent interlocutor.

So Ticineti, Johnny News says, told her this thing—he told

me about it—this thing that I told you I know that the Communist bastards over in Russia did in the war. Did I tell you about sailing to Murmansk the first time I shipped on a Liberty?

About eighty thousand times, the Sailor says.

Yes, well, O.K. Anyway, here's what happens. The girl—Ruthie—sits at home for an hour every day at noon in a chair facing a window, O.K.? She gets a broomstick, a regular goddam broomstick that you saw the broom part off like when you used to play stickball, and you wrap this stick up all the way up with silver foil.

Silver foil? the Arab says. Just plain and ordinary and mundanely banal silver foil?

Just plain old silver foil like from a pack of cigarettes.

You never bought a pack of cigarettes in your life, the Sailor says.

What does that got to do with it? I'm just saying that *she* wraps the broomstick up in silver foil.

Avanti! the Drummer says.

Very nice, Drummer, the Arab says. A touch of cosmopolite elegance of phrase.

She sits with the stick at a window, and oh yeah, in the other hand she holds an old-fashioned pair of scales like you put one thing in one side and another thing in the other—like the fish man when—

We are aware—pardon me, Johnny, the Arab says—we are aware of how you function with a pair of scales.

O.K. And she has to put on a big bathrobe comes down to her feet.

What's this got to do with Ruthie growing big bosoms? the Sailor says.

Wait a minute. Wait a minute. One thing at a time.

The way this goddam guy tells a goddam story! the Sailor says. Christ!

Now here's the part that Ticineti told me about which I already knew it because of my Russia experience. At noontime the electric currents in the air are really strong, I mean according to Ticineti if you could catch them all and store them up you could light up all the goddam lampposts for a week on just one charge.

Is this true, Arab? the Drummer asks.

The electrical arts and sciences have never been my forte, and I will accept Johnny's posit.

So these really strong electric currents can't fight flowing into this broomstick, see, because the silver foil acts like a whatchamacallit, you know, a thing that pulls electricity in easy. The current flows right into the lady's hand—Ruthie's hand—and through her body. Then they combine with like special female juices and organs and stuff inside of her and a chemical reaction happens that for some reason goes right to the bosoms.

This is shatteringly incredulous! the Arab says. Electric currents? Female juices?

Female organs, the Drummer says. Mmm.

I don't know how it works, Johnny News says. All I know is Ticineti told her her bosoms would grow about an inch a month if she did this every day. And when they get big enough to suit her she can quit and they'll stay that size. And the long robe, oh yeah, is so that the electric currents after they mix up with the female juices and elements and Christ knows what, atoms, won't just like leak out from her skin. The robe keeps all this stuff inside and it goes right to her chest. But I told you I used to see that in Russia. You ever see any Russian broads? Those knockers they got?

An inch per month? the Arab says. In about eight months Bony Ruth should be a vibrant chunk of muliebrity, at least in reference to the mammarian charms.

She don't say hello now and she's still flat as an ironing board, the Sailor says. In eight months she'll go to goddam Hollywood, change her name.

Probably to Ruth Bone, the Drummer says.

But Johnny, the Arab says. Although hanging with raptness on your every word, what of the scales? Those old-fashioned, fish-man order of scales? What do they function as doing? Did Ticineti hint of such?

He didn't say. And to tell you the God's honest truth, I don't know what the scales are for either.

Probably Ruth Bowman, the Drummer says. Or Ruth Brown. Ruthene Brune?

The scales are so one tit don't come out bigger than the other, the Sailor says.

12 Dance of the Hopeless

Isabel and Berta? the Drummer says. Oh God, a couple of honeys.

Restrict and prescribe them from your mind and its fantasies, the Arab says. They are not for you.

I didn't say they were. But God, how I hate to see them headed for dopey marriages with cars out on Long Island.

Maybe Teaneck, Irish Billy says. There's always a chance they'll go to Jersey.

Indeed, the Arab says. If they marry stout hearts whose noble and yearnful eyes glint and flash forever westward!

Jokes can't disguise those sour grapes, Arab, Billy says.

But hearken! And hark! the Arab says. What do we have here?

Willie Wepner dances and struts about in front of Isabel and Berta. Suddenly he executes a brilliant series of cartwheels and comes to rest directly before them.

What a bore, Berta says.

And a boor as well, Isabel says.

Is that Willie Wepner showing off some of his stuff for the luscious lasses? the Arab says.

It *is* Willie Wepner, the Drummer says. How he's grown. The last time I saw him or even thought about him was, I can't even remember when.

Isn't Willie Wepner the guy who when he was a kid fell on a picket fence outside his house and got one up the gool? Irish Billy asks.

The same! the Drummer says. That's what I was trying to remember. The famous picket in the ass.

A day of blistering excitement, the Arab says. Such small

slabs of life thus gleaming make the neighborhood sit up and take notice of the human comedy.

Hey, look at him, Irish Billy says.

Willie Wepner leaps high in the air and comes down on his knees in a garbage can filled with ashes and clinkers. I love you! he shouts. I love both of you or one of you! I love you! Clouds of dust billow around him.

He loves us? Isabel says. *Willie Wepner?*

He's the young fellow had the utterly embarrassing accident years ago, Berta says. *He* loves us?

Let's have some fun! Willie yells. He seems to be near tears.

A falling-down type of guy, Irish Billy says. It's embarrassing to watch this.

True, the Arab says. But now, the clodlike churl, in his ineptness of awkwardness, has tried to turn his penchant for falling down and making a clown of himself, to say nothing of grievious injuries, into a type of passionate mating love act. Of such dumb ideas sprout broken hearts. I should know.

I'd crack my goddam knees to bits and pieces, to powdered waste, if I thought it could help me get inside Berta or Isabel's dress, the Drummer says. Jesus, I can almost feel them now.

What does a guy got to do to get a glance from you girls? Willie asks, staring up at the sky and somersaulting out of the garbage can. Who does a guy got to be? Clark Gable?

Leslie Howard! Isabel and Berta say simultaneously, and giggle.

Staring with vacated glims up at the welkin will not assist the oaf no wise, the Arab says. Their destiny calls them.

Onward to Teaneck for the ladies, the Drummer says. But I'd jump off a moving trolley if I thought it would help me to assist them out of their garments. Either one.

Willie Wepner begins to juggle some eggs and tangerines. The girls look vaguely amused and return to their shared copy of *Silver Screen*.

Santo Tuccio, don't ask me how he knows this, Irish Billy says, says that Berta wears lace pants.

Stop! the Drummer gasps. Or I'll chew this goddam fedora of mine to pieces! Do I need images like this? At my age?

Yes, Billy, the Arab says. It is of an unusual cruelty to fold such thoughts into the head of a passionate *homme* like the Drummer here. He has not fully come to terms with or even grudgedly accepted his crushingly meaningless role in life, I mean amorously speaking, of course.

Lace pants, the Drummer says, and throws his fedora to the ground. Lace pants, he says again, and begins to stamp on it.

How about this? Willie says, and catches all three eggs and two tangerines in his mouth and swallows them. Whole.

That last smacks of hyperbolic fustian, the Arab says.

Willie catches all three eggs and two tangerines in his mouth one at a time and propels them into a cellarway.

That's better, the Arab says. Not perfect, but better. Acceptable.

Did you see something, Berta? Isabel asks.

I thought I saw something, but it was so crude and vulgar that I really couldn't believe my eyes. Let's say we didn't see what we thought we saw.

Willie begins a fast soft shoe to "Tea for Two," then cuts to a buck and wing and finally sails horizontally through the air and disappears into the open door of a hallway.

The goddam fool will kill himself, Irish Billy says.

He's dying of love anyway, the Arab says.

Lace pants, the Drummer says, kicking his fedora into the gutter. Lace *panties,* I'm going to say. *Panties* sounds better, it sounds more like what the beauty Berta would wear to cover her luscious and gorgeous—Jesus Christ!

Willie Wepner rushes out from the hallway and lands in a split on the roof of a Chevrolet coupe. I'll do anything, girls! he yells. Anything!

Isabel and Berta are pointing to a photograph of Myrna Loy and talking about it. Perhaps Miss Loy is beginning to show her age, perhaps her gown is particularly striking, perhaps her coiffure reminds them of one shown in a photograph in the window of Andrew's Beauty Parlor.

Although this young rascallion is a moron of purest blood, the Arab says, I begin to feel a small but true pang of pain in my heart for him.

Suddenly, Willie jumps into the air, twists his body so that his head is pointing directly toward the sidewalk and his feet are jabbing upward at the sky, and hooks his right heel over the bottom rung of a fire-escape ladder. Hanging there, upside down, a dazed look invests his face and a golden nimbus surrounds his head. This may be a manifestation of the spirit of Eros which possesses him.

Anything, he says, anything. And I don't even believe what Santo Tuccio said about you, Berta.

Isabel and Berta begin to walk down the street toward Fifth Avenue.

They're going to gaze upon those louts playing at softballs in the playground, the Arab says. They will be requested of for dates. They will go. I see the inception of the hegira toward Teaneck. A cloudy vision, I confess, yet I place most ponderous trust in it.

Lace *panties,* the Drummer sighs, sloshing his fedora back and forth in a filthy puddle with his foot. Did God mean for me to bear this?

How long is Willie going to hang there upside down? Irish Billy says. Maybe we should help him?

Leave him be, the Arab says. He must allow this embroilment of *l'amour* to cool off by itself.

I know a couple other tricks girls, Willie calls after them. Girls? I know a couple other tricks I can do. Girls?

As it is sometimes penned down, the Arab says, "Silence is his only answer."

13 Prescience

The Magician falls into a trance. Let's call it a trance, anyway, the Magician says, to no one at all. Whatever state this may be . . . certainly, it's a famous state that magicians cannot escape.

In the trance—or whatever—Death suddenly appears as the usual skeleton, but without the usual scythe. Instead, Death is clad in shining black armor and sits astride a white charger. In his left hand, or what's left of it, he holds a staff from which flutters a banner, also black, on which is depicted a white rose.

This white rose must signify Life, the Magician murmurs. Or it may simply be an ad for that string of sleazy bars. Certainly Death is banal and tiresome enough to do something like that.

He laughs, but he is quite uncomfortable. He stares at the banner and as he does so the white rose fades and its place is taken by a slowly changing series of printed statements. The Magician tries not to read them, but he is forced to. This is a legitimate trance, inescapable. The statements read:

Richie, on the beach in Miami in his late seventies, coronary occlusion; Dolores, while a nurse supervisor at Mount Sinai, uterine cancer; Big Duck, killed in action with the Seventh Division fourteen miles south of the Yalu River, North Korea; Gene Phillips, a coronary occlusion as he walks one evening to get the first edition of the *News*; Dorothy Phillips, cirrhosis of the liver; Marjorie Phillips, at ninety-one, septicemia, in a nursing home in Oakland, California; Sergeant Nick Carruthers, cause of death unknown; Major Gentry, self-inflicted gunshot wound in a San Francisco rooming house; Master Sergeant James Gentry, mosquito-borne encephalitis contracted at Fort Sam Houston, Texas; Helen Walsh, diabetic coma in the Swedish Hospital, Brooklyn; Curtin, at forty-three, of teaching high-school social studies and bleeding ulcers; Santo Tuccio, colonic cancer in Akron, Ohio; Little Mickey's mother, wood alcohol poisoning in Detroit; Big Mickey, killed in action on Iwo Jima; Red Miller, shot to death by mistake in a saloon near Third Avenue and President Street; Little Mickey, cirrhosis of the liver at fifty; the Arab, of Bright's disease, the history of which fascinates him; Fat Frankie, of leukemia, but not before he sees a grandchild born; Doc Friday, ruptured aneurism, misdiagnosed as a bad blow to the head by an intern at the Jersey City Medical Center; Irish Billy, bacterial endocarditis at sixty-one; Cheech, after sixteen weeks of hospitalization for malignant hypertension; Professor Kooba, of apoplexy, while working on "The Curse"; the Drummer, of hypertension in Kings County; Pepper, of a stroke one week after he joins AA; the Sailor, stabbed to death in a fight over a crap game; Isabel, cause of death unknown; Berta, of viral pneumonia at seventy-six; Miss America, leukemia, which she calls "thin blood"; Tania Crosse *née* Thelma Krulicewicz, thirty pheno-barbitals, eighty-three aspirins, and a pint of vodka; Constance Glynn, in an automobile accident on the way home from Jones Beach with her new husband; Mark Glynn, of rectal cancer, in New York Hospital; Bony Ruth, botulism, source unknown; Ticineti, hepatitis, in his sleep; Cookie LaNord, pernicious anemia, in Reno, Nevada; Mr. Huckle, of a massive coronary after hitting the double for $804.74; Irma Huckle, eighteen years later of tuberculosis; George Huckle, seven years before Irma, of Hodgkin's disease; Henny the bartender, cirrhosis of the liver and a perforated ulcer; Phil Vogler, peritonitis after a routine appendectomy; Mrs. Elkstrom, heat exhaustion, shock, and despair, on the street; Joycie Lunde, with her head in the oven and all the windows closed, at twenty-nine; Burly, uremia and malnutrition, in his cellar; Lizzie Mulvaney, uterine cancer at fifty-three; Jo-Jo, diabetes; Johnny News, of drowning after falling off a fishing boat four miles out of Sheepshead Bay; Eddy the tire man, of a heart attack while cursing at a wrench; Eddy Ellsworth, of an asthma attack in a drive-in movie outside Baltimore.

The last words fade from Death's banner and the white rose appears again. Death rides off. The Magician comes out of his trance.

From this time on, he says, I'll . . . I'll . . . what? What will I do with all this useless information no one wants to hear anyway? I'll look at them differently, anyway. With more kindness. Maybe. But after all I still have to do my magician things. But with a little more kindness.

14 The Postulate of Superposition

I'm telling you, Johnny News says, I was stuck on the ferry for eight hours once in a fog and when it lifted the boat was about fifteen miles past Sandy Hook out in the goddam ocean.

Johnny has taken his usual position just inside the door next to the newsstand, arms folded, on his head a stained fedora. His craven and nondescript dog shivers at his feet. Noteworthy too is his cracked and stained leather jacket.

Oh for Christ sake Johnny, Irish Billy says. I'm talking about something I saw at a country fair and you come up with another ferry story.

More like a fish story, Red Miller laughs.

Johnny leans against the door, smug and silent.

Go ahead Billy, Red says. The ferry can wait out in the fog for a while.

What I wanted to say is I saw this weird guy—maybe it was a woman even—maybe he was some kind of fruit, I saw him at this country fair over in Jersey a few years ago. He's got some kind of white robe on and long blond hair with a gold headband. He's standing at the edge of a pond with one foot in ... I remember it really clear because the sun was going down and shining really bright over some mountains, these Watchung Mountains they call them, far away. I mean it was *shining*. And then he does this I guess trick.

This was an entertainment? the Drummer asks. An act to separate the rubes from their shekels?

No, I don't think so, I mean, nobody paid. We all just watched him.

Maybe more like twenty miles past Sandy Hook, Johnny News says.

Fuck Sandy Hook! Red Miller says. For Christ sake!

This guy, Billy says, this fruit or whatever he was, he has these two cups, one in each hand, and with water in them. O.K. And he's pouring water from one cup into the other.

This is a trick? the Drummer says.

Wait a minute. Wait just a minute. Yeah, he's pouring the water, *but* the water goes from one cup to another and then back to the first cup and then back to the other cup and so on. The guy doesn't really pour the water, the damn water just flows all by itself, he don't move his hands or his arms or anything. They're just still and the water is flowing back and forth from cup to cup. He don't look at anybody, he don't look up. He just stands there with the goddam water zipping back and forth. It was really weird! And I forgot too, this guy's got big phony wings on, like he's impersonating an angel.

A bona fide rube snarer, the Drummer says. I once worked in vaudeville with a guy just like this, the Great Professor Aquarini. He had at least a dozen tricks with water he'd perform. This one was in his repertoire too. He did it by flicking his wrists up and down so it looked like the water was moving all by itself. He was terrific at it, perfect, but who cared? I think he finally packed the act in and teamed up as a clown with a couple of acrobats, the Tumbling Zitos, I believe.

No, Drummer, this guy was on the level. I was standing about five feet away from the guy for about a half an hour. That water flowed, I mean, it just goddam well flowed.

I conducted an experiment like that in the Army with a couple bottles of 3.2 beer, Johnny News says.

Hey terrific, Johnny! Really tee-riff-ic! Red Miller applauds.

God! the Drummer says. As if that leather jacket wasn't an offensive enough eyesore, we get experiments too, plus that mangy dog with his worms and bleary eyes.

I don't even remember Johnny having a dog that ugly, Cheech says. I mean I knew he was ugly, but now that I take a good look at him I see that he is really *ugly*.

You are certainly and irrevocably assured, Billy, the Arab says, that this odd creature did not trick you by diverse sleight-of-hands and feats of legerdemain as known to professional magicians?

I can swear it, Arab. This fruit was strictly the McCoy.

Just a moment, gentlemen, a moment, Doc Friday says. All of this is clearly explainable by the immutable laws of physics.

Physics? the Drummer says. You know about the science of physics? I find this a hard nut to crack, let alone swallow.

Sh, the Arab says. The Doc, as anyone may testify—am I correct?—was a scholar at night school for a few annums a few years back in order to attain to his high school sheepskin. Speak, Doctor, and cast down the beams of learning's light. I pray you.

As I said, Doc Friday says, the laws of physics can explain all these mysteries that are not so mysterious after all. In this case of the strangely flowing liquid, this can be explained by what is called the postulate of superposition. Simply put, this a theorem that states briefly—perhaps, I admit, too briefly—that kinematic vectors may be superposed according to the parallelogram law—although it is well to remember that this method is not convincing when applied to accelerations. When used in such cases it often leads, in fact, to *serious mistakes.*

Wow! the Drummer shouts and tosses his fedora in the air. Wahoo! Kin-e-mat-ic-vec-tors! Wow!

Trenchantly and profoundishly penetrant, the Arab says, grasping Doc Friday by the hand. Incision-like. Even, may I expound addendly, *mordant.*

Doc Friday looks around modestly, then turns to Irish Billy. You didn't suggest, did you Billy, that this oddball homo accelerated the speed of the water's flow from cup to cup, did you?

What accelerated? The water went back and forth back and forth like I told you.

Doubletalk, Red Miller says. The laws of physics, my ass.

Then, Billy, the Doc says, this phenomenon may indeed be

explained through employing the parallelogram law. If you had only jotted down some simple—simple but necessary—data we might well have worked out the principle of this feat right here in the store. A shame.

Jee-zuss Kee-rist! the Drummer says, kicking his hat over the greeting card display. Necessary data! Of course!

It nudges and bunks into the tragic that you did not consider gleaning this data, Billy, the Arab says. Plotting the equation of this aquatical activity might have made for an amusing evening indeed.

Oh God, Billy says. Oh God.

Let's go shoot some Chicago up in Sal's, Billy, Red Miller says, and they exit hurriedly.

I'm telling you, Johnny News says. I performed the exact same experiment with 3.2 beer in the PX.

Yes? the Drummer says. Yes? Then state the parallelogram law! Go ahead, state it.

You state it, Johnny says.

No. You. You, the great experimenter.

Gentlemen, the Arab says. *Pax vobiscum.* Pure science is supposed to stand aloofly remote from heated quarrelsome passions. Am I correct, Doctor?

Absolutely, Doc Friday says. And remotely aloof as well.

You don't have to know these paragram laws to do things, Johnny News says, dragging his dog out into the street.

15 Pittsburgh. The Devil. Yellow Mustard

So Little Mickey's in Pittsburgh, Richie says. What a place to be. I wonder if he'll stay long.

What? Curtin says. Pittsburgh? You're crazy.

I think he's in Pittsburgh. Why do you say I'm crazy?

Because I saw him yesterday crabbing off the 69th Street pier.

Well. Let's just *say* he's in Pittsburgh then. I heard that his mother took him there so they could get away from Santo Tuccio. And another story goes that his aunt took him to live with her there so he could get away from Santo *and* his mother.

I'm telling you—he's here. Where do you get this Pittsburgh business?

Imagine how strange it must be for Little Mickey to be in Pittsburgh. Assuming that he's in Pittsburgh. Which I do. Little Mickey never even went to Queens before.

Goddamnit, he's here in Brooklyn. *You* assume. *You.* I don't assume, I know.

Let's assume that I am in Pittsburgh, Little Mickey says.

Has anybody heard him?

That's what I like to hear. Way to go! Richie says.

We may assume that Richie has heard him.

Assuming this, Little Mickey says, let's further assume that I don't like Pittsburgh. I never even went to the Bronx before.

Not even to see the Yankees? Richie asks.

The Yankees? Who the hell cares about the Yankees? Little Mickey says, from Pittsburgh. Assuming assumptions, the story that assumes that my aunt took me here to get me away from my mother and that rotten son of a bitch rat bastard Santo Tuccio, is the right story.

Aha! Richie says.

I don't like Pittsburgh, Little Mickey says. It's smoky and dark. Pirates fans are loudmouth sore losers. Also, I don't understand the streets and the bus routes. All the names of the streets are funny too. There's no ocean, there's no beaches, you can't go crabbing. Assuming I'm here, which I say I am, because where in hell else am I, I won't be here too long I hope. As soon as my mother throws out that bastard deadbeat she'll remember me and take me home again. I get sick to my stomach a lot here. They don't have any barbecue sandwiches like in the Surprise for a dime. Even if they did you'd get sick from them probably. I have a lot of bad dreams. One I have all the time, over and over.

They call that a recurrent dream, Curtin says. Like in *White Rain* was it called? Where crazy Chester Morris always dreams the same dream. When they find out what it means, bang! he's cured.

I dream of the Devil, Little Mickey says. He's this real ugly bastard with a beard and horns and he's all hairy below the waist with big claws where his feet should be. He's sitting on a perch. Standing in front of him chained to the perch with this big chain around their necks like the chains on the Staten Island ferry I see my mother and Mister Bastard Louse Santo Tuccio. They have big horns just like the Devil and they don't have, well, they haven't got, any clothes on. When Santo starts to smile over at my mother and she starts to smile back I always wake up and I'm crying. I'm ashamed to say I'm crying, but I am. That bastard with his Seagram's 7!

Curtin, Richie says, is this or is this not Little Mickey telling us all these things from Pittsburgh?

I saw him yesterday crabbing off the pier. This is some kind of a trick. Some shitty bush league trick like Ticineti would pull. Or the Magician.

Mick, Richie says. Settle something, will you please? Are you really in Pittsburgh?

Yesterday I had a hot dog and they had this funny yellow

mustard that you can't taste worth a goddam on it, Little
Mickey says.

What about it, Mick? Richie says. Where are you?

Yellow mustard! Little Mickey says. God!

The pier, Curtin says. I even saw him pull up a bunch of
crabs, those little tiny ones.

Yeah, but how about the yellow mustard? Richie says.

What does that mean? Curtin says. The yellow mustard.
What does that mean?

I saw a swell picture, Little Mickey says. *Dr. Ehrlich's Magic
Bullet* with Edward G. Robinson. About this great doctor who
invents some terrific medicine to cure horrible diseases.

You really don't know what a hot dog with lousy yellow
mustard on it means? Richie asks.

No, I don't know what a lousy hot dog with yellow mustard
on it means, Curtin replies.

If I had a different kind of magic bullet, Little Mickey says, I
maybe could meet Santo somewhere . . .

Think! Richie says. Think, damnit. *Yellow* mustard.

My aunt told me to say three extra Hail Marys before I go to
bed and I won't have the dream anymore. So long, guys.

I really don't know what you're driving at, Curtin says.

Mickey's gone anyway, Richie says.

A cheap bush trick, Curtin says. Some real Ticineti bullshit.

Hey, Cheech says. What's this I hear about Little Mickey
moving to Chicago?

Chicago? Curtin says. Now it's Chicago for God's sake.

Cheech, Richie says, if I say I had a hot dog with yellow
mustard on it, what does that mean to you?

It means you probably ate a dog in Pittsburgh for some
goddam reason or other, Cheech answers. What were you doing
in Pittsburgh?

Sweet mother of God! Curtin says, slapping his forehead as
Richie takes a bow.

16 Arab Stew

While it is not my wont to discuss my philosophy of life willy-nilly and in whatever environings at all—particularly on this offensive and odiously cockaroachish street corner, the Arab says, you tempt me sorely to present a briefly compendous sketch of my basic creedo because of your remarks anent the vague nature of good and evil and their effect upon the homo known as sapiens, in short, us.

Go ahead, Fat Frankie says. Me and Big Duck are all ears. Right, Duck?

Big Duck grunts into a glassful of vanilla malted.

Allow and permit me then to present my ideas in simple wise, and the Arab takes up a position midway between the candy counter and the soda cooler. Psychologocal behaviorism suggests with stern puissance that people who tread paths of evil, however disguised, tend to fall, or get pushed, a posteriori, into disrepute. Holistically, and tautologically, this is sometimes given the terminology of "falling on evil days"—odd contradiction! Allow me then, for a brief sec, to give you a rather puerilitous phenomogical example, invented out of wholesome cloth, yet still basically a mere outline. Still and yet, it obtains a certain odd logic that draws me. May I go on?

Onward! Fat Frankie says, keeping his place in *Sexology* with an index finger.

Let us suppose that what mere mankind takes to be success—in terms, of course, of ethical objectivism—may be presented paradigmantically, as an enormously high tower built upon an equally high or maybe perhaps even a higher mountain. This homely image comes from certain obscurant works on dialectic materials, yet it will suffice to serve our purpose. Take then this skyscraper of looming—nirvana!

Holy Moses! Big Duck says.

Upon, so to speak, this beetling scarp, two men, pure products of the raging debate between the forces of appearance and
those of reality, climb up, flushed with victory. They are suc-
cessfully, or so they think, assaulting the tower of Aristotelian
nous with pick and hook and rope and grappanels and heavy-
cleated hobnail clunkish boots, all of which have been made in
the small yet renowned workshop down in the valley that I
might as well entitle Neo-Platonic, Inc., if you follow my anal-
agous metaphor?

Holy cow! Big Duck says.

Go on, Arab, Fat Frankie says. This is getting pretty good.

What's up? Irish Billy asks, entering the store with Curtin.

Sh, Fat Frankie says. The Arab is explaining his philosophy.

Oh boy, Irish Billy says. Oh boy oh boy oh boy.

Saint Augustine says . . . Curtin begins.

I am not speaking of Saint Augustine and all that *cogito* and
such attitudes that replete his thought, the Arab says. May I
continue, *Frankie?*

Of course, Arab.

Irish Billy and Curtin sit at the fountain, grinning.

Our two hearty gents attain the very apex of the mountain,
and versed as they are in arcanic webs of positivist rationale,
enter the tower itself and go clumping up the winding stairs to
the very pinnacle—their journey, though tortoisely slow and
packed full of sighs and panting, is, unfortunately, slopsistic.
Wherefore? you ask. I answer: Who can prove utterly and mis-
feasibly that the stairs are really there? Who can even prove
that the tower itself is really there? Certain disciples and aco-
lytes of Berkeley trekked and trudged this route—and were
never heard from again!

Holy God! Big Duck says.

In all events, they reach the top, despite the possibility of
phantom stairs in a phantom tower that exist as true objects
only in their mucky and muddled and post-Kantian, if I may be
so cruelly wroth as to so term it, brains. Certainly it is clear that

they did not reach the paradigmantic summit of the tower via vitalism.

Surely not, Irish Billy says.

Nor through some spatialistic transfer of Bergsonian *durée*.

Perish the thought! Curtin says.

So let me suspend and hang it—though there is an iota of room for bitter argument—upon the post-Kantian—neo-Kantian, if you prefer.

I prefer, Irish Billy says. Curtin?

I prefer as well, Curtin says. Let's make it neo-Kantian absolutely.

So, the Arab goes on, they have, a fortiori, attained to the good, despite the epistemologicalism of the ethos of evil. Or so they suppose, deluded clods. But chaos and cosmos are not so easily averted from or aborted unto. They rage, if you will allow, in a continuum of metaphysic continuity, regular as clockwork in a superior genre of syllogism of being.

Holy mackerel! Big Duck says.

I couldn't have put it better myself, Duck, Irish Billy says.

The man is a bona fide grade-A Jesuit, Curtin says.

They are at the alp, yes, but only in the *existential* type of way. Certainly, no one would seriously consider these two to inhabit this locale deterministically. Not even devotees and apologists of mysticalism! For what is the efficient cause of their climb? Utilitarianism? Bah! A priori emanationism? Ha! Only a dodderish cretinic would accept such a transparent explanation. No. The only sole thing that might be considered to be the efficient cause of their lumberishly dopey climb is panpsychism!

I might have guessed! Irish Billy says, and punches himself in the head.

What else? Curtin says. What else indeed? Dazzling in its simplicity.

However, when it comes to good and evil and their powerful strength to affect the human animal, the Prime Mover, the Super Being, or whatever monicker you deign to impute to this

supremely brainy intelligence, is not impressed by such shanigans of derring-do. They smack of what is a genus of deviant
pantheism. In effects, this centeristic intelligent creature is not
amused, if I may be for a moment levitous.

By all means be levitous, Curtin says. Levitism is the soul of
discourse.

Pantheism, to this mammoth intelligence, conjures up an-
noying and pestering visions of what was once labeled diabol-
ism, but which less direct and spook-crazy thinkers of moder-
nity like to call the physis and nomos—as if mere semantic-
ness of words can change the face of the Evil One!

Holy Jesus! Big Duck says.

Assuming then that the two antagonists, good and evil, are
inextrically locked, in Spinozic terms, in the psyches of the two
tower climbers, huffing and puffing, there is nothing for a self-
respecting Prime Mover to do but to harness the powers of the
cosmos in order to assert his infinite rights, not only to his absolute hemegony over monism but also over plurism. And so
what is the only recourse, the only route left to this brute force
that oversees the entire shebang? Mind you, I speak not of the
Prime Mover of Thomists' ideas, but the entire absolute idea of
all things, the Supreme Chief!

Holy shit! Big Duck says.

What, for Christ sake? Irish Billy says.

This power decides *against* the triumph of evil, even though
this evil does not or will not actually triumph except in that it
will survive as part and parcels of the good. Its survival is disgusting to the Supreme Chief, no matter how you cut it, and
more or less fills him up crammed with nausea. So he ropes and
lassoes the great destructive powers of the cosmos like Jupiter
of aeons back and blasts and cannonades the tower with a bolt
of lightning, a thunderbolt of huge and intractable strength, a
Jovean bolt from the blue, if you will, since these men are
sotted up with hubris, they reek disgustingly with it hidden
underneath their savantish masks, and knocks them ass over
heels out of the tower and into the pit of Cartesian fumble and

erratic mistakes. To hew true to the metaphorical comparative we have constructed, jerry-built though it may appear to a naked eye, the thunderbolt from the blue heaven is an indexical sign of the Absolute Idea. Thus, Frankie, my philosophy has worked out the curious business of good and evil. I admit with humbleness and hanging head to a loose end here and there and now and again, but there it is, in essentialness.

Fantastic! Fat Frankie says.

Cogent and incisive, Irish Billy says. Big Duck?

It scares me, Big Duck says.

It scares me, too, Duck, Billy says. This, however, is how truth works. It strikes the eye of the soul like a blinding white light. It is nature's own bomb. Hey, Curtin, what about it? You're—

Strangely silent? Curtin says. Yes I am. Strangely and even—eerily?—silent.

Yes, Curtin, the Arab says. I am acrave with curiosity about your opinion.

Well, Curtin says. I agree in essence, and yet, and yet . . . the whole exposition seems to me merely a rehash of the adiaphoristic controversy.

The *what!* the Arab almost shouts.

The adiaphoristic controversy. So it seems to me in any case.

Rubbish! the Arab says. Trash and effluvia! This is my own idea, worked out in its basic tenets and saliencies over years of silent and glum brooding on life. You made this thing that you just uttered up.

The Arab leaves the store, scowling and muttering.

Curtin, my friend, Billy says. What *is* this controversy? Its essential tenets and saliencies, I mean. I ask in all humbleness and hanging head.

The adiaphoristic controversy? It's an ancient stoic argument over whether or not people from the land of Araby should hang out in corner candy stores.

It's the part about the lightning that scares me, Big Duck says. I never did like lightning.

17 Her Name a Star

In Hungary once, or in Bulgaria or Estonia—somewhere—Professor Kooba was young and the world seemed a less intransigent—good word—place. At least I imagine this was the case, Richie says.

You speak the truth, Professor Kooba replies. He seems utterly exhausted today. The August heat has emptied the streets of all save the iceman and some boys sitting in the shade of Flynn's Tavern playing Knuckles.

Let's say you knew love, Richie goes on. Did you know love?

Who doesn't? Even the Arab, the Drummer, and Fat Frankie have known it. Futile, for the most part, I admit. Bitter, impossible, wounding also, I admit. But definitely and absolutely there. Yes, I have known love.

Do you want to tell me? Pass the time?

No. But I will tell you about a vision of love, or should I say a memory of love, that often comes to me. It's so clear that I distrust it and feel that it could never have happened. Yet it comes over and over, always the same. As a matter of fact, it seems so absolutely legitimate that I have never dared include it in "The Curse." That, as you know, is a book of fact, a book of truth, and this vision of mine is too good to be true. Kooba pauses and lights a Wings.

Let's hear it true or not.

The vision is abrupt, that is, there is no hint as to how things begin or how they turn out. Sudden. Suddenly it's before me and I'm transfixed by its beauty. You understand that in this vision I'm a participant, but my role is that of a viewer. Yet I know that I *belong* there. I'm not playing the part of a Peeping Tim.

Peeping Tom.

Yes, all right. The vision is before me. A beautiful blond young woman, completely nude, is in a field, down on one knee. She is my beloved—I know that she is my beloved—but she doesn't look at me. I feel, as the vision gets clearer, as if we have just made love. Yet I also feel, very sadly, that this beautiful woman has forgotten me and that I'll never see her again.

The Sailor enters the store and buys a Trojan, five loose Old Golds, and a Forever Yours. Hey Kooba! he says. Getting much? Hot enough for you? He leaves, and Kooba looks after him.

Even the Sailor, he says, may have such memories or visions as this, but they leave him—or they would leave him—enraged at the fact of what his life really is. Beauty is really insupportable, after all. It's much simpler to do without it altogether.

Professor . . . ?

Ah, yes. Forgive me. Her breasts are youthfully firm, the nipples rosy pink, her body is golden brown from the sun. She kneels in such a way, out of modesty, that her pudendum is not visible to me, but I know it like I know—this hat, he says, taking from his head an old straw with a rip in the crown. It is delicately and symmetrically haired. The field is sparsely dotted here and there with small, shy red flowers. On a hill over her left shoulder there is a tree in whose branches a large and rather ugly bird has just alighted. My love does not look at me or at anything else except a pitcher of water which, for some reason, she is pouring from into a pool just in front of her. In her left hand there is an identical pitcher and she is also pouring its contents out—perhaps inadvertently—but onto the ground beside her. This pool . . . this pool . . .

Maybe she's drawing the water?

Forget the water! Kooba snaps, annoyed. It became clear to me years ago that the water and the pitchers have nothing to do with anything. It's the pool! The pool itself. In such a field, on such a day, one would expect the water in this pool to be a clear blue, maybe even what you call azure—or sapphire. But it's grey, grey and icy, and I know, as I see this lovely creature, that she's drunk this water and it's made her forget everything, like the water in that mythology, the water from that river, I forget what it's called. I look at her, my heart is bursting, churning with love and adoration, burning. She is intent on her meaningless labors. But I decide to speak. As I do, my words change from sound to images, to real pictures. Her beloved and beautiful name, which I speak, but which I will not allow to pass my lips in *this* foul world, is transmuted into a golden-yellow star of eight points, one for each letter. My other words, which I always forget because of the sudden blazing appearance of the star in the air over her lovely head, turn into smaller, silver stars, each one also having eight points. They surround the golden star. Professor Kooba falls silent.

And? Richie asks. What happens then?

Nothing happens. The vision fades away. I'm alone in my room or wherever the hell I am. She exists among the dead. I am certain of this. Why am I certain of this? Because I'm certain that this is a true story—I mean a *true* story, much more than mere facts, what *happened,* and so forth. I am certain that this lovely woman married, had children, grew old, and died. She never remembered me again after that particular afternoon, wherever and whenever it was.

And this was in the old country?

In the old country. And in a language that I have almost forgotten. The Professor sighs and grinds his Wings out. Blinded by beauty! Absolutely! And now I have to listen to people like the Sailor buy prophylactics, which he cannot pronounce, in order to satisfy himself with some slut in the park or on some filthy roof. Satisfy! Ha!

Can I buy you a Pepsi, Professor? Or something?

Professor Kooba walks to the magazine rack and gestures toward the movie magazines, from the covers of which smile, pout, and scowl erotically sex goddesses, sex bombs, and starlets, all nearly hysterically vivacious.

Pigs and sluts, Kooba murmurs. Sluts and trash and pigs. He turns toward Richie. The form of her kneeling body, he says. The exquisite form of . . . the strange icy heat from that golden star. Her remote and dreaming face. All too clear, all too clear to be merely—a fact! Yes, yes, Richie, yes. I'll have a Tropical Punch, if you please.

18 Black Coffee, First Love,
the Lake, Etc.

I don't care, Doc Friday says. You think I care about what you think about what I say? Or anybody damn else? I know what I know. Too goddam subtle for you people.

Who said anything, Doc? the Drummer says. All I said was you look like you could use some black coffee.

Black coffee, black coffee! That's all anybody can say when a man has a few drinks. Black coffee! Like a goddam scene in some dumb old movie they resurrect to life like a goddam zombie with Jack Holt or some other old fart out in the jungle, Bruce Cabot, with a pith helmet on. Here, drink this black coffee, they say. God!

All I said, I mean, all I meant . . .

You meant: you're drunk. Well, why not? Why the hell not? Why should I be sober? So I can stand here and talk about opening a heliport with you to deliver greeting cards to the suckers who will buy the goddam shit? Hear your friend, the Arab, talk his twisty words like he knows what he's saying? Or how about Kooba there, at his old stand behind the godforsaken soda cooler, read me selected passages from his damn unfinished novel, saga, whatever he calls it?

I don't read to those who have no wish to hear, Professor Kooba says. Particularly to you, Doc. I know how *you* feel about the art of letters.

Hear, hear, the Doc says. You and your stories. Not a decent goddam one in the bunch. You should have experienced that. My mother. You ever imagine a big moon waxing? A night made for young lovers? A night you take a girl for a walk down to the lake, sweet young girl? Sweet night?

"The Curse," my friend, Kooba says, has amorous passages aplenty. Aplenty.

Handled with taste and restraint, right Professor? Irish Billy says. Ho hum. Ho ho ho hum.

Really Doc, I didn't mean by black coffee any kind of insult, the Drummer says. We all take a drink.

But while you sit there, Doc Friday says, and you can smell her perfume, and the night. The night is silent. Absolutely silent. It's silent. Like the old song. You know? Are the stars out tonight? Well, hell, yes, plenty of goddam stars but the moon's so bright might as well not be any at all.

Taste. And restraint, Irish Billy says and gets a penny's worth of pumpkin seeds out of the machine.

I observe candidly that good Doctor the Honorable Friday is at his cups again! the Arab says

At his cups, the Doc says. Right. There you go, Arab. *Le mot juste.* Terrific!

He's mad about my mentioning some black coffee maybe at the Royal, the Drummer says.

But! Doc Friday says. But! Something happens but you don't know what. You feel that even though at this minute life is absolutely and terrifically—what? Possible. Right. That life is absolutely possible. You *know* this and yet, and but, while you *know* this you also know—something happens and you also know you're not going to achieve anything with this girl. Like we say in America here, you're not going to get goddam *anywhere.* Christ. You remember forever how her mouth tasted. You know, with the moon shining down and love is all around you. Oh yeah, yeah yeah yeah. Go ahead, call it mystical bullshit, but I'm telling you. My mother said it a long time ago when I was a kid. Something passes.

The sapient wisdom of mothers is legendary fare, the Arab says. In a word, they know. What, by the way, is that *mot juste,* Doc?

After years, the Doc says, the feeling that whatever you think you have or had down there by the goddam beautiful lake, that's probably still there but who the hell could bear to look at it now, all of us so goddamned old now, she must be forty, for Christ sake. But I'm telling you, she was a pearl, sweet sixteen.

The memory of first love . . . Kooba begins.

Oh Christ, who's talking about first love? the Doc says. I'm talking, I'm talking about having it there and feeling it over before it even damn well begins. Jesus Christ, Kooba.

What was that movie with the guy with the girl who was something, I can't remember, Santo Tuccio says. You know he's about to fall in love with her even though he's married. I can't remember.

Santo, I don't think the Doc means precisely that, the Drummer says.

Santo can't remember the movie because he only saw it eight times, Irish Billy says.

I mean, damn it, Doc Friday says, I mean it's only later, like tonight when I was down at Gallagher's with all these goddam assholes watching Uncle Miltie with the grey beards on his fucking jokes, I found this image for what happened years ago. Jesus, it scared me almost sober. Almost. You're with this lovely, lovely girl, just a kid, both of you just kids, you don't know a goddam thing, and like I said before, the whole thing is possible. The moon and the lake. And then you get this feeling that it's all dead.

I only saw that movie *twice*, Billy, Santo says. It had a lake in it too like the Doc mentions. Or maybe the Ocean.

These things, Santo, the Arab says, are merest supernumary addendas. But trifling footnotes and glossies.

So tonight—listen, Kooba—you can put it in your goddam novel, the Doc says, tonight I get this image made me almost sober. These dogs, these horrible mangy dogs, stand on the shore of the lake howling at the moon, terrible howls. And this desolate path. Leading off to these bleak grim mountains. Out of the lake comes this horrible thing like a slimy lobster but it's not really a lobster, a kind of big spider coming up to—Jesus! to eat the dogs. Two towers there where like the lifeguard platforms are but you know somebody is in there looking down at you and the girl, he's pushing these buttons to fuck up your life, to fuck up everything that's possible. But there's really nothing there, it's just that this is the feeling that you get and goddamnit, tonight this feeling turns itself into this horrible scene right at the bar in Gallagher's. That's what happened. Now you see, right? Now any damn fool can understand why the moon is supposed to make you crazy. Jesus Christ, she must be forty now. I wonder if she felt this too like I did? You see what I mean?

Of course, Kooba says. And thank you for the idea but "The Curse" is to be wholly my own thoughts and experiences, Doc.

In literature, this narration of the Doc's image is known as an object of correlation, I believe, the Arab says.

You want to buy me that black coffee now, Drummer? the Doc asks.

Sure. Good. And a bow tie too.

Doc? *Mot juste?* the Arab asks.

19 The Drummer, Discovered Alone

Well, she left me. How long ago it was. Or seems it was anyway. You're not supposed to be able to remember faces clear? I remember hers! Like she was here next to me. When she wore that black dress. For what? I can't remember anymore. Something about money. Who the hell knows how to earn money? Is this the be-all and end-all of life? I could have shown her—other things. Look at the Arab! A great mechanic who quit for his studies and his wife left him too. Men of a higher calling. Schemes—schemes. That was her great goddam paradigm of a word. Schemes. Every goddam thing I did was not a job or an interest or anything else but part of a goddam master scheme. The humiliation, that she thought I was just a schemer like a truck driver or a mailman for Christ sake. The dog act she didn't like. Too silly. All right. It wasn't a big thing but they were good dogs, especially the little fox terrier. Then there was the novelty act with a little patter, some nice, I mean it was really nice soft shoe, a couple of nice old songs but nice arrangements, modern, then the finale with her coming out for the ending together with me on "Shine On Harvest Moon," to knock the rubes' eyes out. Small, I admit, small but with some class, a classy kind of small. No good finally either! She didn't want everybody staring at her in tights and opera stockings. Miss Modesty. As if she was showing her bare ass off, Christ! She didn't even show it to me after a year or two. Once that time I broke my foot in the dark in that fleabag in Utica. Schenectady. Right. Not even a little light from the bathroom! No, the goddam blackness of stygian darkness for Christ sake. The drumming which was also no soap. The jobs were few and far between. Lousy little clubs at crummy lakes in New Jersey, those corny bands always with an accordion and the polkas. Oh yes! And I had to *practice* too much! What was I a goddam Toscanini I don't have to practice? With some luck and a break or two who knows? Lester Lanin maybe? Vincent Lopez? Maybe even a permanent spot with them, or even, Christ, Blue goddam Barron. I could read with the best of them, anything at all, still can. Too much drumming. Too much practice. How do we eat while you wait for a job? And blah-blah. Couldn't have got into those damn tights by then with all the potato chips and beer, damn lucky vaudeville was dead. And how can I listen to Lux with your drumming? And Mr. District Attorney? And Fibber fucking McGee and Molly! The merchant marine—no good either with her. First she can't stand me always here with the drumming, then she can't stand it with me being away on trips. Spent the money on clothes and Chink food anyway as fast as I goddam made it. Quit! Quit! Quit! For Christ sake, we were better off with the mutts and the novelty act. The tune changed quick, very quick. She forgot about the tights all of a sudden and showing her legs to the hayseed scumbags in the first row. They look up my crotch, she says. Then, all of a sudden—we were better off, we were better off. Don't go to sea no more, we'll manage. Greeting cards? Selling *greeting cards!* What a joke, what a humiliation! I can't go around telling people my husband sells greeting cards! Jesus Christ. You should have kept shipping out, why the hell did you stop shipping out? So you could go around from door to door with your damn sample boxes of greeting cards? The rubes looked up *her* crotch? Hers? All the beer and chips, God almighty. When I first started to mention the heliport seriously that's when she figured I was completely apeshit and packed up. But it could have worked fine, by Christ, and it can *still* work. All a man needs is a little capital, that's all. Maybe if we'd had a kid. I used to tell her—what?—I used to tell her, a nice house out in the country on the Island or in Jersey with a garden with all those big flowers, those big tall daisies—sunflowers! That was it. A lot of sunflowers and the sun shining down like it does in the comics with a smiling face and all those rays shining out of it. And our kid with goddam flowers in his hair, free as a bird. Free, do what he wants, no novelty acts or bullshit dogs running up and down ladders and hiding their eyes for *him*. I could tell him a lot of things, give him books, he could talk to the Arab and Kooba. Give him a horse even. Sure, she said, a horse. Make sure it's a white horse like Gene Autry or the Lone Ranger. Well, why not? He could ride around in the sunshine. Why not a white horse? She yelled as soon as I mentioned it. Quick. A kid? Here? While you sit up half the night drumming? A kid whose mother used to have to expose her private parts of her body to strangers drooling in their Cracker Jacks and doing Christ knows what else in the dark? No thanks! We'll get him a grey horse! I'd say, a joke. Something, some joke. Get him anything he wants but just let's *have* him. A kid whose father sells greeting cards? Can you imagine what the other kids in school would say? Ride under the smiling shining sun, naked on his white or grey or any goddam color he wants horse, flowers in his hair. Let him carry a big red banner even, for God's sake, to show the world. Looking up into her crotch! Jesus Christ! Packed up the one goddam suitcase with the broken lock, how many years ago? Let him ride any goddam color horse he wants. Anything he wants! Harvard. Princeton. Yale. Massachusetts Institute of Technicians. Ivy College. Anything. Silk ties and convertibles. She *could* have stopped with the beer and all the other shit she swilled. Till she couldn't even get her girdle on and wouldn't buy a bigger size. *That* was my fault too, oh yeah. I *made* her eat all those chips and cake. I can't stand you—and then she slammed the door like in a goddam movie and took a cab Christ knows where. And with the last sawbuck in the house. She was something in those black tights and opera stockings. Anything he wanted. Riding naked in the sun with flowers in his hair and a big red banner, those big sunflowers in the garden. Make sure it's a *white* horse, she said, Mr. Rockefeller. Something in those tights. So many years ago now. I mean really *something*.

20 Free Movies

The gas station's outdoor movie tonight is an Abbott and Costello and also how to put out an incendiary bomb, Little Mickey says.

That's what *he* thinks, the Magician smiles.

I gleaned up the informational data earlier this week, the Arab says, that it was, on the contrary tack, some stelliar pair of Hollywood thespians in a comedy of romance and genteel laughter.

And that's what *he* thinks, the Magician says.

Too many of the vox populi milling about, the Drummer says.

Goddam air-raid wardens couldn't put out a goddam cigarette, Irish Billy says.

You coming over, Pepper? Fat Frankie asks.

Me? Who the hell wants to see Bette Davis? Every time I go to the movies all I see is Bette Davis, Bette Davis. It's like looking at my wife by now.

Bette Davis? Fat Frankie says. It's a Western.

And you know my comment on *that* remark, the Magician says.

Santo Tuccio, in the front row center for two hours, says, I don't give a good goddam *what's* playing.

The twilight deepens, as it will. Men in white helmets and armbands move about the gas station.

Couldn't blow out a match! Irish Billy sneers. Incendiary bombs, my ass.

I find personally the cinema to be stultificating, the Arab says. But still.

But still, it's free, right? Pepper says.

73

Let's go! Santo shouts, stamping his feet. It's dark enough!

Not that it costs nary a copper, Pepper, the Arab says. That is not it at all. Such base considerations are not of my ken. Although at core an effusion of moron-ness, yet I find the cinema highly preceptive, and thusly instructive, in so far as terminologic of the regular type of American mind.

And besides, he likes Abbott and Costello, Irish Billy says.

Abbott and who? the Arab sniffs.

Abbott and who, Irish Billy says. Abbott and goddam incendiary bomb! Look at those jerks with their tin hats on. Couldn't put out a spark, for Christ sake.

Abbott and Costello appear on the screen above the gas station's fence.

That's a Western? Santo Tuccio says.

I don't see any Clark Gables or Bette Davises either, the Arab says. Good.

The Magician stands at the edge of the crowd in an air-raid warden's helmet and armband. He winks an eye and Abbott and Costello are transformed into an angel blowing a long horn. Summoning, perhaps.

This looks like the handiwork of the Magician, the Drummer says.

He's more fun than a barrel of monkeys, Pepper says. The goddam bum.

The angel, dazed of eye, continues to blow his horn, summoning, summoning.

Its horn! the Magician says. Not *his* horn!

I never saw this picture, Santo Tuccio says. That guy looks like Leslie Howard, though.

The audience stands and begins to jeer at the screen.

That's not Abbott *or* Costello, Little Mickey says. Hey!

That angel just doesn't strike me right, the Magician mutters.

This is maybe the incendiary bomb movie, Irish Billy says. This angel is going to set the whole gas station on fire by blowing flames out of that horn he can't play.

It can't play! the Magician says.

His musicological expertism does leave a pittance or an ort or two to be desired, I admit and confess, the Arab says.

Its expertism! the Magician says. Damn it! This is not what I intended, he grumbles. I had thought to fill these plain folk with plenty of fear and awe.

I'm sorry, the angel says. I don't know how to play this trombone or whatever it is. I didn't *ask* for this.

This is absolutely a bush-league angel, Irish Billy says. Jesus. This magician has got to be the biggest dummy in the whole magician's outfit.

Fill them with awe! Fill them with trembling and awe! And fear! the Magician whispers, concentrating on the image on the screen.

Bravely, the angel keeps blowing sour notes on his horn. The audience is shouting and hissing.

It sure ain't Randolph Scott, Santo Tuccio says. Maybe Joel McCrea? But his nose ain't big enough.

Even a stupid air-raid incendiary bomb movie would beat hell out of this, Irish Billy says.

Pepper drifts away. Even Bette Davis, he says. Fucking idiot Magician! Yeah! You! he yells at an air-raid warden. You! The air-raid warden looks around, puzzled, since he is not the Magician, who has left.

The angel disappears from the screen and his place is taken by—

Its place! the Magician shouts. *Its* place! *Its* place!

Its place is taken by two actors spraying water on a burning incendiary bomb while a deep voice describes proper procedures.

I think maybe *that's* Joel McCrea, Santo Tuccio says. Manly voice. Strength.

I think it's Bette Davis, Irish Billy says. You jerk. You think Joel McCrea would have anything to do with the air-raid wardens and their two-bit fucking movie? Wise up.

The audience starts to leave, grumbling. Somebody throws a

pop bottle at the air-raid wardens on the screen, but they continue busily scattering sand.

I won't be around here for a while, the Magician says. What a mess.

One might enlabel this balmy summer eve a fiasco, the Arab says.

I'm going to sit right goddam here and see the movie anyway, Santo says. I don't give a damn if it's The Three Stooges or Deanna Durbin or whoever it is.

Hey Santo! Irish Billy says. If you see Deanna Durbin give her a great big kiss for me, O.K.? You know where.

Santo sits stolidly, his eyes on the busy air-raid wardens, the sole remaining member of the audience. Take a flying fuck for yourself! he yells back, without moving.

I have entertained on varied occasions the opinion that this neighborhood may be too much for the Magician, the Arab says. Grossly crass. Overwhelmingly craggedly rough and unliberal.

Still, the Drummer says, you have to admit that the angel was rather wanting. Rather . . . inane? And simpleton-like. And on who can the blame be lain for the ill-feeling stirred up if not the Magician.

Not *my* fault if I can't play the trombone, the angel says, flying, of course, through the starry heavens.

True, the Arab says. I fear that we have but given as goodly as we have received, unfortunate and tragedic as it may be in terms of the hapless wizard's reputation and honor. That truly bathotic angel—he was, as they say, the ultimate straw.

It! It! It was the ultimate straw! the Magician shouts, perhaps from a cave somewhere in the wilderness. Damn fools.

Did you hear something? the Arab asks.

No, the Drummer says. Except for Santo across the street.

Anything! Santo yells. Anything! Gloria Jean or Kenny Baker even, even a Pete Smith I already seen twenty times! Anything! Ah, come on!

21 A Small Adventure

Little Mickey, who has fought the drudgery and meanness of his life to what is called a standstill, despite . . .

Little Mickey, who has fought against the drudgery and meanness of his life with what is called enormous courage, cannot summon up the strength to confront the fact that Santo Tuccio, now working steadily as an usher at the Roxy, has virtually moved in with his mother and himself and insists that Mickey call him "Dad." Little Mickey decides to run away.

Had life been different for Little Mickey, Richie says, he might be having the sort of childhood that could lead to competition in the Olympics.

Ha! the Arab says.

He might be grooming himself to become, in time, a new Willie Pep.

Preposterous! Fat Frankie says.

Richie falls silent and buys himself a Frank's Orange Nectar. Maybe I'd be better off, he says, if I insisted on an absolute prose. What about Conrad?

What? the Arab says. Who? The name reverberates no memories up in my cerebrum.

I don't know from it either, Fat Frankie says. Is he the guy used to steal rags from the junkman?

Forget it, Richie says.

Little Mickey ran away? Doc Friday asks. Imagine him then, if you will . . .

"If you will" is an example of absolute prose, Richie says.

Like Conrad, Doctor, the Arab adds. Yes, yes, now I seem to fasten and batten on the name. Of course! Conrad.

Imagine him, the Doc continues, if you will, in a coat from

the Salvation Army that must have been made to fit Finn
MacCool, yellow good-morning shoes on his tired feet, shoes, I
need hardly mention, that were stolen from the extensive Sunday wardrobe of Santo Tuccio, Esquire, on a stick over his
shoulder, in the time-honored fashion of Pete the Tramp, a
handkerchief bundle, inside which is a peanut butter and jelly
sandwich wrapped in wax paper. Somewhere he has found a
white paper carnation and he carries it in his left hand.

On Mother's Day you wear a red carnation if your mother is
alive and a white one if she's dead, Irish Billy says.

The young man here is astoundedly versed in matters of alle-
gorical natures, the Arab says.

You've hit on something important, Billy, the Doc says. A
white carnation. You see, of course, what Little Mickey is *saying!*

It's what you might call a kind of absolute prose, Richie says.

Exactly! We may also assume that had he a dog, that dog
would have gone along with his master, in the time-honored
fashion of all prose, absolute or otherwise. At least it's nine to
five. Richie?

Correct!

I should guess that this dog would have been, had there been
one, a small white dog, one that would gambol about Little
Mickey's yellow good-morning shoes.

Like Zero? Fat Frankie asks. That would hit the nail on the
head, along with the bundle à la Pete the Tramp.

Exactly so! Doc Friday says. Terrific, Frankie.

Vulgarity and swilly trash, the Arab says, picking his teeth
with a matchbook.

But, Doc Friday says, Little Mickey has no dog. In any event,
imagine him leaving, walking the Brooklyn streets, crossing
the Brooklyn Bridge, treading the streets of old Manhattan,
going through the Holland Tunnel or over the George Washington Bridge, and emerging into the great world!

Where's my goddam good shoes? Santo Tuccio shouts. I got

to usher today and where's my shoes? Where the hell are they?

Big Mickey, enraged and miserable because of Little Mickey's disappearance, cavorts on one foot on the roof ledge of an apartment house. In daring death, he perhaps feels that he is honoring his friend.

He'll return, the Arab says. In the absolute prose that our amicable friend, Richie, and his colleague in letters studies, Mr. Conrad, speak about and thrash out, it is the rage, as well as it being necessitous, to return.

You're right, Doc Friday says. Wholeness! Harmony!

And a touch of radiance, Richie adds.

22 Willing Suspension of Disbelief

Major Gentry, or so the story goes, has been drummed out of the corps because of some hideous infraction of military regulations, involving, some say, Sergeant Nick Carruthers.

Better than average, Curtin says. But I don't like the antiquated phrase, "drummed out of the corps." Richie?

I have a hunch what's coming and if it's what I think it is, "drummed out of the corps" will do nicely. My objection is to "hideous infraction." That doesn't sound like army talk to me.

Who says it's army talk? Doc Friday says. It's the opening of a Kiplingesque tale, perhaps. What about that old willing suspension of disbelief?

Major Gentry, with a five-day growth of beard, in ragged and stained clothes and broken shoes, is earning an honest dollar working for Eddy the tire man.

Eddy the tire man? Doc Friday asks. Did I say Kipling? Forgive me. I must have been insane.

Willing suspension of disbelief, Curtin says. You said it.

Major Gentry's work entails rummaging through garbage cans in order to rescue deposit bottles for Eddy, as well as rags, old shoes, sodden newspapers, tin cans, and anything else that might conceivably be put to use by the flat fixer and all-around drunken reprobate.

Speaking of such, Gene Phillips just fell in the gutter over there by the Baptist church, Richie says. If he's not careful they'll throw a white robe on him and feed him some vanilla ice cream.

He rummages, muttering, eyes glazed, his gnarled yet still-powerful hands manfully clutching at the mounds of detritus that they encounter. Moving almost as if in a state of trance, he goes from garbage can to garbage can.

There's something about a soldier, Curtin says.

Into the tattered pocket of his overcoat, or ulster, or benny, he quickly thrusts a ripped and ragged pair of pink drawers trimmed with a narrow edging of white lace.

Somewhere then, Doc Friday says, there beats beneath that monumental disaster of a wreck, a passionate heart!

But—hello! What's this?

"Hello what's this?" Curtin says. Maybe this is a Sherlock Holmes story?

Hello! What's this? Major Gentry says, scrabbling feverishly in the leaking and odorous can, disregarding the pain in his gouty, hamlike fists.

Oh Christ, Richie says. Now he's *talking*. You give these guys an inch . . .

A curious picture! Major Gentry says. His hands tremble as he brings the faded photograph close to his rheumy eyes. I wish I had remembered my spectacles. Still . . . I can just make the image out. My God!

Mr. Phillips is making his way hand over hand along the Baptist church's iron-railing fence. Suddenly he sees Major Gentry, raises a hand in fraternal greeting, loses his balance and falls again. The pastor appears at the door of the church.

Oh no! Richie says. Guess who the pastor turns out to be?

It seems quite impossible, yet the pastor appears to be Sergeant Nick Carruthers, late of the 31st Infantry Division.

My God! Major Gentry says. *My—God!*

A Description of the Photograph: A young woman, her full breasts bared, a slight smile on her face, appears to be dancing, or running, or hopping up and down on one foot. In each hand she holds a candle, or perhaps a wand.

A wand? Aha! Doc Friday says. So—this is, after all, the Magician's doing. The story, everything. I thought it was unbearably tedious and corny.

Enter, my son, Pastor Carruthers says to Gene Phillips. We have a beautiful white robe for you and also a nice plate of vanilla ice cream.

Just a little half-glass gin, Father, Gene Phillips says. Say, look familiar.

The Description, Continued: Her—ah—her—sex . . . is modestly covered by a long and loose scarf that is draped over her body from shoulder to waist to belly to buttocks and thence to the ground. Her hair is coiffed in a tight permanent wave.

I am not of the Roman faith, my son, Pastor Carruthers says. You may call me Pastor or Mister or even Nick. But not Father, ha ha.

No beer, Father, no beer. Just a little little gin. Just a little half glass give me a little steam get home to the family.

My God! Major Gentry says yet again, his legs quaking beneath him. This is surely First Lieutenant Anna Gornishe of the Women's Army Corps! How things are rushing back to me! How memory smarts and stings! Oh Anna, Anna! In a "saucy" pose—a "spicy" pose. This must have been "snapped" that night in the Officers' Club when I left early only to bump into—into—oh Nick! Oh Sergeant Carruthers!

Where is that lousy stinking bum? Eddy the tire man says.

Major Gentry's eyes blaze and his shoulders square. His face becomes as handsome and stern as that of his boyhood hero, General Custer, Old Yellow Hair himself, his eyes now piercing as those of a sage old eagle. Power surges through his frame, making him as strong as a young bull, and he becomes as fierce in his determination as a proud lion.

This winner should be living in some other neighborhood, Curtin says.

For the thousandth time, gentlemen, Doc Friday says, forgive my use of the term "Kiplingesque."

I have the strength, stamina, fortitude, courage, and pride to go on with my work! Major Gentry shouts to the heavens. And his arms become a veritable blur of speed as he scavenges madly for his kindly benefactor and employer.

We may even have some pistachio left from Sunday's Bible meeting, Pastor Carruthers says. Though I can't vouch for how frozen it still is, ha ha.

What an odd neighborhood, First Lieutenant Gornishe mutters. Still, an officer is created to serve. When I think of the boys at Fort Hood or Camp Pickett a chill infests my heart and also racks my frame.

So there you are. You fucking bum! Eddy says to Major Gentry. And I'll take that dirty picture of that naked broad and also the pair of lady's drawers you got in your pocket. Wise guy.

Major Gentry falls to his knees and thanks Eddy for rescuing him from remorse and temptation, in that order.

We would have been better off at the Stanley, Curtin says.

Well, O.K., Father. O.K., O.K. Then I'll take a beer if you're going to be, if you're happy to be—certainly and absolutely, Gene Phillips says.

Come in, my son, Pastor Carruthers says. I have an old officer's uniform you can change into so your wife won't know who you are when you finally reel in. Good idea?

O.K. O.K.! No vanilla please?

Hmm, Lieutenant Gornishe muses. I wonder why I'm ordered to report to this little Baptist church here? No matter. An officer—

An officer is created to serve! Doc Friday says. All right, Curtin, come on Richie, let's go to the Stanley. This might all just sort of end if there's nobody here to listen. I hope and trust.

They leave. The corner is deserted.

Major Gentry, trembling with gratitude, is dipping a hard stale crust of bread into

23 Be Prepared

It doesn't surprise me at all, Irish Billy says. Not at all—I always suspected that all adults in the Boy Scouts were crazy. No, not at all. Did I say "adults"?

Surprise or not, Billy, Doc Friday says, it's the truth. The man became another crazed Swede, just like thousands of others.

Carl Krigmann is a Norwegian! Big Duck says, proudly. One might even say he throws his chest out.

How did this mania come about? Billy asks.

How, I can't tell you, the Doc says. *What* . . . that I can tell you.

He was a good Scoutmaster, Big Duck says. I don't care what you bastards think. He was a goddam good Scoutmaster.

Duck, do us a favor and buy a Milky Way and feed your famished acne, Irish Billy says. I want to hear this without testimonials from you—even though I know you were a First Class Scout.

Star! Big Duck says. A Star Scout. With only two more Merit Badges to make Life.

Irish Billy looks around at Big Duck, he studies him. He shakes his head and looks back at Doc Friday. Go ahead, Doc.

Are Duck's raging patriotic fires quenched? May I go on?

Duck grumbles, buys a Mrs. Wagner's pineapple pie and sits at the counter.

You know, of course, Doc Friday says, Crazy Krigmann was always slightly abnormal. "Disturbed," as they call it.

Sure, I've heard the stories. The semaphore contests he organized from Brooklyn to Staten Island.

You heard about the mapmaking classes in Bliss Park in snowstorms? Or teaching the new kids to build fires in torrents of rain? Then he fails them when they can't do it, or whatever they do in the bottle suckers.

Bottle suckers, my ass! Big Duck says, his mouth filled with pie. The Boy Scouts will make a man out of you.

Ignoring this ruffian interruption, Doc Friday says, the gentleman quietly continued conversing with his companion.

And, Irish Billy says, his companion gave him his rapt and undivided attention—also ignoring the meatball intrusion from the peanut gallery.

From the cheapo seats, Doc Friday says.

From deepest bleachers, Billy adds.

You know, I take it, Doc Friday says, about the swimming lessons in the bay among the garbage and the navies—the *armadas*— of Trojans and Sheiks?

I've heard.

The ten-mile hikes of which alternate miles were walked barefoot?

One trembles at the memory.

The meals—meals?—of orange peels and eggshells?

Ucckkh! Billy says, and crosses himself.

At this, Big Duck, his face flaming, leaves the store.

For this relief, thanks, Doc Friday says. Young pimple puss is no doubt on his way home to gambol away a stray hour among his collection of Mallomars and electric trains.

He needs the sugar for his yearning eruptions' health.

But, the Doc says. Running these young saps through their paces wasn't enough for Crazy. He then dishonorably discharged the entire Pine Tree Patrol for looking too Italian. Still not enough. He banned from all fun and games for a month the troop librarian because he refused to sob at a recitation of "Barbara Frietchie" in Swedish. Not enough. Finally—and this is a Hitler you're talking about—he wanted absolute fidelity and faithfulness. One Friday night the troop gathers in the basement of this little asshole Baptist church—even more degenerate than the one across the street—

Yet a hallowed meeting place, Billy says, broken toilet and all.

Hallowed indeed. As the kids file in, the slobs, I should say, in all their sweaty khaki glory, there's Krigmann on a throne—a big chair, anyway, taken from the pastor's office upstairs. And God knows how many young-lady sopranos have been bent over it. He's in some musty and nauseating robes, he's got on a crown made out of oaktag on his head like in a school play in the third grade, he's wearing his mother's or his aunt's or somebody's necklaces, cheap gaudy shit costume jewelry, around his neck. He's got a big branch from the peach tree in the back yard in his mitt. Shall I go on? Or do you get the picture of a man gone totally bananas, wholly apeshit?

I have got the picture.

He's ordering all these little bastards to kiss his feet, he's smacking them with his peach branch, he's telling them they spend too much time at home and that he wants them in the basement every night. He's telling them that he's fucking disgusted with them because not enough of them are Swedes or Norwegians or whatever the goddam hell Scandihoovian he is and he wants them to stop being what they are and turn into Swedes.

Apeshit and bananas are words too mild to describe this yo-yo's condition, Irish Billy says.

Aha! But wait. He has a list of new names for them—all the same—Ivar Andersen. He starts yelling for them—Ivar Andersen! Ivar Andersen! And all the little assholes are milling around while he bashes them with his branch because they're not answering to their names right. He says, you're not Ivar Andersen! *You're* Ivar Andersen! Finally amid all the din and snots and tears the Assistant Scoutmaster, another rawboned Swede, overpowers him and ties him up with a sheepshank or a bowline or some goddam knot and they call the cops. You are not prepared! You are not prepared you guinea mick dago bastards! he's yelling as they cart him away to the big jamboree at Kings County.

Nothing as wacko as a sick Swede, Billy says.

He's *not* crazy! Big Duck shouts into the bathroom mirror at home, pushing chocolate-covered grahams into his mouth. Sobbing? All right, sobbing.

24 Scorcher

A hot afternoon in mid-August. Those who would normally be in Vogler's candy store are, instead, at Gallagher's bar, drinking beer and waiting for the free lunch.

The sun on the street is so bright that it is like a pickax in the eyes, the air like a hot, damp hand over the mouth. Exhausted pedestrians walk like phantoms in a nightmare of hell and cars seem to creep along like wounded insects. Sounds are swallowed in the overwhelming humidity like stones thrown into the sea. Like symbols in an exotic verse by a French decadent, the storefronts in the merciless glare stand out like a *trompe l'oeil* painted in frenzy by a madman sweating in a personal inferno of hallucination, and far-off sounds of ship whistles in the Narrows trudge through the deadening atmosphere like doomed travelers lost in a blizzard in the Klondike of an imagination suffused with a fear so intense as to be as swift and ungraspable and yet as deadly as sheet lightning illuminating a ravaged landscape with a ghastly effulgence like the glow of a sinister moon on an unhallowed graveyard. Brains seem to cook and thrash like lobsters thrust viciously into a pot of boiling—

O.K.! O.K.! Enough! Spare us! Doc Friday says.

You asked me how it is out, Richie says, so I figured I'd tell you. A beer, Martin, he says to the bartender, who is drawing one already.

How hot, yes, Doc Friday says. But do I need a crash course in vivid language? Purple prose? Flimsy similes?

This is technologically known as *furor scribendi*, the Arab says, according to a profound and weighted tome I keep on my desk at all times.

Said tome? the Drummer asks, doing the small shuffle of a straight man.

Richard's Rules of Modern American Mucilage, the Arab says.

Oh, a joke, Richie says. A won-der-ful joke.

The problem that inheres upon all nonfiction is that it is often joky, the Arab says. And who needs laughs in a cosmos of a world that can make gouts of hysteria for the poor human being who just ambles his feet down the street?

Pepper enters the bar, sweating. Jesus Christ, that sun is *bright,* he says.

Like a pickax in the eyes? Doc Friday asks.

What?

Nothing—have a beer. The free lunch will be out soon.

Well, Pepper says. The bastard did it, by the way.

Who did what? Richie asks.

The goddam landlord on 68th—he threw Mrs. Elkstrom out. She's sitting out on the street there in all that hot sun and heat waiting to go—Christ knows where.

Threw her out? Doc Friday says. You mean he *evicted* her? Mrs. Elkstrom? She must be eighty-five.

She's out, whatever she is, Pepper says. You think that bastard cares?

She's got a son, I know, the Drummer says. I remember him when he came back from the war. He was on the "Portland."

That's her grandson, the Arab says. Her son has long wended his way into the pale of the other world.

They stand silently at the bar and nod their thanks as Martin buys a round.

Mrs. Elkstrom sits in the sun, hardly feeling the heat in her old bones. In her mind is a vision of cold Swedish lakes and black-green forests in the northern sunlight. She sits in an old and ornately carved wooden chair from the old country, decorated with exquisitely rendered lions and flowers. In her right hand she holds a small sapling that she has been tending in the back yard, in her left a huge sunflower she has grown. At her feet sits her small black cat, Bjorn.

Icy ponds reflecting black trees and high thin clouds. Cold grey churches. The ghostly sun of midnight. She sees her husband falling falling from the bridge that he has been redleading.

The sun is remorseless and suddenly she feels its power. She lays the sapling and the sunflower on the sidewalk and strokes the cat.

Bjorn, Bjorn, she says. Bjorn. There is no point to it anymore and she leans back in the chair and dies.

He's a bastard, Pepper says. I don't know, maybe we ought to do something? Take her into the ice-cream parlor? I don't know.

The Sailor comes in. My God! he says. It's like walking through a furnace out there.

Like a nightmare of hell? Richie asks.

Right! What?

On 68th Street, Mrs. Elkstrom sits in her chair, as still as death.

25 An Incident at Coney Island

Jimmy Finney? the Arab says. The name is totally alienable to me. I am glutted with tragic sorrow, as is only human, by the news that the gent is demised, but I don't know him.

Sure, Arab, Fat Frankie says. The guy who wanted to be a cop. Georgie Huckle's cousin, a little guy with a funny kind of pointy head?

Ah, Professor Kooba says. I remember him. God rest his soul, but he was the odious young fellow who insisted on mispronouncing the title of my tome and calling it "The Coise." Yes, his head was pointed in more ways than one.

Memory now floods my cranium! the Arab says. Of course. The youth who was wont to hang from a doorframe to stretch out his scrawny body. The youngster who was prone to guzzling himself disgustingly on pounds of bananas and Hershey bars till his teeth were a maze of blackened stumps so that he could gain some weight on his skeletonish frame. This unfortunate dolt has expired?

He once asked me what a drummer did, the Drummer says. Or, to be exact, he asked me what instrument a drummer played. Would you, Arab, call him a churl?

A churl is a meet designation for James Finney, yes. It may be, in fact, too kind, too euphonistic a term for such a knucklehead.

Remember him with that goddam suit he had like kids get for Christmas to play cops? Fat Frankie says.

Ah yes, Kooba replies. It even had a little tin badge that read "Official Police." A simple soul. Hm. "The Coise," indeed!

I would venture the tentacious commentary that he single-handed—or single-mouthed—kept the United Fruit Company in business for at least a year all by himself, the Arab says. But how did he die? Was the hapless moron's shuffling off this mortal coil a natural one?

Or was it caused by a surfeit of bananas? the Drummer asks.

Or perhaps he strangled or otherwise suffocated himself by the wrong pronunciation of words? Kooba adds.

What I heard, Fat Frankie says, I heard from Georgie Huckle. He was so broke up over it that he overlooked to put a couple of beans down on a three-to-one sweetie at Bowie.

He will remember that cursed day for the rest of his obsessed existence, the Arab says.

Son of a bitch will scan the *Morning Telegraph* now, the Drummer says, looking for some dog with the name of Crazy Jim or something. Finney's Ghost. Bananas.

Anyway, Fat Frankie says, two weeks ago, he takes the police test for the tenth time. He can hardly walk from all the goddam bananas he ate, he spent the whole morning hanging from the doorframe, he lays down on his back on the floor then till it's time to get going, then he grabs a taxi and lays down on the back seat. He does everything.

A stout heart despite the idiot brain fizzling within, the Arab says.

So—in he goes. He makes the height by an eighth of an inch. He makes the weight by a quarter of a pound. The doctor looks at him, he looks at him. He takes some tests, some other doctors look at him, they ask him some questions. Then they say they'll let him know.

The statement hangs portentious with doom and failure, the Arab says. When they say they'll let you know you can rend and tear up your stubs.

The tests come in, Fat Frankie says. The cops let him know that from what they can see, he's an alcoholic. No soap. Naturally. The cops don't need no more drunks in the department.

Coals to Newcastle, Kooba says.

Black despair spears its path into young Jimmy's heart, the

Arab says. I see it all now. His poor teeny brain, such as it may be termed, stews and bubbles within his pointed skull.

Yesterday, Fat Frankie says, he steals a horse and gallops the nag down to the beach at Coney with the phony nightstick he made for himself years ago in shop in high school—and of course he's got himself his little toy suit on.

Tears are riveleting down his blankly characterless face, the Arab says.

Also he's drunk as a coot, the Drummer adds.

He gallops around on the beach but there's nobody to see him the middle of winter. So then, according to Georgie, he aims this fruit peddler's nag right at the ocean and charges in, clubbing the waves.

Clearly besides himself with melancholia praecox, the Arab says. A common ailment among horsemen, according to certain findings among . . . among scientists.

The nag staggers out of the drink, Frankie says. But Jimmy Finney, no.

Now *this* is the type of horse that Georgie should put a pound or two on, Professor Kooba says. The horses he bets on are the kind would stand in the ocean and breathe the water in.

They found his little fake hat and jacket, but no Jimmy, Frankie says.

He went as he lived, the Arab says.

You mean dumb as shit? the Drummer asks.

Well, precluding and obviating strongly the vulgarism of the phrase, Drummer, I would say, yes, affirmatively yes. I would be compulsed to harmonize with that opinion, the Arab says.

It's a shame, Kooba says, he never made the acquaintance of that other chowderhead who comes in here and who's always off to Delaware or some odd spot like that, God only knows why. I cannot think of his name—the tall one with no idea of personal hygiene?

You mean Eddy Ellsworth, the Drummer says. Christ yes, they would have made a fine pair.

Sort of like a real-life Mutt and Jeff, Fat Frankie says.

Yet, the Arab says, it behooves a devilish advocate, if you will so allow me, to hint that did the young numbskull become a member of New York's Finest he might slowly but surely have gotten sane, or else at leastwise smart enough to carry off his functional duties. Let us say, normal. What is your opinion, Professor?

My opinion? My opinion is that you can't make a silk poice out of pig's ass.

Bravo! the Drummer says.

Bravo and double bravo! the Arab cries, clapping his hands. Cute and trenchant! *And* perceptible! Bravimisso!

26 Jo-Jo Speaks

Jo-Jo hold stick.
Mikky Way! Mikky Way!
Could say bella wonderbar!
Big stick for Jo-Jo.
Smell movie nice candy.

Jo-Jo have nickel.
Banella ice-cream cone.
Wanna hear joobox. Wanna *hear*.
Jo-Jo see Popeye!
Stinky cheese sannich.

I pull off leafs off stick.
Like chawkit soda.
Bella bella. Bella bella. Bella bella.
Green? Leafs.
Jo-Jo smell stick a lot.

I squash Mikky Way.
Jo-Jo likes eat stick.
Boys yell?
I take Popeye book?
Jo-Jo want lollipop smell.

27 Mottoes

There goes Georgie Huckle, Santo Tuccio says. His head is hanging low.

Picked another goddam nag that ran out on him, Pepper says. Without him the bookmakers would croak.

He told me he was putting a sawbuck to win on some dog he's been following for a year and was due.

You see how due he was. If it's the nag I'm remembering, Tootsie Roll, Georgie's dropped about six months' pay on him at every track in the country.

That's called beating a dead horse, Irish Billy says. Or I should say, *not* beating him.

As it is penned in the *Vigils* of the Sheikh Bey Arafir Kadat, the Arab says, "He who carries clubs to a village of scoundrels will be beaten."

This is a horse, Arab, Pepper says. We don't need no goddam wisdom of the East.

Ah, but a moment! the Arab says. "The wild horse mounted remains wild."

A horse that *races*, Arab, Santo says. A regular thoroughbred. Not a wild horse—what do they call them—cayusas? lollapoosas? Just a regular racehorse like they had in *National Velvet*.

The Sheikh Bey Arafir Kadat speaks with sheer clarity of the perceptible on velvet in his *Night Musings*, the Arab says. "To the poor man, velvet is but the rough homespun that sharpens desire."

We're discussing Georgie Huckle, Irish Billy says. World's Greatest Handicapper. What are *you* talking about?

Exactly so, the Arab says. *Exactement! Voilà!* Does not the gigantically losing Huckle, in his usually wonted lope of a loser's posture, carry clubs—the metaphoristical clubs that appear in the *Vigils*—to a village of scoundrels, there to be ultimately beaten and thrashed upon.

He's just going home, Pepper says. What thrashed?

This is an analogistic expression, Pepper, an allegoric turn of the phrase. Am I correct, Professor Kooba?

Don't ask me. I never heard of this sheikh. My only literary concerns are—

You know the only Sheiks he heard of, Santo laughs. Only he's too goddam old to use them.

Professor Kooba turns his back disdainfully and examines the magazine rack.

Watch out you don't hurt your brains with that *Famous Funnies*, Santo says.

"Those who mock at cloudy images of profoundness but mock at the fugitive wind," the Arab says. Also from *Night Musings.*

You can't say a goddam thing around here, Pepper says. God help you if you try and make a little conversation. A little light conversation.

Mercly examine, the Arab says, the aphoristic motto about the clubs in the lights of allegoric meaning. Georgie will be beaten on by the village of scoundrels in so far that the clubs are, in fruitful essentials, most certainly—

Stop, Pepper says. Billy, open the door and let all this gas out. Somebody might by accident light a match and we'll all get our asses blown off. Just a little light conversation, for Christ sake!

"The conversation of the blind is filled with unperfect portraits." Or maybe it's "pictures," the Arab says.

That's from Abou Ben Adhem again, Irish Billy says.

A little light conversation, Pepper murmurs.

Note, gentlemen, note, the Arab says. Note perspicacitously how Georgie's entire corpus of his trembling and abased frame is bent over and bowed down as he approaches his block like a malformed crip. One can puissantly almost envisionate in the mind's eye his onus of clubs. I might go so far as to say his massive fardels of clubs.

Fardels *this*, Santo says. He who talks a lot talks like a man with a paper asshole.

And a hollow barrel makes the most noise, Pepper says.

A stitch in time gathers no moss? Billy asks.

Gentlemen, the Arab says, I admit that you press in close upon me with your arrows of misfortune and pointy darts of mocking palaver. "When rained upon by the rocks and boulders of the foe, the wise man . . . the wise man . . . "

Yeah? The wise man what? Pepper asks. Here's a guy don't even know how his own goddam mottoes go. The wise man, hell.

Mr. Huckle meets Georgie at their apartment door and grabs the losing stubs he proffers. Thirty bucks? Thirty goddam bucks on that three-legged dog? He throws the stubs in Georgie's face. You don't got either brains *or* luck!

So what of the wise man? Irish Billy says. Rained upon by rocks and stones?

Boulders, the Arab says.

He can't remember the sultan's words of wisdom, Pepper scoffs. Jesus.

It is not that, the Arab says. It is that the translational interpretation is slightly askewed and, I fear, slightly levitous. "When rained upon by the rocks and boulders of the foe, the wise man calmly dips bread in his chowder." That is how it transfers across into the English tongue.

Georgie Huckle sits on the steps leading to the roof and bites his knuckles. Tootsie Roll, he sobs. Tootsie goddamned fucking Roll.

Dips bread in his chowder? Pepper says. This sage sultan of yours sounds like a momo. Chowder? In goddam Arabia? Don't make me laugh.

They ain't even got no clams in Arabia, Santo says.

28 Symbolism

I read this story, the Sailor says, talk about *luck*. This guy was so broke and he figures he'll put his last pound on a long shot so as he starts to look at the entries he knocks some book down and there's this name he sees, Golden Delights. And by Jesus there's a horse running that day with the same name and goddamnit if it don't win and pay almost three hundred bucks. Talk about luck!

Very nice, the Drummer says. But these things, as you said, happen in stories only. Not in the reality of life.

I agree with my good friend, the Arab says. Though crushed with ruth as I am to breathe it, I have never yet played a hunch that did not leave me out of my pockets. Such things occur only in fictional writings, made, I am sorry to emote, for slobs and patsies strictly.

It *could* happen, the Sailor says. Things in stories happen in real life all the time.

The Sailor's right, Johnny News says. I mean I don't know about stories but those things happen. Did I ever tell you about the time I didn't know what I should do about asking my wife to marry me when we were keeping company? I had this lousy job, no money in the bank, and I didn't know. Damn it, one day I look up at the sky and there's a cloud shaped like a L. A L! You get it? Louise. That's my wife's name, so that night I ask her to marry me.

I cannot desist congratulating you that the cloud didn't say R, the Arab says. Or else your beloved spouse of a helpmate might at this moment well be Bony Ruth.

Oh come on, Johnny News says. You know what I mean.

Louise, on the roof of their apartment house hanging the

wash, stops, three clothespins in her mouth. The son of bitch! she says. A lover! A Clark Gable! A cloud? That's what he saw to ask me?

Truth is stranger than fiction, as the old proverb goes, the Arab says. Although I speedily tag upon this pronunciation, if it *is* truth!

I swear on my mother! Johnny News says.

A goddamned regular William Powell! Louise says, looking over toward the distant gas tanks.

Gentlemen, Doc Friday says. In the Army once, during the war, when I chanced, by ill luck, to spend a few weeks in the stockade at glorious Camp Pickett in sunny and aristocratic old Virginia, I noticed that the wooden stakes used to support the stockade commander's tomato plants—which us poor bastards had to deworm and deweed every day—these stakes seemed to grow taller when you weren't looking. And one day, by God, if they didn't start to sprout leaves. I mean real green leaves. Live leaves.

I don't understand comprehendingly the esoterical allusions of agriculture, Doc, the Arab says. Is this a wonderful phenomena?

Wonderful? Christ, these were little goddam sticks, I mean dead wood, like a popsicle stick. And they sprouted. Leaves! You'd turn your back on them and quick look to see if you could catch one sprouting. Never. But they sprouted when you looked away.

What is the analogousness in this tale to long shots finishing in the money and marrying Lois? the Arab asks.

Louise, Johnny News says. Lois is my daughter.

Spencer Tracy in disguise, Louise says. That's who he is, the rat.

Symbolism! Symbolic truths, the Doc says. I knew, I mean I just knew these green leaves meant new life for me. That I'd soon be free from the humiliation of the stockade and the unwanted company of, ah, criminal elements within the military. And sure enough, a week later, they cut my sentence short.

This, the Arab says, is a hard nut to swallow, Doc.

I admit they shipped my ass to Europe just in time for the Bulge, but . . . the symbolism was true.

Symbolism, the Arab says, smiling. I've never really cogitated deeply on such a thing. Quite wondrous and repleted with interest. Is it a new species of idea?

See? the Sailor says. In stories you get all these ideas. I mean they may not be really true but they might as well be true.

I swear to God I saw a cloud like a L, Johnny News says.

Who says you didn't? the Drummer asks.

Mister Robert Taylor Rotten Bastard no less, Louise says.

Symbolism, eh? the Arab says. I shall avail some tomes on this subject from the library. *Symbolism.*

Louise? Hey, Louise! You on the roof? Johnny News calls.

Yeah! I'm on the roof, Mister George Brent. I'm having some cocktails and highballs and little hot dogs on toothpicks and caviar with Bette Davis. Come on and join us, Mister Romantic!

What? Johnny asks, pushing open the roof door.

You can uncover and incarth these symbolisms in fictitious tales a lot? the Arab asks. What types of genres of tales?

29 Palm Sunday Maybe

How about the way the light of early spring shimmered on the lake on that long ago—well, not too long ago—Easter Sunday? Richie says. Or was it Palm Sunday? The girls were in their pastel spring suits, they even had veils on their hats.

It was one may impute a vision of loveliness, the Arab says, if you will be so kind as to overlook the banalness of such a trite cliché.

A vision of past loveliness, Richie says.

What girls? the Drummer asks.

In any event, Richie says, the thing I remember most clearly is the darning needles flying in squadrons over the lake. At the time I wished—and how I wished—them to be symbols.

Ah! the Arab says, symbols! Wonderous phenomenons. I have of late recently decided to research them soon.

Now I think that there are no symbols at all, Richie says. Or let's say that there *are* symbols but that they're real as anything else.

What girls? the Drummer asks.

Suppose, Richie says, you have a piece of pie that stands for a triangle.

A wedge of pie is more smacking of exactness, the Arab says.

A wedge of pie then. Suppose you have it and that it stands for a triangle. Suddenly, Big Duck, let's say, comes along, his acne is goddam growling. And he stuffs the pie into his mouth. What about that?

As real as reality itself in the flesh, the Arab says.

Girls from the neighborhood? the Drummer asks.

It must have been Palm Sunday though because all the guys wore crosses made of palm in their lapels. But the suits were new like they would be on Easter Sunday, Richie says.

The memory tricks and trumps up the brain often, the Arab says. Sundays in the gentle springtime are often much the exact same as each other.

I kept thinking that some of us would probably marry each other. It doesn't look like it though.

I like girls in suits, the Drummer says. They look so chaste you can hardly goddam stand it to keep your hands off them!

Those darning needles over the lake probably had something to do with it, Richie says. That bright blue lake and the darning needles flying exactly parallel to each other. Dolores had on a suit that was dusty rose, was what they used to call that color. I remember her saying "I don't know, Richie." What did I ask her that she didn't know, I wonder?

The term "dusty rose" crams me up with some nameless emotion myself, the Arab says. I tentatively touch your nostalgia of being young together. The giggling smiles and the Brownies click-clicking snapping pictures. Ah.

That's right! Richie says. Somebody had a Brownie and took pictures of everybody. Now I remember.

I like the skirts to come just to the knee, the Drummer says, so that when they sit down and cross their legs—

But what about, I wonder, the green landscape and rolling foothills just beyond the lake that I remember? Richie says. Foothills in Prospect Park? Maybe I'm mixing all this up with some movie I saw.

That could be bashing the nail squarely, the Arab says. Pictures often cause such an impingement on the memory that you could vow is so real that it happened.

That was the day Dolores and Big Duck disappeared together, Richie says. Big Duck! I'll never understand it.

Then when they sit down and cross their legs, the Drummer says. Jesus Christ! When they sit down and cross their *legs*.

You don't have to tender informational datas to me, Richie, about automotive mechanics, the Arab says. Chalk it on to experience.

Big Duck though. My God.

30 Daydreaming Plus

Big Duck stands on the crest of the hill in his baggy green sweater, his face set in a determined frown, wielding a long two-by-four against the attacking thrusts of a half-dozen other two-by-fours held by faceless opponents on the hill's slope beneath him.

Behind Big Duck, out of sight on the other side of the grassy hill, Dolores reclines in fear, pride, and love.

Big Duck is defending her.

Donald is defending my honor, she sighs.

The sun glances brilliantly off Big Duck's acne-ravaged face.

Aha! he yells. Aha! And again—Aha! Dull thunk of wood against wood.

One might well imagine what the attacking forces are saying. A lot of Oofs! Ohhs! Ows! Ughs!

Dolores is clad in a diaphanous gown of powdery blue that clings provocatively to her young, beautifully shaped body. She studies her Latin verbs to take her mind off the sounds of combat.

Don't get all this wrong now, Big Duck says. I'm not defending Dolores because of her *body*. She's a lady.

Ooof! a foe grunts as Duck bangs him on the head.

Dolores adjusts her dusty-rose peignoir under which her limbs stir languorously. Oh, Donald! she gasps. Maybe it's the strange and yet lovely green of his baggy sweater that has so filled me with love. She plucks at a jeweled lace garter around her swelling thigh and smooths her black silk stockings over her long legs.

Now don't think it's her *legs* that get me! Big Duck shouts. No Sir!

Thwack! Crack! Thunk! The usual haze of dust, etc. Sweat and blood and so on.

Ugghhh, a brutal voice groans as Big Duck batters a lewd face. A lewd and lecherous face.

Dolores settles an ermine robe about her bare shoulders as the sun goes behind a cloud.

Don't think it's the *shoulders*, Big Duck pleads. This is a lady. She might as well be my mother or my sister if I had a sister.

Pimply slob! a guttural voice rasps as Duck thrusts his two-by-four into a soft belly.

The hill is silent. The air is clear. The shouts and curses of battle—all departed.

Big Duck holds Dolores close, trying desperately not to notice that she is in nothing but white lace underclothes.

I can't imagine what happened to my dress, Donald, she whispers, blushing.

Don't think it's because she's got no *dress* on, damn it, Duck says. I respect this girl, I mean I really respect her a lot.

I'm a Catholic, Dolores says. And Donald knows that.

I don't understand, dear, Big Duck says, how you get *these* on under these straps—I mean, once you got the stockings attached, how do you manage to get– to get these on underneath these?

Oh Donald, Dolores laughs softly. These aren't underneath these, don't you see? You put this on first and then you put these on over it, see? That way you can take these off without having to unclasp—Oh, Donald!

Meanwhile, the stars have come out.

Pepper and Red Miller stand at the base of the opposite side of the hill from where the young lovers are reclining.

Don't ask me, Pepper, Red says. The Magician said to wait until dark and then shoot off these skyrockets and Roman candles.

O.K., Pepper says. I'm not worried. It's an easy fin.

They set up the fireworks at the base of the hill and commence shooting them off.

Skyrockets and Roman candles burst in multicolored splendor and effulgence all across the night sky, rivaling the very stars themselves in grandeur and beauty and etc., etc.

Be careful, Donald. They're caught—they're caught on my heel there—oh, there, oh, all right.

O.K.? Big Duck gasps. O.K.?

Yes.

Look at all the fireworks, Big Duck pants. I wonder what—

Oh. Donald. Oh. Donald. Donald. Donald. Donald.

O.K., Red Miller says. Let's set off the last big batch and call it a day.

Right, Pepper says. Goddamnedest silliest thing I ever did.

The night is warm and windless. Of course.

Skyrockets and Roman candles burst in multicolored splendor and effulgence all across the night sky, rivaling the very stars themselves in grandeur and beauty and etc., etc.

One is almost the precise shade of green as Big Duck's sweater. Believe it or not.

Don't think it's just *this* I want, Big Duck moans. I really respect this girl. I really respect you, Dolores. Oh. Oh. Oh Jesus.

31 Riding the Carrousel

Big Mickey, with money from the sale of fountain pens stolen from a boxcar in the freight yards, goes to Coney Island.

Coney Island? Red Miller says. With all that money he should have gone to Rye Beach! Or at least Rockaway Playland.

All *what* money? Big Mickey says. And what's this about fountain pens? I took a dollar or so in change from a goddam newsstand.

How he loves Coney! The Cyclone, the Whip, Steeplechase, and Luna Park! Hot dogs and french fries and buttered corn! Not to mention frozen custard.

Coney's not what it was years ago, Professor Kooba says. I well remember when all the ladies walked with parasols on the boardwalk, all in white dresses, and when Feltman's had—

But especially he loves the merry-go-round. The oddly haunting, joyous yet curiously poignant –almost sad—melodies of the pipe organ as the brightly colored horses—

Silent movies outdoors in Feltman's for a nickel, Kooba says. Those were *movies*. Those were *stars*.

Ahh, they all had these goddam fruity voices, Santo Tuccio says. I read about it.

The meetest and supremely exact word, the one that bespeaks and affirms elegant thought and cultured know-how, is carrousel, the Arab says.

How Big Mickey would ride! There was one merry-go-round just off the Bowery that had a grey horse of noble frame that he particularly loved. He rode and rode. And rode again.

Maybe *less* than a dollar, Big Mickey says. And this guy is talking Playland. Rye Beach!

The Hudson River Dayline, Kooba says. My God. I don't think I've even thought about that in years.

I was on one of those Hudson River Dayline boats one day years ago and we got rammed by a submarine, Johnny News says. I swear to God.

Sitting there in the saddle he imagines himself a conquering hero, surrounded by a select bodyguard of troops, his staff sporting a wreath of laurel, another wreath on his head. Hail, Caesar!

Is it feasibly proper for submarines to navigate the environings of the Hudson River, Johnny? the Arab asks.

Then how come the cops were all over the place asking questions about who saw anybody down in the yards? Red Miller says. Newsstand, the guy says.

A schooner of beer for a nickel, Kooba says. Granted, they were almost all head, but still. A nickel!

Arab, I don't know how it got there or why, Johnny News says. All I know is we got rammed. It was in the *News*. Some people thought it was a Nazi U-boat.

You ever see that movie about the U-boats with Charles Laughton and Gary Cooper? Santo Tuccio says. I think that Charles Laughton gets drowned because he's so fat he can't swim or something?

That day I went to see my aunt up in the Bronx, Big Mickey says. You can ask anybody. I wasn't even *here*.

Not only does he ride twice and thrice—he rides seven times, and pays for each ride, disdaining to try for the metal ring whose successful seizure is worth one free ride.

Did you glimpse at any Teutonic gobs upon the maindeck or poop? the Arab asks. Or were they seelfully locked into their submersing craft?

Big Mickey, all his money gone but for a nickel for the Sea Beach, starts home.

O.K.? Big Mickey says. Convinced?

You did go to Coney though, Red Miller says.

The singing waiters in Feltman's, Kooba says. Ah, it's not the same. Too many trashy people there now. Not a parasol in sight.

The hoi pollois, the Arab says. Is that what you infer about, Professor? Still on Coney Island?

Maybe they thought the excursion boat was a subchaser, Johnny News says.

As the train roars homeward—

Yes, Coney. And you've got it right, Arab, Kooba says. Too many of the hoi polloi.

I wonder who did steal those fountain pens, Red Miller says.

In Beirut, the Arab says, much the same identity of events transpired. Occurring in such a mode as to change certain enclaves and purlieus of the great cosmopolis from veritable Edens and Valhallas into stews, cesspools, and septic tanks of teeming humankind. Chatter, chatter, chatter.

Or maybe they said it was an Italian submarine, Johnny News says. I should check that old *News*.

I remember when well-off people actually rented little cabins for the summer at Coney, Professor Kooba says. Actually rented little summer houses.

Bungalows is the more claritous word, the Arab says.

Yet even the roar of the train does not completely obscure his sweet remembrance of imagined victory and honor.

32 A Farrago

What's all that noise? Irish Billy says. It sounds like a bunch of maniacs.

These potent decibels are of ill-use to the human ear, the Arab says. Am I right, sir? he asks the Drummer.

Well it's not "Canadian Capers," that's for sure.

A bunch of Norwegian seamen, drunk, Cheech says. And some yo-yo in a soldier suit is leading them down the street.

It's Master Sergeant Jim Gentry!

The military leaves a large fragment to be desired, the Arab says. It *is* Gentry, and five Norsk seamen in their cups as well as their glasses and goblets. Goblets is probably most felicious vis-à-vis Vikings, yes?

And all of them carrying flagpoles except the beloved sarge, Irish Billy says.

It must have something to do with his brother, that idiot who swabs the floors in Pat's and Gallagher's for a buck or two and a morning eye-opener, the Drummer says. Hear what he's saying?

I demand an explanation! Sergeant Gentry shouts. An explanation for my elder brother's—an officer and a gentleman!—my elder brother's debasement!

Ja! Ja! the seamen shout in chorus, brandishing their flagpoles. One falls down and rolls around for a moment or two, at a loss to discover his feet.

Can this be, the Arab says, a kind of vanguard to the Protestant Day parade? But where are all the rosy-cheeked maids in their profligantly embroidered old-country handmade skirts and blouses and caps? If this is so?

Where? Maids? Where? the Drummer says.

Pepper, across the street, yells Hey! Just right down the block for some free vanilla ice cream and a Bible lesson! Goddam fools!

Ja! Ja! One seaman accidentally hits another in the head with his staff and in a moment they all begin to flail away at each other in murderous good humor.

Looks like Finn Hall on Saturday night, Irish Billy says.

Debasement! Sergeant Gentry cries. Ignominy! Shame and degradation! Is it for this lousy horseshit treatment of my beloved brother that I busted my ass studying all those skeeters?

The young noncom has slipped a gasket, the Drummer says. What did you say about those maids and their profligant cheeks?

Just keep going, champs! Pepper yells. Just file right into any church you come to that don't have any nuns around. Pound cake! They got pound cake to put the vanilla ice cream on! Yum! Yum! Yummy yum!

Ja! Ja! a seaman says, blubbering through a bloody nose and mouth.

Pepper is besides himself, the Arab says. Filled to the brimful with a demonish and anticleric rage to fling invectives.

I could use a little pound cake and vanilla ice cream, Cheech says.

For *this* raw deal that I wound up one of the most mean and rotten NCO's in the whole goddam First Army? Sergeant Gentry shouts. Hah?

Major Gentry is sleeping off a muscatel and stout drunk in the cellar underneath Pat's and hears none of this.

Such is always the ironical twists and darts of the cloudy plot of life, the Arab says.

The seamen stop smashing at each other and, slowly milling about, begin walking down the street again after Sergeant Gentry.

Lingonberries! Pepper yells. Lingonberry custard, by Jesus! Lutefiske with chocolate sauce on it! Hotcha! Super-sprinkled headcheese! Attaboy! You name it they got it! Just keep walking toward that first cross down there, the one with all the little light bulbs on it!

Major, Major! Sergeant Gentry cries. Major big brother! Oh God!

Burly wakes Major Gentry up, holding the mouth of an open bottle of white port under his nose.

Am I dead yet? Major Gentry asks. Burly? Stand up, soldier, goddamnit! when you offer an officer a slug of sweet wine!

What I don't get, Cheech says, is why all these Norwegians with the sarge? What the hell are *they* doing?

Ingenuous stripling, the Arab says. It is a banalous and clichéish truism, trite though it may be to utter same, that if something can happen it will happen sooner or later. Do you know that if we were to stand all nonchalant and insoucious on this corner for perhaps a million years, *everything* would happen?

Malarkey, malarkey, Irish Billy says.

Ah, not so, the Arab says. When Professor Kooba arrives, ask him about the curious parallelogramisms of this theory—or law—in letters and their art and practice. In short essence, Kooba states inequivocably that an author who could write at the same book for a million or ten million or infinitudesimal centuries, would write about everything and everybody doing anything you can think up, despite humble talents. This is of apparence a well-known literary and philosophical veridical-ism.

Onward, gentlemen! Sergeant Gentry shouts. Onward! I feel the presence of my drunken brother nearby! Oh, onward!

Ice cream! Lutefiske! the seamen cry. Lingonberry custard! Light-bulb cross! Ignoring Sergeant Gentry's commands, they reel and stagger toward a church on the next corner.

Gentlemen, gentlemen! Sergeant Gentry screams. You goddam squareheads! But the drunken seamen continue their advance on the church and its unsuspecting pastor, their flag-staffs clattering against each other.

Atta babies! Pepper yells. Don't forget to ask for the bluefish steeped in whipped cream! Accept no substitutes!

I think they entitle such an odd assemblage a charivari, the Arab says. Charivari? Perhaps not.

This way, you yardbirds! Sergeant Gentry screeches, stamping his foot on the sidewalk. God damn it to hell!

Burly, Major Gentry says, I'm making you acting corporal for this devotion to duty on your part.

Charivari? the Arab muses. Rigadoon? Perhaps farrago?

I'm giving up mosquito research forever, Sergeant Gentry mumbles as he walks over the very spot underneath which his brother is taking a long swallow of white port.

Ahhh.

33 The Whole Story

The two girls are too far away for me to make out who they are, Richie says, but I suspect that one is Berta and the other Isabel. You may wonder what they are doing together, since Isabel lives right down on Colonial Road and Berta lives in the Bronx on Shakespeare Avenue. I assume that they've just graduated from high school, where they were classmates.

I don't even know them anyway, Irish Billy says. Now, if you want to talk about Helen Walsh, say . . .

Helen Walsh long ago married a checker for the Penn Railroad. Name of Vince. He checks big manifests off trailers to the neglect of small independent truckers who dash to the platform with one or two pieces. For this attention he is given a number of weekly, ah, envelopes.

Gotcha! Cheech says. She was hot stuff anyway though, old Helen.

Now, Richie says, she's a good Irish-Catholic wife and mother, spreading a little in the hips, sagging a little in the bust, and sporting a bouffant hairdo. On Saturdays she shops with her hair in large pink plastic curlers. She doesn't know it but to many people she represents a "class."

I don't get it, Irish Billy says. And what's wrong with Irish Catholics?

All these years in school together and we hardly know each other, Isabel, Berta says.

Yes. It seems so silly. And I *knew* that I'd like you.

There's something the matter here, Doc Friday says. Isabel and Berta both grew up on Senator Street. They know each other well. They did not go to the same high school. Irish Billy knows them too. And *I* don't know of any Helen Walsh. What is all this? Shakespeare Avenue?

Sh, Richie says. It's better this way. Who cares about two girls who spent their childhood playing jacks in front of Lambui's Car Rental? A little mystery!

O.K., the Doc says. He may be said to say it "wearily."

They stand outside the main entrance to the high school, Richie goes on, a monumental edifice designed to look like a medieval castle, complete with a bridge over a moat. This motif is slightly sullied by the presence of orange peels, candy-bar wrappers, chocolate-milk containers, and a condom in the water of the moat.

And the water itself's no bargain either if it's the school I think it is, Irish Billy says.

Are you going to the prom? Isabel asks. I am.

Yes, Berta answers. With a boy I went steady with last summer. My mother had a fit when I told him yes . . . the religion thing. You know?

I hope it works out for you.

Oh, we're not really *serious*. But my mother thought it was all over at Labor Day and then he called up during the winter and we started dating and she started in on me.

Well, I'm going with a boy I more or less grew up with on a block I lived on for a long time. I don't think you know him? Donald Halvorsen?

Donald Halvorsen! Cheech says. For Christ sake, that's Big Duck!

The son of a bitch can't even dance, Irish Billy says.

What's he going to do, sit in the corner all night and show her his goddam callouses? Cheech says. Big Duck!

They are swept by jealousy, for Isabel is lovely, and both Billy and Cheech have for years wallowed in sexual fantasies concerning her.

Well, the school did its best for the graduates, Richie says. At the edge of the lawn you can see they put up a kind of rough archway through which the girls passed on their way to the folding chairs on the lawn—which the school likes to call "the green." From four shaggy-barked poles hammered into the ground, a garland of flowers is hung like a kind of awning. The arch still stands there in the late afternoon sun, the flowers now a little wilted. The girls are waving their bouquets at their parents, who approach them. They probably have watches and pen-and-pencil sets in their hands. Isabel will go to a commercial school in the city and Berta will go to Smith. See? They smile at their parents.

They smile flashingly at their parents. They really are very beautiful girls, caught in what many believe to be absolute feminine perfection at seventeen. Many do not believe this.

Big Duck, believe it or not, does sit in the corner with Isabel all night, not only showing her his callouses and the greasy and ground-in dirt of his knuckles, but droning on about lube jobs, points, plugs, ring jobs, transmissions, differentials, and on. And on. On the way home from the prom he parks his Studebaker at Plumb Beach and Isabel quickly and inexpertly masturbates him so that she can get away from him early.

Isabel? Irish Billy says. Isabel? Isabel jerked that bastard off? He is furious and red with shame.

What can I tell you? Richie says. That's what happened. I can't tell you a lie.

Sure you can, Cheech says. Sure you can.

Right, Billy says. You're goddam right you can.

Big Duck parks at Plumb Beach, Richie says. He starts to paw Isabel and tries to pull her skirt up. She's pale and says she thinks she's going to be sick. She gets out of the car. All right? What the hell can I tell you guys? She *does* get sick, Big Duck takes her home. All right?

Better, Richie says. I don't like the idea of her getting sick in front of that son of a bitch.

Neither do I, Cheech says.

Berta, by the way, Richie says, puts her gardenia corsage in her underwear drawer that night. Nice?

Fine. Good, Irish Billy says.

But what else happens? Cheech says. I mean, what *about* all this?

It has a point, Richie says. I just need a kind of ending for it. With a decent ending it has a point, it does have a point, I swear.

34 An Esoteric Item

The Drummer is selling greeting cards again. He enters Vogler's with a small overnight bag full of sample boxes. He opens his bag and takes out a box—an "all occasions" selection, birthdays to anniversaries, christenings to condolences.

This one I love! he says, displaying a horribly colored card.

A man in a red cloak stands on a cliff in front of three meagerly leaved saplings, one of which he leans against with his hand. His back is to the viewer of the card and he faces into the setting sun. Far below him, on the sea, three ships sail from right to left. When the card is opened, these words are revealed on the recto:

I'll be
SEAING
you soon

Love it! the Drummer says. Filled with tenderness, meaning, nostalgia, wit, *and* a certain *wistful* quality. I always put this baby on top of the others and aim my pitch at the tenderest spots in the hearts of my prospective suckers. This one makes them feel like a movie with Bette Davis. Whammo! Bam! This hooks them and then I follow up with a couple of kitties and some goddam puppies sticking their heads out of an old boot and they part with a buck in a trice! A cinch.

Interestingly voiced, the Arab says. You, as they say, plink upon their heartstrings.

Perfecto, camerado. Who can resist a sunset, an ocean, the briny deeps, then a kitty, a puppy? In a boot? Nobody.

Hey Drummer, the Sailor says. Let me see that card, O.K.?

The Drummer shows him the card and the Sailor looks at it carefully.

Jesus Christ, he says, slapping his brow with an open palm rather theatrically. I had a dream a few weeks ago and this is exactly what I dreamed. Even the colors were the same.

Rather leaning toward garishment, said colors, the Arab says. Not to offend, Drummer.

The hell with the colors, the Sailor says. The main thing is this picture is my dream. I can't get over it.

I would be pleased to interpret this dream for you, Sailor, Professor Kooba says, leaning forward over the soda cooler. In my youth, before I began my labors on my epic, "The Curse," I compiled a dream-interpretation book, based on the ageless and ancient folk wisdom of the peasant as well as the latest psychological findings.

Oh for Christ sake, Kooba, the Sailor says. Everything anybody says you either know about it or you saw it or you wrote it. Dream book my ass.

Kooba leans back against the magazine rack and folds his arms.

Pay him little or for that matter no heed, my dear Professor Kooba, the Arab says. I am sure that I emote for all lovers of knowledge when I say that I am fraught with interest and nibbling curiosity anent your expatiation and dissection of this dream—despite it being the dream of one whose coin is naught but the scoff and the cynical jest.

Amen! the Drummer says. I know that *my* curiosity is wetted.

In that case, Kooba says. In that case, for the benefit of you gentlemen at least I'll try to penetrate to the core of hidden meanings in the cloudy images of this dream. And picture.

Andiamo! the Arab says. Grade A!

The fact that a man stands with his back to you in a dream, Kooba begins, means that he doesn't wish for you to see his

face. That means treachery and sadness, or, if the man happens
to be a woman, hidden revenge that is being contemplated. The
hidden face usually means concealment of actual motives.
However, the three saplings, although skimpy and skinny, have
a leaf and a branch here and there and that always means a possibility of hope and goodness. As a matter of fact, in this con-
text, I cannot do otherwise than to consider these three little
trees as symbols of a blossoming and growing faith, hope, and
charity, three of the cardinal virtues of Western mankind. The
man peers obdurately into the sunset—*not* the sunrise, and *not*
high noon and so on. This betokens the end of youthful fool-
ishness and the beginning of mature wisdom, maybe even
more than just mature, more like the wisdom of age, like the
sunset years, you see? The sea is not blue or green like we expect, but golden from the setting sun—or, as my reading and
penetration of the dream insists—*yellow.* Therefore, it is the
Yellow Sea, why not? Just off the coast of China, if I remember
my geography, a land that by its very history, not to speak of its
nature, is also replete with wisdom, most of it mature and hallowed, not to say even ancient and grizzled. The three ships are
misleading, because it is easy to err and take them to mean
hopes and wishes coming to pass, but that is absolutely incor-
rect, since that can only be so if the ships are entering port like
in the old maxim about when your ship comes in, which I'm
sure you are familiar with. But these ships are sailing *out* to sea
as can be read from the fact that the man is leaning on a sapling
as if he needs support because he is worrying about their fate.
And why shouldn't he? For these ships represent *discovery.* As
a matter of fact, it is clear by the dream that they are none other
than the three ships of Columbus, whose names I can't recall,
but you know the three little tiny vessels I refer to, setting off to
discover the United States! A final warning is given by the
symbol of the man standing right on the edge of this sickening
cliff, where one false step will propel him down into the foam-

ing briny to his inescapable doom. All together, the dream is one of hope for a brilliant future of wisdom and discovery—*if* you're careful and don't make a misstep and *if* you keep whatever treachery you feel in your heart and which is also etched in your face, well hidden from those prying enemies who would as soon sink your three brave little boats as look at you.

Fantastique! the Arab says. A rendering of the most arcanic symbolistic images with preceptive acuteness and language soaked and steeped with clarity so that even the layman can understand it without tears.

Bullshit, the Sailor says. I didn't have any dream like that anyway. I made it up just for fun.

Fun, the Arab says. Fun to the besotted Sailor is hurtling cynicism at things he doesn't understand.

For shame, Sailor! the Drummer says.

I expected as much, gentlemen, Professor Kooba says, trying to hide his annoyance. I'm not a bit surprised by this uncouth and vulgar jape that the Sailor has turned. However and however. The fact that the Sailor now denies having this dream doesn't change the legitimateness of my interpretation. Had he had this dream the interpretation would be exact. And anybody who happens to have this dream can use my interpretation with no fear of putting his intellectual foot in his mouth.

Bullshit, the Sailor says again, more weakly this time.

Jesus, the Drummer says, I think it's terrific! I can use your dream interpretation, my wonderful friend, as a kind of esoteric come-on to sell my cards. For instance, this card was based on a dream that Christopher Columbus had when he didn't even goddam well yet know that the world is round. And then work the whole rest of the dream meaning in. Intellectual stuff. Hook the suckers so they think they're getting an item that's top drawer and also make them think they have to be smart to even buy an item like this. What about it, Professor? What do you think?

You may, as they say, be my guest.

I feel that it hews and cleaves close enough to the truth to be used to primal advantage in the commercial world, the Arab says. Close but not too close.

A quality item, the Drummer laughs, delighted. An item of sheer esoterica!

35 Mundus Marzipani

The Magician, terrifically bored—again—turns himself into some kind of ancient nobleman and stands on the roof of a building looking over his lands—somebody's lands, anyway.

Do we need the Magician again? He's really bush league one hundred per cent, Doc Friday says.

It's a cinch he don't like himself worth a damn, Cheech says. He's always somebody else.

Gene Phillips walks by and waves gently, drunkenly, hopelessly.

Seven to five that paper bag has a quart of Gordon's in it, the Sailor says.

Nobody takes the Sailor's odds, which is too bad for them. The bag has a quart of Dixie Belle in it.

The quirks of fate.

The odd transmutations.

The things not said, the things not done.

And what if Freud had not had "that" toothache?

Toothache? Professor Kooba says. What toothache? What—for that matter—Freud? The tailor on 68th across from Bloom's drugstore?

The Magician doesn't quite know what to do with himself here in his new-found domain. He's got a funny-looking hat on . . .

Like Huckle's homburg? Cheech asks.

. . . and a doublet and such all. A cloak. All that old-time costuming. Knights and pages and so on. He has two staffs of office.

Mr. Phillips has crossed the street and is engaged in conversation with Eddy the tire man. Eddy is pointing at the paper bag and waving a copy of the *Brooklyn Eagle*. The two gestures are totally unrelated.

Just for the hell of it, and either because it looks good or he thinks it looks good, the Magician is contemplating a model of the globe that he holds in his right hand.

Size? Doc Friday asks. He is half asleep in the languor of this hazy October afternoon.

The size of a large grapefruit.

But imagine his awkward shock of amaze when it strikes him that there is something odd about this globe, Professor Kooba says.

What? Doc Friday asks.

A shock of amaze? Cheech says.

Something odd, something very very odd, Kooba says.

At this moment, this very moment, the Magician discovers that the substance of the globe he contemplates is made of marzipan. Yes, marzipan!

A custom-made specialty deluxe item from Mariane Gade's chic sweete shoppe, Doc Friday says, finishing a lime rickey.

Since when do you get lime rickeys in Vogler's? Cheech says. Come on.

Doc Friday is finishing a lemon-lime with a squirt of cherry syrup.

Marzipan! the Magician utters to the wind blowing off the sea and over the waters of the calm, bright-blue bay, the bright-blue, mountain-girdled bay, and across the brilliant green trees and foliage and red thatched roofs of the little town over which the Duke gazes. For this is the Duke's domain.

The Duke is the Magician? Cheech asks.

Too goddam sweet, Doc Friday says. Too much cherry syrup.

Correct. He is the Duke. Or the Duke is he.

Eddy the tire man is escorting Gene Phillips into his cramped and filthy shop for the express purpose of having a long swallow or two of the Dixie Belle in the paper bag.

Marzipan indeed, the Duke murmurs. Wherefore, sugared

globe? How now, sweet world, 'pon which the nations melt into each other like doth the honey in a tyke's mouth? Ho!

This is the Magician? Cheech says. What the hell is he doing?

He's doing his best, Professor Kooba says.

Boredom, Doc Friday says. Boredom and heat and humidity and languor.

Smiling grandly, the Duke shifts his sparkling hawklike gaze and sweeps it over the small and peaceful village beneath his aerie.

Oh tender town, belike unto a kitten's mewl whose milk-be-spattered phiz doth fright itself agazing in a glass, the Duke says.

This town, I fear, Doc Friday says, is one in which all the men talk like Jean Hersholt or S. Z. Sakall, and a chorus boy in a jerkin or whatever they call it lurks around every corner ready to leap out, do a cartwheel, and rip into a novelty song. God! This *is* a bush-league magician. God! If I were still married I'd go home.

Wait a second, the Sailor says. This Jean Hersholt and Essie Zakall and chorus boy in a jerkin shit. Who can follow this? You expect ordinary people to know what the fuck you're talking about? This is strictly private stuff, special stuff.

Oh town! the Duke says. Oh globe of succulent and dulcet composition, oh world whose massy stuff doth compose itself o' the choicest sweetmeats o' the Mistress Gade, oh globe . . .

Gene Phillips leaves Eddy's shop and walks very carefully across the street toward the Cities Service station. He enters the office. In a moment he comes out, carrying a grapefruit, re-crosses the street, and returns to Eddy's shop.

Where the hell did Mr. Phillips get a grapefruit in the gas station? Cheech says.

This whole goddam thing is too goddam fucking much for me, the Sailor says.

The sun is beginning to set on the Duke's town. Domain.

Professor, Doc Friday says, do you think it worthwhile for

the two of us to stroll across the street and accidentally pay a visit to Eddy—good old Eddy—and Gene Phillips?

An excellent suggestion, my good doctor, Professor Kooba says.

The wind from the sea is getting stronger . . . lights are winking and blinking all up and down the cobblestoned village streets, and the nutty smell of evening fires is issuing from the chimneys of the cottages. They puff immaculate white puffs. Jean Hersholts and S. Z. Sakalls are in front of each door, smoking their pipes on benches in the golden technicolor twilight. The pipes have curved stems and silver covers over hand-carved bowls. Chorus boys by the score are turning cartwheels down every crooked street. Plenty of urchins. Odor of cabbage soup.

Oh globe of sweets compacted! Oh delicious nations! Battling fiercely with questions of state that are plaguing him, the Duke begins nibbling on Sicily.

Oh honeyed isle! he says, bored to tears.

36 Group Therapy

The Magician, undisguised, and in his shabby and nondescript robes and scarfs and hung with talismanic pendants, wearing his anonymous face, sits with Dolores, Helen Walsh, Isabel, Berta, Cookie LaNord, Tania Crosse, and Joycie Lunde. A devastating aura of femininity pervades the room.

Why all these women happen to be together

The reason these women have gathered

These women have decided to meet

The Magician has asked (asked!) these women to a particular place in order to talk to them. Or something.

The opening is turgid and unnecessarily melodramatic, Doc Friday says.

It commenced off with beneficiousness, the Arab says. "Talismanic," "anonymous face," and such fragrances.

By the employment of necromantic, not to say goetic arts, the Magician persuades these young women to reveal their most secret dreams. As a matter of record, in fact, that is exactly how he puts it.

Reveal to me, O young women, your most secret dreams.

The old bastard is not one for beating around the bush, Doc Friday says.

I see Donald Halvorsen through the window of a castle, Dolores says. He is on a faraway hillock.

Dolores must be plunged into the grip of spell, the Arab says. "Hillock" is not the genus of word the young lady would ordinarily use.

So do I, Helen Walsh says. Except that I see Red Miller.

Isabel and Berta speak. The same dream but with different men appearing to each on the hillock. Cookie, Tania, and Joycie

127

also agree. One cannot tell if the Magician is pleased or annoyed.

Stone-faced son of a bitch, Doc Friday says.

And? the Magician says. What else appears in your dreams?

A giant hand in what appears to be a grey sky, Tania says. Or I should say, a giant hand issuing from what seems to be a grey cloud in a grey sky.

"Issuing" is sheerest delight, the Arab says. The sheerest nicetiness of verbality.

And? the Magician says. And? And?

The old crock of shit is beside himself, Doc Friday says.

Well . . . the Arab says. All that pulchritudious flesh gathered close about him with their knees and things and murmurious garments. For that I cannot blame him.

And, Tania says, and in this gigantic hand which in my dream happens to be dead white . . .

All the other women nod.

. . . there appears . . . oh dear, I don't think I'll say what appears.

You then! the Magician shouts disgustedly at Isabel. Your dream!

The hand, Isabel says. The sky. The cloud. And in the hand— Forget about it. I can't say what I see, it's too private.

None of the other women will tell the Magician any more than that they too have seen the hand, the sky, the cloud. He is extremely irritated, but refuses to give way to his anger, an anger capable of transforming them to frogs, trees, streams, and a myriad other things, on a good day, that is. Instead, he swiftly disguises himself as a psychiatrist, complete with carefully trimmed Vandyke, pince-nez, and file folder.

How will you ever get well, he says to Berta, gently, gently, if you don't *want* to? How can I help you if you won't allow me to? He says many other things dear to the hearts of those in the profession, all of them too trite to record.

Thank God for that! Doc Friday says.

Charlatan! the Arab says. Knave, phony, blowhard. Rake!

Tania breaks the silence, although it is not true silence, the breathing of all the women being faintly audible. In the giant hand in the sky, she says, there is a long, sturdy club, ending in a knob at the top.

Would you say that it—? the Magician begins.

I would say, Tania says, from what I have learned from reading, listening, and conversation, that the stout club, with knob atop, is a bona fide phallic symbol.

There is assent from the other women, the rustling of feminine garments as legs are crossed and uncrossed, some discreet throat-clearing, and not a few blushes.

They blush! the Arab says. They blush! What a pig! Cagliostro!

Now that we have confronted the source, the Magician says, the root, as it were the wellspring and matrix of your disturbances, he goes on, expertly fiddling with a gold pen, perhaps we'll be able to come to grips with specifics, so that you all may be better equipped to deal with the realities of life in a responsible and mature, a *womanly* manner.

He is really good, Doc Friday says. You have got to admit that the bastard is very good. He sounds like a whole goddam clinic.

And now ladies, the Magician says, you may go. Except—except that I would like you, Miss Crosse, to remain so that we may begin our therapy immediately. As Freud said, *"Entbehren sollst Du! Sollst entbehren!"* His false quote is followed by a fatherly chuckle and a brisk rubbing of his hands together.

Oh boy, Doc Friday says. Oh boy oh brother.

Pig! the Arab says. Beastly porcine maggot! Begrimed filth of a scumbag!

Oh boy, Doc Friday says. With the phony chuckle and the handrubbing even. I'll give the poor kid about fifteen minutes before she's bent over the desk.

Hog swine of a garbageish swill can! the Arab says. And this, *this* with a young woman who says "issuing."

37 Water of Life

Mr. Phillips, on a weekend visit with his family to a friend's house on Breezy Point, sits on the beach in a canvas folding chair. In his left hand he holds a curiously shaped piece of driftwood, in his right a tall glass of whiskey and water.

That's Gene Phillips all right, Pepper says.

No ice, right? Santo Tuccio says.

The mysterious Ticineti drifts in and out of the scene, saying nothing, but listening, listening. Or perhaps he drifts on and off the beach at Breezy Point.

In his left hand, Gene Phillips holds this oddly shaped piece of driftwood.

Made so by the natural action of the wind and water? Pepper asks.

How the hell do I know? Santo says. Hey, remember the waves at the beach in that scene in *From Here to Eternity* when Montgomery Clift is boffing Deborah Kerr?

Santo is delighted when he thinks he finds parallels for experience in art, Richie says. Right, Santo?

What?

It *is* curiously shaped, Richie goes on. In his right hand, he has this tall whiskey and water, easy on the water, no ice, in a glass provided by his hostess. The glass is decorated with what proves, on closer inspection, to be daisies, symmetrically arranged. These glasses may be bought in hardware stores, five and tens, and other retail outlets specializing in sundries, dry goods, and plain goddam junk.

Years ago, Santo says, when I was a little kid, I remember that my mother used to get them in the movies on Wednesday night. Or Tuesday night?

Santo, Richie says, is of the unshakeable opinion that all of Western experience can be explained or glossed by the cinema and all its extensions—right, Santo?

What?

I'll take a shot, Richie says, and guess that his drink is about four parts booze to one part water. I'll guess it's Paul Jones or Kinsey Silver Label. A cheap blend, a potent blend, a rotgut, as some say, often sailors. Paul Jones is probably right, speaking of sailors.

Remember *Action in the North Atlantic?* Santo says. The big sensational panorama of the unsung heroes of the global conflict? The colorful canvas—

The curiously shaped piece of driftwood in Gene Phillips's left hand, Richie says, looks like a scepter. Ah, his eyes are blank. He seems at once to be gazing out over the water and into the depths of his soul.

That's the way rotgut booze makes your eyes look, Pepper says. You take your congenital idiot, your lamebrained salesman, your asshole congressman, your dumb office manager, and fill the son of a bitch up with a pint of blended rye and his eyes will get all serious and deep and poetic. Meantime, he's the same goddam jerk he always was.

Ticineti, the mysterious, stands at Santo's elbow. His eyes are blank and inward gazing too but he doesn't look out over the water.

I can't, Ticineti says. At the moment I am not at the beach.

Remember how weird Edward G. Robinson's eyes were in *The Sea Wolf?* Santo says.

No hot tears on celluloid for Santo, Richie says. No complications, no eructations, odors, embarrassing swellings, pimples, or putrefaction. All is clean and neat—right, Santo?

What?

How about no furious blushes! Pepper says. No vomit, no death rattle?

O.K., Richie says. I'll buy it.

The mysterious Ticineti, furiously blushing for no apparent reason, drifts out of sight. Santo might think of him as drifting out of camera range, or off the set.

Far out to sea, Richie says, there is a fish leaping and also a sailing ship sailing. Looking more carefully, the fish is seen to be a dolphin and the sailing ship is seen to be, indeed, a sailing ship.

Green Dolphin Street! Santo says. I saw it twenty-six times when I used to work at the Fox.

What do these aquatic symbols mean? Pepper asks.

At the word "symbols" Ticineti looms clear, dazzlingly clear, ready, as it might be, to set up his old, creaking shop, so to speak. To their credit, everyone leaves, Pepper in the lead.

Gene Phillips remains seated—he is debating whether to go up to the house and freshen up his drink or call Dorothy to perform this homely chore. Just then he catches sight of the dolphin and the sailing ship.

What can these symbols mean? he mutters. Ticineti, smiling faintly, trudges across the sand toward him, arranging an opening line in his mind.

38 Paris

Big Mickey, after running away from reform school for the sixth time, finds himself in the city of light, Paris. After a light snack of croissants and café au lait at a sidewalk cafe that, with its red-and-white-checked tablecloths would make your heart break, he wanders toward the Seine.

At the edge of the beach, he finds a woman sitting in a large wing chair, gazing into a rather ornate cup filled to the brim with Sanka.

What is your name, young man? the woman says, in French.

Big Duck, Big Mickey says.

You are, ah, French? she says, smiling.

But of course.

It has not been mentioned that the woman has been paddling in the water with her bare feet. Behind her, the rough walls of a cliff plunge almost straight down into the river.

At this moment, Paris seems—almost, almost—forgotten . . . Is it not so, Big Duck? she says.

So it would seem, Madame, Big Mickey replies. That's a really terrific hat you're wearing.

A René Pedersen, she whispers. As a matter of fact, my entire wardrobe was created by Pedersen.

Gorgeousness in action, Big Mickey says. The silvery blues. The odd yet how piquant touches of scarlet. Or is it vermillion?

I prefer to think of it as *rouge*, she says, gazing again into her golden cup.

Don't let me prevent you from enjoying your coffee, Big Mickey says.

She grins girlishly at him, her teeth a sparkling mélange of alabaster, meringue, and snow. You don't want eggies on the coffee? she says.

Good Lord! Big Mickey says. For what kind of uncouth beast do you take me? I learned *something* at the reform school! He reddens in anger and embarrassment.

Don't be angry, Big Duck, she says. Beneath my chic ensemble my firm flesh cries out, yearning, panting for *amour*.

Take it slow, Big Mickey says, and runs, stumbling, to the Metro. He is pleased when the Sea Beach pulls in a moment later.

I didn't know they had a Sea Beach in Paris, Red Miller says.

It's a *story*, for Christ sake, the Sailor says. Right, Richie?

Right, Richie says. Big Mickey doesn't know a word of French.

I don't like it so much that he called himself me, Big Duck grumbles.

Oh what the hell, Duck, Big Mickey says. You ain't going to no Paris anyway.

I can't believe this guy turned down an easy piece, Red Miller says.

Now it is clear why Theodore Dreiser called Paris "a lamp lit for lovers in the wood of the world," Doc Friday says.

All right, all right, the Sailor says. Now. Who'll fade this lonesome three bucks?

The woman finishes her Sanka and gazes across the Seine at the Tuileries, where she believes that somebody important was born, perhaps Flaubert.

Big Duck, she muses. Big Duck. What a monicker. *Incroyable! Zut!* And yet . . . he had a certain *élan*, an undefinable chic . . .

39 *Leif Eriksson's Memorial*

It happened, Richie says, that a group of civic-minded, proud, and patriotic Norwegian-Americans decided to place a stone—a huge, rugged piece of granite about twelve feet tall—in the middle of the lawn in Triangle Park. It's still there, but this is the story behind it that I heard.

You know the name of that park is not *really* Triangle Park, Irish Billy says. It's really Leif Eriksson Park.

I thought it was Owl's Head Park, the Drummer says.

No. Owl's Head Park is the part of the park down by the Narrows, Irish Billy says.

That's Bliss Park, Cheech says.

You're *all* wrong, Professor Kooba says. The park from 8th Avenue down to Colonial Road is Leif Eriksson Park. Then, the little part of the park from Colonial down to the water is Owl's Head Park. Triangle Park and Bliss Park are time-honored neighborhood names—not official names.

The way I always call it, Big Mickey says, is this. From the water up to Colonial, Bliss Park. From Colonial to 4th Avenue, Leif Eriksson Park. From 4th to almost 5th Avenue, Triangle Park. Then just at 5th you have the softball field. Across the street from 5th to 6th, you have the playground and the big softball field. From 6th to 7th, that's the 6th Avenue Park and from 7th to 8th, that's the 8th Avenue Park or else you can call it the end of Leif Eriksson Park if you want.

Actually, and officially, Professor Kooba says, I think the entire thing is Leif Eriksson Park.

Wait a minute, Richie says. Can I tell this story? You all wanted to hear it and now this and that and this and that about the park. I'm talking about Triangle Park! We agree we all know what and where I'm talking about no matter what they call it?

There is general assent.

O.K., Richie says. The Norwegians, I don't know who was the boss in all this, Maybe Mariane Gade and the *Nordiske Tidende*—I don't know, they put up this big stone with a plaque on it commemorating Leif Eriksson's discovery of America— you know, a plaque with one of these Viking ships, with the dragon on the prow, lots of oars, a big striped sail.

Columbus! Cheech says. Columbus!

Sit down, Cheech, the Drummer says. Who cares?

O.K., Richie says. They've got the stone, they've got the big plaque. They unveil the thing on Brooklyn Day when the Protestants march up and down and then eat ice cream in the churchyards.

I thought that was called Protestant Day, Professor Kooba says.

Sister Augustine told us that if we even looked at the parade by accident we'd probably go blind, Cheech says.

Instead you just got ugly and dumb, Irish Billy says.

Bands they've got, Richie says. They've got bands and firecrackers and girls in their Norwegian costumes with all the embroidery and beads and little Hans Brinker caps on.

Wasn't he Dutch? the Drummer says. The kid who stuck his teeny little finger in the goddam dike?

He's the guy with the magic skates, Hans Brinker, Cheech says. For Christ sake.

Lemonade they've got, ice cream, Richie says. A bunch of drunk Norwegians making speeches. O.K. There's the stone, to sit there a thousand years, forever, I don't know. But some guy gets the idea a few years later to take the stone down and move it somewhere else where they have a lot of Norwegians, Minnesota or someplace.

That's Swedes in Minnesota, Kooba says. I happen to know that for a fact. Swedes.

They're all the same damn thing, the Drummer says. A mongrel bunch.

They take the stone down, Richie says, and ship it out. The reason they do this is because this rich guy, a Norwegian-American—who turns out to be the guy who paid to ship the stone out—gets this idea to put up a statue of Leif Eriksson holding a sword. He figures it's more artistic. O.K. They get some sculptor to make the statue. They put it up where the stone used to be and unveil it, again on Brooklyn Day.

Sister Augustine used to say that even if you didn't mean to and you got a glimpse of the Protestants marching, like if you looked out your window by mistake, your eyes would probably fall out, Cheech says. And if you went and got some free ice cream in the back yard of a Protestant church, oh Jesus! Your legs would fall off, your mouth would catch on fire, your—

Again on Brooklyn Day, as I was saying! Richie says. More lemonade and beads and Hans Brinker hats and everything else. More Norwegians making long speeches about the fjords. Native dances.

Accordions too, probably, the Drummer says, and grimaces.

So here's the statue, Richie says. Leif Eriksson on a horse. The sculptor has him all decked out in armor like a knight. He's got a winged helmet on, the visor is up. Goddamned if his face doesn't look just like George Raft. Yeah! In his right hand he's carrying a sword sticking straight up in the air. The Norwegians are not too goddam happy and thrilled, since this guy, believe me, doesn't look much like a Viking. He looks like some bust-out gambler in an iron suit. But they don't say anything, they figure, I guess, what the hell. What do they know about sculpture? Besides, the base of the statue *says* this joker is Leif Eriksson.

Maybe he did wear armor, Professor Kooba says. Stranger things have happened. In "The Curse" I tell of a Pope who wore corsets and petticoats.

I wonder if Sister Augustine wore a corset? Cheech says.

Time goes by, a few months, maybe a year, Richie says. Then, one morning, and again on Brooklyn Day, people start gathering in Triangle Park—

You didn't say they put the *statue* in Triangle Park, Irish Billy says.

Oh yes, Richie says. I said—and my exact words were—"they put it up where the stone used to be."

Sorry.

They gather in the park. The same old goddam caps and beads and lemonade and vanilla ice cream. Then they take a look at the statue. Somebody's broken the sword off—actually, sawed it off—and cemented a bottle of Pabst Blue Ribbon into old Leif's hand. The Norwegians go absolutely apeshit. Insult! Insult! they yell and scream. They throw lutefiske around at each other, they try to shield their daughters' eyes from the sight.

A cultural truth is often greeted with consternation and fury, Professor Kooba says. In "The Curse," I speak of the anguish of the Jewish community in Cracow where a maverick rabbinical student proved that Moses and company, in their flight from Egypt, probably ate, at least once a week, the rough equivalent of pork lo mein.

So they take the whole statue down, Richie says, and sell it to some guy in Coney Island for a come-on for an attraction on Surf Avenue. They get the stone back from Minnesota and set it up again. Now they can get juiced in peace on Brooklyn Day.

Sister Agustine said if you ever looked in the door of a Protestant church—you didn't even have to go in—your teeth would all get cavities and rot out of your mouth before you even got home, Cheech says.

40 In Sheepshead Bay

One day Mrs. Glynn travels out to Sheepshead Bay to see
Ticineti about her son, Mark. The boy has been associating
with bad companions, she says. Staying out till all hours of the
morning, in trouble at his job as a clerk with the Fidelity and
Casualty, and drinking to excess. Mrs. Glynn, who was born
Constance D'Amato, is deeply upset by all this, especially the
drinking. Alcoholism seems to her, as it does to all Italians, totally incomprehensible, as puzzling as parents who don't care
about their children.

Must we again tolerate with benignous good nature and bon-
homie in the extreme these clichéd and unfounded mindless
cracks about Italians? the Arab says.

Mindless my ass, Bony Ruth says.

Excusez-moi? the Arab says. I failed to auriculate your *mot*,
cadaverous one.

Bony Ruth is often called "M.B.," or "Mosquito Bites," a
cruel sobriquet that refers to the size of her breasts.

What a character, she says. Ugh.

Anyway, Ticineti, is there any way you can help me out with
this kid of mine? Connie says.

A phony touch of delirium tremens might straighten the lad
out, he says.

I'll bet you a half a buck Ticineti didn't say "lad," Bony Ruth
says.

I have to chime in agreement with you, osseous one, on that,
the Arab says.

After a moment or two of silence, "lad" remains the word uttered by Ticineti. The Arab and Ruth grumble but do not pro-
test.

Delirium tremens? Connie says.

The shakes, Ticineti explains. The screaming meemies, the fear, the horrors, the terror. A harsh step, yes, but in this case I believe it to be a perfectly valid one. He is looking hoodedly at Connie's legs. They are sturdy and with lusciously swelling calves and slender ankles.

If this is the same Constance Glynn, bursted into the sad world as D'Amato, who domiciles herself over the Italian Products Company store on 69th Street, I do not blame or fling censure in any way or shape at Ticineti, the Arab says. Mrs. Glynn is, as the figure runs, a fine figure of a woman. It astounds me into an almost catatoniac trance that she ever wedded that beery lump of a lout of a stevedore, Jack Glynn. Even I, who rarely—

Oh for Christ *sake!* Ruth says. The Arab's phrase, "fine figure of a woman," fills her with anger and frustration, understandably so. Although Ruth's sex life is full and somewhat varied, this is because she will never, as the phrase goes, say no.

As I was attempting to articulate, the Arab says, even I, who rarely looks up from his midnight oil except to study the ways of the human creature in an artificial environings, to wit, this great metropolis, even I have oft plucked a moment or two out from the rigors of intellectual labor to ogle upon the swing of that lady's hips, the roll of her buttocks, and the smooth line of her remarkable legs—not to mention, if you will, her firmness and fullness of bosom.

I don't have too much money, Connie says, standing up and undoing the buttons of her dress.

Ticineti locks the door and pulls down the shade.

Aha! the Arab says. Aha! Now, let us see . . .

But the shade is all the way down to the windowsill.

Oh curses and rats! the Arab says. But, but, to *imagine,* in the arena of the pulsating cerebellum, the gentle semi-darkness in Ticineti's kitchen, Constance Glynn in a posture of abandon, sweating just a small trickle, her unmentionables utterly deshabille—it pushes and prods me into a state quite uncomfortably nervous!

All you goddam men are the same, Bony Ruth says. But at the same time she wonders what it must be like to have the sort of body that one can bargain with.

Mrs. Glynn soon leaves and Ticineti takes a nap. Some few nights later, the Magician rows into Sheepshead Bay in a punt.

Rows? the Arab says. Rows? One *poles* a punt.

The Magician *arrives* in Sheepshead Bay, at Ticineti's invitation. Over spaghetti with red clam sauce, breadsticks, and a cheap and tinny Chianti, they talk. Two nights later, Mark Glynn, about to down his tenth stein of beer of the evening in an Irishtown bar in Rockaway Park, suddenly sees a fish pop its head out from the foaming head and look at him sadly yet penetratingly.

Holy sweet Mother of God! Mark says. He drops the stein and runs out of the bar, leaving his companions calling drunkenly after him.

And now he's a Jesuit, Bony Ruth says mockingly.

Who? Richie says.

Mark Glynn, Ruth says. The fucking miracle of Irishtown in the fucking flesh.

What? Richie says.

Tender the wench little heed, Richie, the Arab says. She mocks, slanders, and traduces. She drags the name of Mark Glynn through the mucky slimeness of blasphemious gossipry as a joke. Joke! Ha!

I don't know where she got the Jesuit, Richie says. Mark just got a promotion at his job in the insurance company and I hear he's studying accounting at night and he's engaged to that Italian girl used to live in Flagg Court.

Ticineti, meanwhile, has rented a second apartment right next door to Flynn's Tavern, right around the corner from—

Don't utter it! the Arab says. I cannot bear the broiling lusts such thoughts awaken! I must rush home and to my lonesome oil, my solitudinary pen. Am I just a lump of frying flesh like everyone else? Or what? As he rushes out the door he sees Constance Glynn across the street in front of Flynn's. She is bending over to pick up a coin.

Oh Jesus Christ Almighty, he says, and rips the lapels off his tropical worsted suit.

41 Magic Rainbow

Gene and Dorothy Phillips, along with their small daughter, Marjorie, and their neighbors' son, Willie Wepner, go to the country for a two-week "vacation," Richie says.

Why the quotes I seem to "hear"? Pepper asks.

Because the "vacation" is not really a vacation. The Phillipses go to the country in order to dry out. They feel that in the supposed peace of the countryside they will be able to stop drinking—to stop drinking and to fill the terrifying chasm that this will create in their lives with tranquillity. The night before they leave they finish off a quart and a half of Gordon's gin before supper. With supper, which Dorothy puts on the table at ten o'clock, as usual, they drink three quarts of beer. After supper, they polish off what's left of the second bottle of gin. The next morning, trembling and sick, they board a coach of the Erie and start for the country. The trip, although essentially uneventful, does have a few interesting, even entertaining things about it. For one, Gene and Dorothy decide to—

Could we cut out all the fancy stuff and get to the country so you can get said what you want to get said? Pepper asks.

Say what you wish, Richie, Professor Kooba says. Pepper is unaware of how fiction works.

Who isn't? Irish Billy asks. As far as I'm concerned, fiction is an effort of the will.

He read that somewhere, Kooba says. Probably in a cheap novel. Go ahead, Richie.

It doesn't matter anyway, Richie says. To tell you the truth, I don't know what happens on the train, I just thought I'd fill in the time for them—they're so lonely and forlorn, all those trees make them nervous, the small-town kids staring at them as the train slows at crossings. Their bleary eyes. Their pounding heads. The burning nausea that—

All *right!* Pepper shouts.

They're in the country, Richie says. Maybe a couple of days have passed, maybe a week, I don't know. In all events—

Wait a minute, Irish Billy says. Is this a true part, or is this still a story part?

Who cares? Kooba says.

I like to know these things, Irish Billy says. As a member of the vast working-class audience, I like to know if I'm getting the straight dope.

Working class! Pepper laughs, since Billy has not held a job of any kind for three and a half years. Ever since his discharge from the Navy because of his terror of the water. No one ever mentions this in front of Billy. Occasionally someone will mention this in front of Billy.

This "terror of the water" business seems a bit hyperbolic to me, the Drummer says.

"Hyperbolic" is a word of the quintessence of the gorgeous! the Arab says. Elegant, succinctful, trig, and foursquare.

Jesus Christ, I knew they'd show up, Pepper says.

Allow the man to proceed with his story or fable, Professor Kooba says.

Thank you, Richie says. They're in the country. A couple days, maybe a week has passed. They have been climbing the walls for a drink, but each night they restrain themselves from walking down the road to where it comes out on the highway and where Henny and Mary's roadhouse is. Henny and Mary sell all kinds of hard booze as well as Trommer's on draft. But they don't go. They try to talk the nights away, they sit on the porch of their little cottage and watch the stars, they listen to the crickets, they play gin and five hundred and checkers. They even attempt to make love, an activity that their alcoholism and its attendant problems has made into a kind of nostalgic memory—almost like something that involved two different people.

Do they succeed? Irish Billy asks.

Let's say so-so. Let's say fifty-fifty. Let's say their knees don't get weak and they don't feel their spines dissolving—but let's say they give it a shake anyway, what the hell. However. One morning—one bright and fine morning, as they say—they get up and they feel good. They eat, by Jesus, they eat breakfast. I mean they eat *breakfast*. Eggs, bacon, rolls, jam, milk, coffee, orange juice, the works. At night they still want a drink but it's not life and death. Marjorie, feeling this change, plays happily with Willie Wepner in the fields under a bright sun in cool, dry air.

Now we're getting nature descriptions, Irish Billy says. This must be the fiction part

Ignore the hooligan, the Drummer says.

"Hooligan," the Arab says. Paragonical!

Gene and Dorothy decide to take a walk a day or so later and are caught in a sudden summer shower. From which they shelter in a—in a—

In a gazebo? the Drummer asks.

O.K., Richie says. In a gazebo.

How could such a cynosuric word have oozed out of my brains? the Arab says. "Gazebo!" Superlative!

The shower ends and Gene and Dorothy emerge into the laved and crystal air and walk toward Marjorie and Willie who are dancing hand in hand around and around in a circle. Suddenly they look up to see a fantastic and perfect rainbow arching magnificently across the deep azure sky.

Now you're cooking with gas! Pepper says. Shaking his head, Irish Billy leaves.

They look up at it in awe and wonder, their hearts filled with an almost tangible gratitude to the country, its peace, and so on and so forth. The children continue dancing.

Richie stops and sits at the fountain.

That's it? Pepper says.

Well . . . yes.

That's not enough, Pepper says.

Well . . . there's a kind of coda but it really doesn't end the story anyway. I mean I can tell you what happened next but then—*that's* it, *that's* the end.

Tell anyway, Pepper says.

Enounce indeed the peroration, Richie, the Arab says.

All right. From a little red-roofed cottage in the distance, the Magician has been watching this scene. Some think that he created the rainbow, or the illusion of the rainbow, but I don't think it matters. But anyway, for some reason, his idea of a joke, boredom, something, he causes Gene and Dorothy to see, stretched across the entire goddam arc of the rainbow, ten bottles—gigantic, monstrous bottles—of gin. They stand there, looking up. Gene puts his right arm around Dorothy's waist, perhaps in support. Almost somnambulistically, they raise their arms, Gene his left, Dorothy her right, and—what? I don't know. They salute the rainbow? They try to ward it off? Maybe they're trying to block their vision of it? Perhaps it's a gesture of despair?

Or maybe, Professor Kooba says, it's a gesture that says "Ha ha! Who cares!"

Maybe.

That's the end? Pepper says.

I'm afraid so, Pepper. I told you it didn't end. Or, I mean, it's a coda that doesn't really end anything at all.

I tend to think of the whole rainbow-gin thing as a rather obvious and crude objective correlative, the Drummer says.

"Objective correlative"! the Arab cries, and leans ecstatically against the soda cooler, clapping.

42 A Strange Occurrence in the Melody Room

For some reason, Master Sergeant Gentry, in suntans and with all his rows of ribbons gleaming, is roaming the neighborhood. Far from the military posts, forts, and camps he has called home for almost twenty years, O far! Perhaps he is searching for a rare species of the *Culex* mosquito spotted in Brooklyn and duly reported to the Bureau of Diptera Studies.

The bureau of what? Big Duck says, shiny black bits of Nibs flying from his mouth.

But enough of this. How curious, how curious indeed that Master Sergeant Gentry should enter the Melody Room at the exact moment that Henny is losing his balance—because of his usual drunkenness—and pitching forward into the refrigerator cabinet wherein is stored the bottled Carling's Red Cap Ale.

In front of a dark semicircular table in the rear of the Melody Room sits Santo Tuccio, facing the noisy, crowded bar. On the table are ranged nine full bottles of this same Carling's Ale. He sits stolidly, his arms folded, as if he is guarding the ale. Perhaps he is. Yet there is a small hint of a contented smile on his face. He seems to be amused at the crash that Henny makes as he falls into the cabinet. God knows, it has happened before.

Jesus Christ! That's some *hat* Santo's wearing, Little Mickey says.

It certainly is, Richie agrees. Where the hell did he get it?

An impartial observer would be forced to agree with Mickey and Richie that it is, indeed, some hat.

Master Sergeant Gentry stands at the bar, and addressing the prone form of Henny, orders a Four Roses and a bottle of Carling's. Henny stirs, then rises to general applause.

The chances are good that someone has somehow been to the table at which Santo sits, because although the nine bottles are still there, they are now empty. This has occurred in the flash of time it took for Little Mickey to remark on Santo's peculiar hat. Yet Santo still smiles. Little Mickey says nothing, but it is quite possible that he attributes Santo's smile to a musing upon the new movie that will open at the Roxy the next day.

If the truth were to be told, which it here will not be in order to spare Little Mickey's feelings, Santo is smiling because he is dwelling upon a certain memory having to do with Little Mickey's mother. One might call it a naughty memory.

The Magician, disguised as a drunken businessman, has been at the bar all this time, swilling Gordon's and 7-Up. He glances at the table in the rear and the bottles are once again filled with ale. No one knows why he is doing this. No one knows, in fact, that he *is* doing this. For that matter, no one knows that this tired figure is the Magician. He smiles the famous tired businessman's smile. At times like these—granted, they are rare—he transcends his limitations.

See much action? he asks Master Sergeant Gentry. The Sergeant scowls and says, Enough, turning so that the dazzle of his ribbons squarely confronts the Magician.

You look like a man with an eye for the mosquito, the Magician smiles, at which remark Master Sergeant Gentry starts and knocks his ale over. Henny approaches and swabs the bar in front of him as the Magician hastens to buy the sergeant another drink.

And another for myself, Henny, he says.

Master Sergeant Gentry nods his thanks, drinks his whiskey and ale quickly, and leaves the bar. Entering a telephone booth, he places a call to the FBI and tells them of a spy who has somehow gotten wind of his secret Brooklyn mission for the Department of Biological Warfare.

In a few moments, agents of the Bureau and a group of Military Policemen enter the Melody Room—but the businessman has disappeared and the Magician has entered Henny's body, causing him to once again pitch forward, face first, into the refrigerator cabinet.

The MP Captain, a choleric man, gazes around and orders his men to place Santo Tuccio under arrest. Although he doesn't know it, and would deny it if he did, the captain's ire toward Santo is based upon the sight of his remarkable hat.

And also because he's drunk as a coot, the captain says. Look at that! *Nine* empty bottles.

Well, that *is* some hat, Little Mickey says. He is beside himself with glee.

I agree, Richie says, lounging against a lamppost as Master Sergeant Gentry rushes by, heading for the park.

I don't understand exactly what happened, Big Duck says, opening another box of Nibs, his black teeth gleaming.

43 *An Example of Metaphor*

A metaphor? Professor Kooba says. A metaphor is the explanation of something deeply hidden and darkly deep, something profound, by using something simple as its emblematic, symbolic surface. It is *not* a simile, which is what dummies use to make themselves look smart when they are at a loss for words.

I revel and wax gladsome at your explanation and differentiation of these two items, the Arab says. But things might partake of the clarific if you were to give us an example.

A wrongo thing to say, Arab, Doc Friday whispers. Now he's going to talk about "The Curse."

Wrongo to you! Professor Kooba says. I shall *not* talk about "The Curse," even though it is bursting with models of metaphor. No. I will invent an example out of whole cloth.

An old song—even the words are familiar, Doc Friday says.

Let's hear, Professor, the Drummer says. I've always wanted to understand this. I never have come across a definition—in my reading—or example either, that suffices to stick in my mind.

What sticks in his mind is fourteen-year-old girls in short skirts, Cheech says.

The Drummer ignores him and "strains every fiber of his being" toward Professor Kooba.

It's a great relief to me that that phrase is in quotes, Curtin says. A *great* relief.

Imagine a man out in LaTourette Park in Staten Island, Kooba says. He's hiking along, keeping close to the bank of a small stream. A tributary of Richmond Creek, or perhaps Fresh Kills Creek.

This is a metaphor? Cheech says.

It is early night and the moon has risen, Professor Kooba goes on. It is a full moon and the man in it stares benignly down upon the hiker. He trudges, he trudges. He carries a stick in his hand to assist him in his trudging. At his back—and let me make it clear that he has his face turned toward the stream—there are, let's say, eight—eight cans of Heinz Beans. It is obvious that he ignores them—I mean to say that he knows that they are there but he pays them no heed. On he trudges, while the man in the moon glances down at his lonely figure.

The scene is weightily freighted with possibilities, the Arab says.

Is this a YMHA campsite? Curtin asks.

Campsite? Kooba says. Who said it was a campsite?

Well, who the hell would leave a bunch of beans just out in the woods? Curtin says. It must be a campsite.

All right, Kooba says. Excellent. Fine. Your nitpicking does not diminish my paradigm a jot. All right, yes, it's a campsite.

A YMHA campsite? Curtin persists.

What the hell does it matter or not what it is? the Drummer says, "fuming."

Thanks again for the invaluable quotes, Curtin says. It matters because if it is, you know that the beans have to be Heinz Vegetarian Beans—without pork. That's why I ask.

All right, Kooba says. It is *not* a YMHA campsite. These are cans of *pork* and beans.

That's better, Curtin says. I just want to get the picture clearly.

He trudges, Kooba says. Making his way doggedly along the stream—upstream. That is, on his way to a different campsite.

I always remember a guy named Seligman in the Pine Tree Patrol, Cheech says. For some goddam reason I always remember him one day when we were all playing Capture the Flag, running through the woods in a drizzle eating raw weenies.

Do we have to hear nostalgic tales of your days with the Boy Scouts? Doc Friday says. Let the good Professor go on—allow him enough rope.

Humph! the Arab says. He has waited for several weeks for the correct time to try this expletive out—in the field, as it were. He is pleased but conceals it.

Now, Kooba says, rope or not, Doctor, the man trudges along—he is on his way to a different campsite where, he assumes, there is hamburger steak, eggs, stew, and coffee for the evening meal. He eschews the eight cans of beans just a few dozen feet away from him and plunges on toward a greater reward, a more pleasant prize.

You remember how everybody used to get pink eyes from the goddam chlorine in the Tottenville pool? Cheech says to no one.

The moon gazes down, blasé, Kooba says. The night grows deeper. The man's figure slowly recedes in the gloom. The moonlight gleams gently on the cans of beans, now forlorn.

And those grass and brush fires out there in the meadows? Cheech says. Somebody's going to get killed out there someday.

Professor Kooba stops and lights a Wings. Well, he says. How does that sit as an example of metaphor, Arab? Drummer?

Example? the Arab says. I fear that I cannot pierce tellingly the meaning of—

Simple, Doc Friday says. The metaphor here is the old tried and true one about the man who ignores the bird in the hand and goes seeking the two in the bush, or, the grass is always greener in the other campsite. Professor?

An interesting theory, Doctor, Professor Kooba says. But, I must confess, one that never entered my mind. May I be so gross as to say that you are reading between the lines?

I am sorely afraid that I lack absorption of the content at all, Professor, the Arab says. What is the explication?

I thought it was a back yard the grass was always greener in, the Drummer says.

Quite clear, quite clear, Kooba says. Simply, and I trust, lucidly, this small anecdote is a metaphor to show the placid workings of nature in the face of man's petty greed and ambition and his striving for—how shall I put it?—pie in the sky.

You mean, the Arab says, the moon—?

Exactly! Kooba says. While mankind sweats, the moon "sails" on.

Bravo! Curtin says, and applauds. "Sails."

The moon "sails" on. The stream "babbles." The trees "tremble" and the wind "whispers," "soughs," and "sighs." All these phenomena go on doing what it is their natural bent to do, Kooba says. Thus, the metaphor is constructed to show a profound truth—often ignored—through the employment of a simple and superficially obvious thing. In this case, the small tale about the hiker who ignores the beans.

Lucid! the Arab says. Pellucidly clear and an example that will stick gluishly to my memory forever.

How simple but how true, the Drummer says. A small burst of genius, Professor. Brilliant!

Yes, Doc Friday says. "Brilliant!"

And a double and triple cheer for you, Doc, Curtin says.

44 The Vision of Bela Mukosa

There would have been a softball game except for this damn rain, Cheech says.

Softball! the Drummer sneers. A pastime for morons. Did Lester Lanin get where he is by playing softball? Guy Lombardo?

Blue Barron? the Arab adds.

Kooba's got his book with him, Irish Billy says. This is the kind of day he ought to read us something.

Regale us with something, Fat Frankie says.

Professor Kooba scowls from behind the soda cooler. He fingers his tie. He places his huge, ragged manuscript on the cooler.

Read something? he says. Really?

Regale, regale, Fat Frankie says.

A choice selection, the Arab says. A dazzlingly lambentish glitter of a paragraph, an elegantishly turned anecdote, a sturdy feuilleton, a dab or shard of belles lettres.

Professor Kooba riffles through the pages of the manuscript and clears his throat.

He always clears his throat, Cheech says.

From, says Professor Kooba, "The Curse." Book Six, Chapter Eighty-four, "The Vision of Bela Mukosa." He clears his throat again and places a pack of Wings and a book of matches next to the manuscript on the soda cooler. He looks up and then down and begins to read.

Bela Mukosa was a young and handsome swineherd who lived on a houseboat on the Morava River just outside the village of Svilajnac in the old country. As the gentle tides and currents of the ancient river rocked and swayed his finely composed corse, tense in its potency, how he cogitated on life! How he wool-gathered! Often he would smile to himself as in a dream of Utopia as he thought of gold and riches beyond compare, and of what he might do with such wealth in relation to certain fanta-sies he had of nights and in the long summer afternoons as he watched the swines root and grunt in their eternal search for a scrap of orange peel or a fragment of Hershey bar some carefree peasant lad had dropped on his way home from school. These fantasies often found themselves centered on the gaily laugh-ing, rosy-cheeked, and high-breasted maidens who partook of knowledge at Svilajnac High. How sorely he missed an educa-tion! It was a constant recrimination to him that he knew he was rather dense.

One hazy afternoon in late autumn, when the trees and bushes and shrubs and all the other foliage and floras of the for-est that was to Bela Mukosa an open book that he could read as easily as falling off a log, or, as he often put it to his friends around the roaring fire of a winter's night, as easily as falling into the Morava! For Bela, laughter and jest were the salt, sauce, and relish of his life without which there was no food for thought worth the eating, or even the cooking. This fall day, turning chill and grey now as the sun began its journey into the waters far beyond Svilajnac, yet but with the floras all carmine and gold and russet to bring a pinch of color to Nature's grim cheek, Bela heard a splashing and a moaning above the roar of the waterfall he happened to sit down next to the better to ob-serve the rooting and snuffling hogs and sows and their fellow swines in his charge.

"What?" Bela inquired of the blank and unpitying sky, the silent forest. But the Morava only stretched away into the dis-tance like a cruel and ambiguous jape! Still the splashing and moaning continued. Rising, Bela forged through the densely packed herd of swines to the very lips of the waterfall, when what to his amazed stare should greet him but the sight of a tiny man all dressed in brown and with a long white beard and pointed cap standing under the torrent of water that the Morava unleashed in its ceaseless fury.

As quickly as he would kick a hog attempting to filch his lunch from his kit bag, Bela made a stout rope from some vines growing in the nearby furze and brambles and cast it into the gnashing teeth of the mighty falls toward the thrashing figure of the tiny man who, with a mien of fixed determination, shot his tiny, skinny arms out and grasped the slippery helping hand the vine rope dangerously offered him, regardless. Swiftly, young Mukosa pulled heartily, the tiny man held on for dear life, and with the sound of a cork being pulled from a bottle of champagne, the tiny man was wrenched free from the roaring flood.

The recipient of Bela Mukosa's Good Samaritan act stomped and stamped about the shore, frightening many of the swines off into the thick gorse that grew in healthy profusion all about the little glade. Bela offered the tiny being a portion of his humble lunch, a tuna salad sandwich on whole wheat with lettuce and mayo and a thermos of coffee and after they had, in silence, refreshed themselves and lit up the cigarettes that Bela had wisely cached in his lunch pail, the tiny man, his beard waggling impishly, spoke up.

"Bela Mukosa," he said, "you have saved me even though to do so meant to endanger your own life, or to risk a bad case of poison ivy by stumbling around in the furze and brambles in order to make a rope out of vines, or to chance losing some of your swines in the almost impenetrable gorse that grows in such profusion hereabouts"—and he swept his tiny hand in an arc to indicate the thick gorse from which came the squealing sounds of swines suddenly discovering themselves lost or stuck.

"I am," he went on, "as you may have guessed to gaze upon my little frame, a gnome from the Dinaric Alps, a far piece from here even as the crow flies or the bull charges. Why I was ensconced in that waterfall it is not for me to say—suffice it that I found myself there, drenched and in imminent danger of an immediate battering to pieces, when you performed your warmly heroic act of sheer valor and selflessness. As a reward for this I am empowered to grant you a magical choice of something beauteous and in all ways terrific. I will show you, in a vision, seven marvels, and you may choose one of them for your own to have and keep forever. It is to be hoped that your purity of heart will enable you to choose the correct one."

Young Bela stared gape-mouthed at the gnome, who was making some strange magical passes in front of his bewildered face. The frightened and angry squeals of the swines and hogs and sows receded into a murmur as gentle as rain falling on the ancient roofs of Bucharest as his sight began to cloud over, then sharpen itself like the blade of a dirk. A strange vision was before him, and as it became clearer and clearer, he heard the gnome's gentle rasp.

"Bela Mukosa, before you you see seven glorious chalices, and in each a gift seemingly fit for an emperor—for a god! You may choose any one of these things and it shall be yours. However, let me warn you that only *one* of them is, as they say in the United States, the McCoy. The other six have flaws which render them useless, if not downright disgusting, malicious, and et cetera.

"The first chalice holds a glorious girl, perfect in all ways, gentle, curvaceous, modest in public and lascivious at home. Yet—she may have an incurable dose of the venereal disease known to sailors as the 'bull clap.'

"The second chalice holds another young woman whose body is that of Aphrodite on one of her better days. Over her head, however, is a mantle, so that you, Bela, cannot see her face. Is this modesty? Or does the young woman have a face that could, as they say, stop a clock?

"In the third chalice is a golden snake, of a species that gives birth to its young alive, so that its owner is assured of a continuing supply of the highest-quality gold—the offspring also have the ability to give birth to gold snakes, and so on and so on. Yet all that glitters, eh? And who is to say that this snake is not packed full of poison and mean as a bitch to boot?

"The fourth chalice shows a castle on a mountaintop. Wow! you seem to say. But how can you know that this castle isn't haunted by ghosts or inhabited by vampires and werewolves and such ilk? This *is* Rumania, is it not?

"The fifth chalice is filled to overflowing with jewels of all kinds, a king's ransom, as they are wont to say in the public prints. May I have your permission to utter one word? Glass.

"The sixth shows naught but a fresh laurel wreath, the time-honored symbol of fame, glory, and honor. But there seems to flitter and flutter and glimmer and shimmer on the chalice itself the horrifying skull of old Death himself—yet perhaps, *perhaps* it is but a trick of the light? Perhaps.

"The seventh chalice contains a vile-looking little dragon crawling out of it, ugly as sin. Yet allow me to tell you that this is but one of the millions of manifestations of an extremely powerful genie, one who will do your bidding for the rest of your life. But there is—there exists the chance that this genie may be maleficent and vengeful and make your life a hell on earth full of pain and misery.

"One, brave Bela Mukosa, one vision of the supreme is legitimate and carries no 'catch,' as they say. If your heart is good and pure, you will choose the right one, if not, you will be, sad to say, stuck."

The little gnome lapsed into a silence as profound as the grave. Bela stared longingly at the objects that shone before him, his eyes sparkling, his breath coming in gasps. Nothing could be heard but the sound of the rushing waterfall and the squealing of the swines in a fit of pique as they crashed about in the entrapping gorse.

Professor Kooba pauses, lights a Wings, and continues.

Book Six, he says. Chapter Eighty-five, "The Odd Behavior at the Millrace."

The reader will remember Bela's half-sister, Craiova Mukosa, snatched from the Mukosa cabin as an infant by ravening gypsies, and later sold into white slavery in Budapest, where, as a young woman of eighteen, she became the wife of the Archduke Reginaldo of Warsaw, brother-in-law to the English nobleman, the Earl of Cadwallader. As we return to her adventures, we find her preparing to board a zeppelin for Bucharest, where she is to attend a ball in honor of the marriage—

Wait a minute, Professor, Fat Frankie says. What about the choice? What did this guy choose and how does it all work out?

Indeed, Professor, the Arab says. We swing wildly on tentered hooks!

Kooba looks around. The choice is not revealed, he says. That is, not explicitly. When next we meet Bela Mukosa, in Book Eleven, it is clear from his actions and circumstances what his choice was. But I have nowhere provided for anything so crass as a "choice" to be made *obviously* in this work. My God! He grinds out his Wings in disgust. This is not mere *fiction*, he says.

Bull! Shit! Fat Frankie says.

Should have played ball in the goddam rain anyway, Checch says.

The Professor, with authorial dignity, begins to pack up his manuscript.

45 Cheech's Composition

MY FAVORITE CHILDHOOD HOLIDAY

My favorite childhood holiday was Easter. It might sound surprising for, many people especially children, always say Christmas is their favorite childhood holiday. They think about the presence and the candy and the joyous Spirit of the Christmas Season when they mention "why." I, am not trying to say that Christmas is not a real favorite childhood holiday of mine because, when I was a little boy I looked forward excitely to the visit of the jolly Elf known to all children all over the world by the same name which is, Sandy Clause or Chris Kringel. I remember laying in bed and waiting for him while visions of sugar plums danced in my head and there was always presence under the tree for me and my brother and sisters. Once I remember I got a brand new Flexible flyer sled, which we shared together, my brother and me. Actually it was a present for the both of us because it was expensive and my father did not happen to be working at the moment.

Yet still Christmas, with all its cheery Christmas Spirit was not my favorite but, Easter Sunday always was. You may wonder why?

I and my family would always without fail travel to my Uncle Joe's house in Bath Beach on Easter Sunday for our dinner. It was a regular tredition. It was exciting especially after, Sunday Mass, when the Church is so beautiful with big bouqueuts of lillies and me and my brother and sisters would always have some kind of new clothes for Easter Sunday. And always, their was something that we didn't expect. I once got a yellow tie with a picture of a rabbit on it eating a carrot. It was fun to wear! Such is the kind of thing that makes a little boy happy.

But anyway my Uncle Joe and Aunt Mary in Bath Beach would always welcome the whole family with smiles and hugs for all of us and Aunt Mary would then, let us color Easter Eggs in the kitchen. Their would be a big choclate egg for us too, and a special Italian kind of loaf of bread for Easter time with hard boiled eggs all around the edge. The bread was shaped in a circle. I have to laugh when I think of the fights I would have with my brother Rocky (Rocco) and my sisters BeeBee (Beatrice) and Connie, over the extra egg because, their always seemed to be one odd egg in the loaf of bread. I am sure, that sometimes we even cried about who got the extra egg but it seems to me that we usually had more fun than fighting and crying and also, my Aunt Mary would give who didn't get the extra egg a nickel apiece.

We'd go in Uncle Joe's back yard that I always remember for some reason was sandy, not, like on the beach but with a little sand scattered around in the grass. And my Uncle Joe would unwrap the fig tree then. Which was a big deal because you had to first take off a layer of old kitchen linoleum and then a layer of burlap from potatoe sacks and then newspapers that the tree was all wrapped up in because of the cold of the winter that kills fig trees. But don't get me wrong, it was only if Easter was late and the weather looked like it would stay warm that my Uncle Joe unwrapped the fig tree. In other words if we had a cold Easter he wouldn't unwrap it until later on in the Spring, not just Easter Sunday.

We'd get out old baseball gloves and my Uncle Joe and Rocky and me would have a catch with a hard ball for a while since my Uncle Joe used to play semi-pro ball when he was young for a team that I think played in the Parade Grounds called the Nathan's Red Hots. Sometimes my father would catch too, but he usually sat outside on a kitchen chair and smoked and watched and told Rocky and me not to be afraid of the ball because that's how you get hurt by a hard ball and read the News. He liked the rotagravur section the best. Sometimes he would yell things like put a little pepper on the ball to my Uncle Joe and then he would throw the ball to me and Rocky a little bit harder and faster and my Uncle Joe had some arm.

I would go into the house once in a while and smell the dinner cooking. If you ever smelled those Easter dinners my Aunt Mary would cook you would almost go crazy from it. She would be cooking brajole and chicken cachatori and big raviolis, I mean the big ones, and a lot of other delicious Italian delicasies.

What I also loved about this childhood holiday of Easter Sunday was that I would play with my cousin Florrie whose real name was Fiorenza, in the Italian language, in the back yard after we had a catch. She was really a nice girl and I liked to play with her and she liked to play with me more even than she liked to play with my sisters BeeBee and Connie. My Uncle Joe once had a lot of lillies in the back yard I remember, in pots wrapped up in gold silver foil, and Florrie and me spent almost the whole time before dinner playing that we were florrists and a florrists' customer, and had a lot of fun.

At dinner time we ate all those things I mentioned that my Aunt Mary cooked plus, a lot of other things like boccalla which is some kind of a fish which I didn't like too much, and still don't, and salads and veal scaloppeni and veal cutlets and we'd have an Italian plant sort of, at the end of the meal that tastes like licorich called fenoke, and then fruit and Italian pastry of which my favorite when I was little was one called conoli but, I also liked sfilleeatel. There was also rum bobbas and of course milk for the children. The grownups drank wine and anizette with black coffee with little pieces of lemon peel in it. When us kids got older by the way, we would get some coffee too called, half and half, which means with a lot of milk in it. Then the grownups would sit and talk and laugh about things that happened to the family and then the men would play cards, usually hearts, or sometimes peenockle or an Italian card game that I don't really remember but, I think it was called breeshk or something like that. This was after dinner when some of my other relatives would come over usually, my Uncle Tom and my Uncle Julius and my Uncle Patsy and my Uncle Angelo, and, their wives and kids. Their wives which were my aunts were, Aunt Mary, and three Aunt Roses which seems funny but it is true.

All the kids would hang around the house and play or read and I'd try and play alone again with my cousin Florrie, but by that time, their would be the other cousins their like my cousin Frank and my cousins Ralphie, two different ones, and Carmine. But we got along all right.

At night we'd all leave and take the trolley home and usually then have coffee and cake at home before we had to go to bed or, we were allowed to eat some of the choclate egg we got. So, for me as you can tell, Easter was my favorite childhood holiday even though, Christmas was also good. But Easter was some way much better and it always made me feel happy. And, to this day, when I see my cousin Florrie who is now a Freshman at Fontbonne Hall I always ask her, if she'd like to buy some beautiful lillies to take home to the family. She always laughs. Then she asks me who got the extra egg from the Italian bread last Easter. And then, it's my turn to laugh.

Maybe, Easter is my favorite childhood holiday because we laughed more than we did at Christmas it seems. But I don't really know.

46 Mr. Huckle's Homburg

Mr. Huckle, in his famous black benny, stands, head lowered, looking at the three bottles of milk that, tearing through the bottom of his grocery bag, have fallen to the ground and smashed. Behind him, he has carefully set down two other bottles, as yet unbroken. Perhaps he was carrying them in another bag. Perhaps it is just luck.

But he is bareheaded. Where is his grey homburg?

The day is grey and still with the smell of snow in the air. The sort of day into which Mr. Huckle would never venture without his hat.

Is it Mr. Huckle after all? There is certainly no one near who can tell us, and the man's face is averted. Perhaps he doesn't want us—or anyone—to see that he is crying over spilt milk.

I think that "spilt milk" is going a little too far, Fat Frankie says.

I agree, Mr. Huckle says.

It is Mr. Huckle after all.

Where is your famous, not to say legendary, homburg? the Drummer asks, smiling. One might call it an "infuriating" smile. Many do.

Mr. Huckle ignores the question. Though he has spilled three quarts of milk, and his benny is shiny and threadbare, he has some dignity.

I asked Georgie to help me, he says. I *asked* him. But he couldn't be bothered.

In domicile and poring with sedulousness over the *Morning Telegraph*, I trust? the Arab says.

The Drummer is still smiling.

What else? Mr. Huckle says. He studies, he pores, he figures, he calculates, he adds and subtracts, he dopes out, he pores some more—for hours. And then . . .

And then wagers a few meager shekels on four dogs to show, all of which crippled equines are last seen hobbling in the stretch as the glowing orb of the moon rises up, the Arab concludes.

Mr. Huckle sighs. It wouldn't be so intolerable to have a dumb and deadbeat horseplayer for a son, he says, if my wife did not look like a cartoon.

Everyone stands absolutely still, amazed and silent. It's absolutely true. Irma Huckle looks as if she was invented by Cliff Sterrett, the creator of *Polly and Her Pals.* For some reason, nobody ever noticed this before.

What about your homburg? Fat Frankie says, to break the silence. The day is growing colder and greyer and one can almost taste the snow that will soon be falling.

Two weeks ago, Mr. Huckle says, Georgie, for what he called a "lark"—whatever the hell that may be—don't ask me, I was born and raised in Greenpoint—wore it while he did his daily handicapping, if you'll be so kind as to let the expression slide. He'd picked a horse to place in a maiden at Hialeah, name of Miss Zero, and she paid $6.80. From that day to this, the moron won't give me back my homburg, but wears it even to bed. I've begged, cajoled, yelled, threatened. I've even thrown myself on the floor, but he will not budge an inch—and Irma backs him up!

Various exclamations: What? God! Jesus Christ! Son of a bitch! Crueler than a serpent's tongue!

To think, Mr. Huckle goes on, that I once was employed as something or other and earned a decent salary. On Maiden Lane. The Exchange Buffet! fondly known as the Eat It and Beat It, fresh plump packs of Lucky Strikes, starched white shirts, silk mufflers, grey suede gloves, my own Ticonderoga pencils, and a fresh crisp copy of the *Daily News* on the Fourth Avenue Local every morning.

He turns as if to pick up the two unbroken bottles of milk, but then resumes his original position, crestfallen in his shapeless benny, his uncovered head grey in the grey air.

I often think, he says, of building a raft out of Georgie's old back issues of the *Telegraph,* placing him and Irma on it, and letting them float down that river there to the open sea.

River? What river? the Arab says, and then stands, in awe, as does everyone else, for sure enough, some hundred yards or so in front of Mr. Huckle, a blue-black river flows quietly, disappearing beneath an arched bridge on the horizon. A little afraid, the group breaks up and drifts away, leaving Mr. Huckle alone as the snow begins to fall.

47 Sudden Change

Irish Billy took to spending all his time in the park under a tree back in those days, Curtin says. Sometimes with a book or a magazine, sometimes without, but always with wine and beer.

I remember it clearly, Fat Frankie says. A bottle of muscatel or white port and two quarts of beer. He'd sit there in a daze looking at nothing, that hard Irish map of his so sad.

Even cynics get hit like a ton of bricks with love, Professor Kooba says. It's all old-hat material. I myself outline such a case in "The Curse," as some of you know.

It is not exactly what one would declaim an original matter, Professor, the Arab says. I mean Faust, Romeo, Hamlet—the roster is lengthily endless of those poor waifs smited down by the stygian powers of Eros.

Only Billy could have managed to fall in love with Thelma just as she was falling in love with herself, Fat Frankie says.

You got to admit the lady has a lot of class, the Drummer says. Nice dresses, slouch hats, elegant perfume, and shoes and handbags that match.

You are considering and envisionating her as she is now as the acmeic Tania Crosse, the Arab says. A sterling editor in the world of glamour and moundish heaps of shekels, well paid, well spoken, and well fixed up. Irish Billy adored and worshiped her as the humble and non-chic Thelma Krulicewicz.

Yes, but, Fat Frankie says. Even then, when she was just one of the girls, she was classy. I always told Billy she thought she was too good for the neighborhood but the poor bastard couldn't help himself.

Her dark eyes! the Drummer says.

She was, I must accord, possessed by deep-seated muliebrity, the Arab says.

And Billy with his jug of cheap wine and two quarts of beer, Curtin says, waiting for Thelma to come and find him sitting there, drunk and miserable and dying from love.

Although it is an old cliché of life, Professor Kooba says, still, it wrenches the heart to remember the poor young man wrapped in that drunken fantasy that she would come to him.

Indeed, it burdens the very aorta with pangish pain, the Arab says.

I remember that Billy didn't care after a while if we made fun of him, the Drummer says.

Now I feel ashamed about it, Fat Frankie says.

Well, he's all right now, the Arab says. As a matter of sheerest fact, something deeply entombed within him became very tough and impregnated through his experience.

Impregnable? the Drummer says.

Impregnable. Correct. Forgive my gaffe, dear camerado.

Ah, tripe to her! Professor Kooba says. From a simple beauty of the streets and of the people she became a snob—it was a sad day for Billy when she first realized she had a good figure for clothes and a nice voice . . .

Urgently packed with truth, Professor, the Arab says. Indeed it was. From there it was but a hopping skip and a jump to *Vogue* and Bonwit and Teller, Goodman Bergman, and a falsificated accent imported out of Smith University or some other finishing school. And then it was but a moment to the time when she should vocabulate *avatque vali* to Billy—a broth of a beamish boy, a strap of a figure of a man, who now and perhaps evermore is filled up to his back teeth with—how do you say it?—cholera?

Choler, the Drummer says.

Choler, yes, the Arab says. Once again, my thanks, *caro mio.*

After a while, Fat Frankie says, remember how she started to break dates with him or stand him up? And she criticized his Windsor knots and his haircut.

She assaulted his Flagg Brothers shoes, Curtin says.

The vicious savagery of her crushing stomps anent his pegged pants! the Arab says.

She'd only have a drink in the goddam White Shutter with all the goddam junior executives in their blue straw hats and repp-stripe ties, Fat Frankie says. Then when she bought that sport car—whammo! That was absolutely the old eighty-six for Billy.

The footgear from I. Miller bootery to flatter her feet, the Arab says.

What about the scarfs from Peck, Peck and Son? the Drummer says.

What I recall best is the French purse by Louis Vooton, Professor Kooba says, nodding. Ah, the whole phenomenon is here in "The Curse." Except that my rendition deals with a pair of young lovers in Prague, years and years ago.

The really big crusher was when she changed her name even before she left the neighborhood, Fat Frankie says. Tania Crosse! Remember how poor old Miss America almost went crazy, crying and yelling?

I remember, the Drummer says. I was on the block one day when the old lady was on the stoop yelling at her "You *love* kielbasa! You *love* kielbasa!" and Thelma was hopping into her little toy car showing off those goddam legs of hers up to her belly in those five-dollar nylons and acting like her mother was some kind of maniac lady she never saw before in her life.

What of the bruising blow that tragedic evening when she refused to acknowledgeate Billy's presence unless he called her Tania? the Arab says. This is a mammoth fardel of misery for any man to bear up, believe me. My own experience of life and love with the fair sex gives me the right to opine thusly, believe me.

That was the time that the next day he went to the park drunk before he got there, Fat Frankie says. And after he drinks the whole bottle of wine and the two quarts of beer—Billy told me this a couple of years later, that's how I know it—he said that some voice came to him from nowhere offering him a way to get out of it all by drinking a bottle of special booze. Yeah. Really. He told me. And he said that he saw a hand sort of swim through the air with a bottle in it and the voice kept on talking and talking. And he also said the voice was familiar too.

The DT's, Professor Kooba says. Plain and simple.

That's when he knew, he said, that he had to get this broad off his mind or he'd go crazy, Fat Frankie says. And from that minute on he started to straighten out.

She *did* have class, the Drummer says. To tell you the God's honest truth, I couldn't ever see her standing at the bar in Pat's or Gallagher's. Billy should have known these things. I mean this wasn't any Bony Ruth or Joycie Lunde you can take to Finn Hall or the 802 Club and then down to Imbriale's beer garden for a few pitchers of brew and a couple dozen cherrystones.

It was that it occurred with such a swiftness of celerity, dear friend, the Arab says. One day the lady was crampacking her maw with greasy cabbage and day-old Silvercup and the next—change-o, presto!—she was racked with anxietyness about whether her undergarments matched her ascot.

Le snobbisme, Professor Kooba says, is a potent force, and no respecter of companionship, old buddies, or love.

I would not be shatteringly shocked with surprise, the Arab says mysteriously, if Ticineti was involved in some mode in her speedy zippiness of metamorphosis.

Ticineti? Kooba says. Ticineti? Why would he get involved?

Fires of Eros, the Arab says. Broiling lusts. Unholy loves. Secret desires. Filthy fantasies. And, don't allow it to sneak out from your minds—*familiar voice,* eh? I just would not be smacked down in surprise.

48 Joycie's Dream

What do you mean "The dreams of beautiful souls and virtuous people"? Doc Friday asks.

Exactly what I said, Professor Kooba says. Literature is filled with examples of the good and the noble having wondrous dreams of beautiful and marvelous things. Dreams that certified to them that they were living lives beyond reproach.

Anybody can have a beautiful dream, the Doc says. And I mean anybody.

I doubt this very much. "Anybody," on investigation, usually turns out to be Galahad, Schweitzer, Joan of Arc, Saint Francis of Assisi, and so on. Not your usual run-of-the-mill person who spends his life hanging out on the corner or in a candy store. Can you imagine, for instance, Aram Kurkjian having a beautiful dream? A dream of making all the money balls in a game of acey-five is about the extent of his concept of the beautiful. How about, say, Finn Drumm? Maybe he dreams of a fountain of Ballantine's beer splashing on his head as he paddles his feet in a vat of Three Feathers. Or Cookie LaNord? A new pair of transparent panties maybe? Rhinestone pasties? A silk corset? But who would call this beautiful?

What about Joycie Lunde?

Joycie Lunde? Kooba laughs. The sweetheart of the Atlantic Fleet? Miss Merchant Marine? The blushing maiden whose unmentionables are forever being stolen from the clothesline? or so she says. Beautiful dreams?

Why not? Listen, Joycie told me a dream she had. She'd had a few boilermakers at the time so her recital of the dream was not completely coherent, but the beauty is there. I was so taken with it that I wrote it down word for word.

Since when does the good Doctor possess and clasp the skills known as the shorthand? the Arab says, looking up from the parlay he is trying to figure.

Word for word, the Doc says.

And how and why and wherefore these boilermakers? the Arab says. You were perhaps plying and stoking up Miss Lunde with alcoholic potations of a fearsome potency in the Lion's Den so that you could perhaps solicitate her favors?

Word for word, the Doc says again. And I've read it so often that I've memorized it.

Saint Jerome maybe, Professor Kooba says. Florence Nightingale. Lucky Lindy. Maybe Babe Ruth or Jim Thorpe or Nick Kenny. Alfred Lord Tennyson and Father Divine and maybe even Billy Sunday. But Joycie Lunde?

Impossible! the Arab says. Aha! Alice Blue Gown at four-to-one leaps upon my orbs as the sturdy little filly who might possibly fill out my parlay.

Joycie Lunde, yes, the Doc says. He takes a position next to the gumball machines, closes his eyes, and begins.

The dream of Joycie Lunde: A garden in the autumn, ripe fruits and vegetables on the ground and even a pumpkin for Halloween or Thanksgiving. And three lovely ladies, really girls, who look like my mother used to look when she was a girl I bet, dancing in a circle like ring-around-a-rosy in long gowns in colors like all the ripe stuff and they have those metal glasses like they have in the movies about the olden times, flasks? Decanters? Goblets! You know, all gold metal and they're toasting each other and pledging and dancing and smiling. Blue sky. Pledging and dancing. Dancing and toasting. Colorful and ripe stuff all ready for harvest. They're a little bit drunk so they must be drinking wine from the ripe grapes made from the sun's rays and their little feet stamping them like Italians in the movies do. One girl even has a bunch of grapes in her hand. Stamping and hopping and dancing and shuffling around. Riping and graping and coloring and bluing. Barefoot. A pumpkin. They're dancing and the music is so nice like when you're just outside the door at the O.L.P.H. dance and you can just about hear maybe Glenn Miller or Tommy Dorsey and you imagine inside it's so great but it's never like that at all. Hopping. Grapey and happy. Flagons, or goblets I mean. They really shine because they're gold and it's all sunny. And it's all blue so you know it's a nice cool day but not so that you're cold. You maybe need just a sweater. They have robes. All of a sudden they sing to me, all at once, all three of them, but not in real words but in the words of dreams so that you know the words before you hear them sort of. You never really hear them anyway, you know? They sing, come and dance! Come and dance! Your father is the King of France! Come and dance! Come and dance! We don't care if you don't wear pants! Come, come! Come, come! Come, come, dance! And then they smile and then I wake up.

This is a beautiful dream? Professor Kooba says. This is the kind of dream dreamt by Mother Cabrini? Do you mean to tell me that Amelia Earhart or Louis Pasteur had a dream like this?

A pedestrian genre of a dream, the Arab says, folding the *Green Sheet*. A prosic dream. The dream of a dope, if you will forgive such a common kind of obloquious word.

It's something . . . something . . . Doc Friday says. Maybe it was the way she told it.

And what, by the way, dear Doctor, occurred post the quaffing down of the boilermakers by Miss Lunde? the Arab says. Did you escort her to your hearth to demonstrate the Gregg method to her? Or perchance—the Pitman method?

49 Crazy Talk

My first wife? the Arab says. Ah, my first wife. You should of needs, howsoever, utter the words "ex-wife," since "first" implicates, with no shred or tatter of correctness, as you know, that I possess or did possess a second spouse. But I have been as freely fancy as a swooping seagull or tern for some space of five and a half years. My first wife? How can I possibly lucidify the deep arcanums of our oddest-ball marriage to you, bosom compañero?

If it's too . . . delicate . . . the Drummer says.

They are sitting at the bar in Pat's Tavern, although Irish Billy implies that the Arab and the Drummer most usually employ Gallagher's Subway Inn as a watering place.

You're goddam right I imply it, Irish Billy says. His voice issues from a booth in the rear of Vogler's, where he is sitting with Lizzie Mulvaney and Bony Ruth.

Not what one would call a brace of queens, Fat Frankie says.

I heard that, Frankie! Billy says, but there is no animosity in his voice. Irish Billy is not the sort of young man who calls a spade a diamond.

No, no, not at all, the Arab says. Allow it to perish on the creeper the thought that this is too "delicate," as *you* so delicately put it, dear comrade. It is simply mysterious. Or, I should elocute that it *was* mysterious. Beyond superficialism of many subloony things of the terra firma we call earth.

Fine, the Drummer says, pulling a bowl of pretzels over in front of them.

Image then in your mind, the Arab says, two people at a festive gala, or, if you prefer, a fete. One of them is myself, the other my future spouse. Who can enumberate the hidden influences, all alabor in the air, benefic or malefical, whatever? We faced each other in despite of the fact, too rugged to be softened over or washed away, that she thought of me—and with what tingling twinges of agonic pain I knew it—as a rather comical figure, a stage Arab, as if so to speak.

A stage Arab? Billy says. I heard of a stage Irishman, but a stage Arab?

We faced each other, the Arab goes on, gazing and peering as best we could through the usual miasmatic air of fetes or galas, into each other's orbs, gleaming and twinkling with love and a tiny pinch, a milligram, of that foul beast named lust. At least so gleamed and twinkled *my* orbs. We pledged and plighted our twainful troths by exchanging cups of the unmixed wine. Perhaps, however, so doth harshest memory dim all, it was *sharbat* we exchanged, nevertheless despite the fact that my beauty, my dear maiden, was, at the time I recollect, a lady of Polish-Italian heritage and extract.

Descent, we say, the Drummer says.

Yes. However and whatever, thus pledged we our twain. I was young and foolish, adeep in salad time, and of a totality of lack of experience in sensual ways, yet how my flesh cried out! How it yelped and yowled in longing pain!

The bastard was thirty-four! Irish Billy says. "Young," he says. Ho! Ho! Ho! And also ha! ha! hee!

Lizzie Mulvaney says something that passes, in her family, for English. Bony Ruth, the soul of wit, answers her. What is said is unknown.

What did I ken? the Arab asks. What, as a fledging babe in the woods, the epitome of callowness, did I know of the straps, the clips, the hooks and the buttons and the dear Christ knows what else other fastening devices and gadgetries of feminine undergarments? What did I seize to my brains as far as an expertism goes anent perfumes and colognes? And about coiffers and frocks and millineries? The merest dim idea of the staggering feats of technogical acumen brought to bear upon the invention of the delicate gewgaw that holds a stocking to a foundation garment was enough to plunge me into blithering doltishness.

Amen! Irish Billy says. And it gets worse with the years. Worse.

Blugga-kow cha mens dird onyla bonze, Lizzie Mulvaney laughs gaily.

How idiotically droll a figment I cut in the eyes of hosts upon dozens upon legions of young ladies as I attempted, for an example, to hoist and bully and haul their brassieres down over their hips, the Arab says.

The Drummer shudders and fills his mouth with pretzels.

The one and only solitary young beauty who managed to control her gouts of laughter at my butterfingerness when it came to but partially relieving her of her unmentionables became my enamorata and later my wife.

You mean . . . ? the Drummer says.

Exactly. *Précisément!* This blooming young heifer with whom I exchanged cups of *sharbat* at this gala—

What the hell is *sharbat!* Irish Billy says.

Junket! Fat Frankie says. Right, Lizzie?

Blazdoo, Lizzie agrees, her silvery chuckle wafting.

"Her silvery chuckle wafting"? Cheech says, and he repairs to Sal's Billiard Academy.

"Repairs," used in that way, is a vulgar middle-class affectation, so I've heard, Irish Billy says.

It was good enough for James Joyce, Doc Friday says, popping his head in the door.

James who? Irish Billy says. Who was that? Kooba?

Once again, Lizzie Mulvaney's laughter chimes among the cases of empty Coke bottles.

Don't forget the cases of empty Dixie Shake bottles, Irish Billy says. Get it all in.

In any events, the Arab says, after the exchanging of *sharbat,* we plaited together our troths.

Troth, without an s, is O.K., the Drummer says, I believe. This remark is spluttered through another mouthful of pretzels.

Check and roger, the Arab says. What could she have espied in me? I, who had on a thousand occasions torn her hosiery to tatters, snapped her garters into shreddings, savaged her petticoats and slips into a veritable chowder, and decimated her panties like unto an Attila the Hun? I should have ogled the bad sign of the lion's head with wings, signifying violent heartbreak, that hovered all afloat in the air above our dizzied heads. I should have peered intensely at the staff of Mercury with the crooked and twined-up snakes that specterally poised between us, signifying poisonous events to come. But I did *not*—or, if I did I cared no whit. I blinded my glims to all but our moment of troth.

I think you mean moment of *truth,* the Drummer says.

Any goddam fool would have paid attention to a flying lion and a couple of floating snakes, Billy laughs, *except* maybe a goddam Arab. Hey, Frankie, why don't Arabs get hemorrhoids?

Frankie shrugs. It is often his wont.

Because God wanted to make them perfect assholes.

Bu, bu, bubba bu, Lizzie Mulvaney titters. Bony Ruth bangs the table with what years ago might have had a chance to be a delicate hand. Bottles and glasses rattle.

As the years passed, the Arab says, I came to sapiently realize that she, my beloved pigeon, although aglut with disgust at my physical frame and all its addendas, had wedded me—for by now we had wedded, as couples are apt to do after *sharbat* pledging—because she descried, in what she supposed to be my intellectualities, a way to be the spouse of a man who would one day be rich, and filled brim-chock with powerfulness, and, although a jerk-like clump like any congressman, a man to who the humble would grovel and toad and lap upon his shoes.

A bitch, the Drummer says.

And yet, the Arab says.

I see odd prefigurings of doom in this story, the Drummer says, scowling at the bartender as he removes the bowl of pretzels.

I *made* money, the Arab says. I bought for her bibelots, adornments, trinkets, and gimcracks. Clothing, goodies, frillies, whatnots, and folderols. As you must of needs be aware, my master mechanicship brought me, as they utter, a heavy paycheck each week.

We say fat, the Drummer says. Fat paycheck.

Fat! Fat! A *fat* paycheck, you Arab asshole, Irish Billy says.

Loudmouth son of a bitch! Cheech curses, as he misses the five ball on a bank shot.

But my grime-enstained hands could not be made up for by the fatness of my money, the Arab says. I glimpsed the disgust and loathingness in her eyeballs as she surveyed the grease-and-oil-caused blackheads on my nose and forehead. One day—whoof!—she was gone, taking everything except my chest of tools.

You're better off, the Drummer says.

Ah, and ah. Now, lonely nights and crepusculated mornings have made me aware that I should have given attention to the curiously phantasmal signs that lurked, at the moment in which we exchanged *sharbat.* I cannot think why I did not . . .

Because, Irish Billy says, you are an Arab and a perfect asshole.

Arckhh, arckhh, Lizzie laughs delightedly.

What can that odd cackle of effusion be? the Arab says, getting up to retrieve the bowl of pretzels.

50 Booze Pond

Visions are symbolical, the Arab says. They arrive unbidden as well as uncalled for and multifarious. Often they conceal truths we can bend our knee in thanks to our lucky stars we are better off in ignorance about.

He read that somewhere, Fat Frankie says. Your trouble, Arab, is you read too much. That's your visions.

The man hurtles doubtful contumely on my visions, the Arab says. It is to laugh. It is to die and collapse all achortle over heels. The Arab looks up at the ceiling, his face a perfect mask of infinite patience and forbearance.

Collapse over your heels? Pepper says. I come all the way over in the fucking rain for the paper for this?

The paper and a few double Wilsons, Doc Friday says.

Carstairs, Pepper says. Wilson tends to give me heartburn.

Seriously, the Arab says. And basically. One must permit one's brains to relax and open up all in bloom like a flower, to stretch upward like the yearning branches and boles of a green, vibracious tree, toward the great sun of mysterious powerfulness, and empty out the cramped and seamily obnoxious cerebellum. And the visions will come!

What if you're like the Sailor? Fat Frankie says. I mean what if your cerebellum is already empty permanently? You must *always* have visions—Jesus! day and night.

Ha and ha, the Arab scowls. Such levitous hilariousness will give me a stroke. Cheers and cheers again to the Milton Berle of the sweaty masses!

I knew a guy in the Army had a vision once, Johnny News says.

Oh God! Pepper says. Give the man a cigar and a ticket for a new fedora.

Fedora? Doc Friday says. Fedora? I thought that odd-shaped lump was part of Johnny's head.

Let the man enounce, the Arab says. Out from the mouths of babes and bullshit artistes often issues forth a modicum of truth, a pinch of insight, sullied over though it may be with hyperbolism and exaggeration. Later we can discuss Johnny's eerily misshaped fedora.

Fedora? Doc Friday says again.

In the Army, yeah, Johnny News says. This buddy of mine in the middle of a battalion inspection, he has this vision. A big hand is holding a cup and out of the cup stream five streams of stuff. Into a pond with those floating flowers?

Water lilies they call them, Johnny, Fat Frankie says. I know it's hard to say. Say wa-ter-lil-ies. Go on, try it.

Don't badger the bull, the Arab says. I sense a profoundly deep symbol here of rejuvenation. So far, in all event.

The guy tells me, Johnny News goes on, that he knows these streams are booze. Gin, scotch, vodka, bourbon, and brandy. They're all pouring into the water. Into the pond, really, of booze too.

This is the craziness of your average drunk speaking, Fat Frankie says. This is not what you would call a vision.

Cease a moment, the Arab says. The whole image is crystallinely lucid to me and to anyone else who possesses a nodding insight into the way that visions function at moments of great mental stresses and strains.

He was in stress all right, Johnny News says. As the colonel reaches his rank he realizes his fly is open.

Total degeneration into a cornball joke, Doc Friday says. A story as old as the Army itself.

Now wait, Johnny News says. I don't know about the vision, but I do know that his fly was open because he got gigged and lost his pass for two weeks and got K.P. for three days straight.

Despite the scoffs and barbs of these heresiarchs, the Arab says, I believe with every fiber of my instinct that this manner of instance is the perfect time for a vision. Besides, it contains unto its core all the symbolical qualities one should have an eyeball peeled open for. These are the nirvanic waters of the ineberation of the senses, all flowing into the quiet pond of sereneness—and on this pond of liquidous fluid float the gorgeous flowers of forgetfulness. In the circumstance, what better time for a vision that would enable Johnny's comrade to forget the putridous situation he discovered himself in?

Right, Johnny says.

Well, I got to admit that Johnny couldn't make it up, Fat Frankie says.

Also, Johnny News says, he said that there was some kind of bird taking a dive headfirst into this cup holding a baseball in his mouth.

Beak, the Arab says. People possess mouths. Birds are decorated with beaks.

And fish got to swim, Doc Friday says.

All the way over in the goddam rain, Pepper says, looking at the clock. Where *is* that goddam *Mirror?* It's always late.

This last ornotholical touch proves the truth of Johnny's story, the Arab says. The bird with the baseball in his beak, diving headfirst into the boozy cup? What else is this but the young soldier's symbol for himself? A symbol of his secretive yearning to plunge into oblivion to escape the militaristic apoplexy of his commander, the voice of doom?

What about the baseball? Fat Frankie says. A symbol of his foot in his mouth? Or his balls in his mouth?

He was a big Detroit fan, Johnny News says.

No, no, no, no, the Arab says. As in all true and foursquare on-the-level visions, there is always something that battles explaining. As a matter of fact, this vision is more of a sticker than most because you have got this baseball in the beak of the bird and you have also got this big hand clutching the cup filled up with booze. Both of these elementaries are of the nature of arcanic mysteries of an absolute sort and type.

Well, Johnny News says, he really *was* a big Detroit fan.

Tut, tut, tut, the Arab says. Don't bother your head about it, Johnny . . . or, *is* that your head?

An oddly ugly lump, Doc Friday says. Within which there beats and pulses a brain of pure lead.

Come on, *Mirror*, Pepper says, Come on, *Mirror*.

51 Minor Difficulties

The Magician disguises himself as a king and sets up a throne at the entrance to the park one afternoon, seats himself, and leans a huge sword against his right shoulder. A king of sorts.

There is a certain number of things a magician must do each year, he apologizes. His magicianly duties, so to speak, more or less, as it were.

An idiot! Professor Kooba says. Each passing day reflects more of the idiot about him—why did *we* get stuck with this sort of moronic magician? In Europe, now . . . in Europe—that's where you get the truly top-flight, the first-rate magicians. Paragons!

The Magician leans back. Two boys of ten or so start to enter the park. Homage! the Magician intones. I must be paid homage. The two boys turn and run.

You see that? Kooba says. Homage! I'll bet a dollar the dullard doesn't even know what homage means. A magician he calls himself. Ha. A disgrace.

Magician? Cheech says. I thought that was Eddy Ellsworth with that old sword of his. That's the kind of uniform Eddy would go for too, in a big way. The Magician? Jesus, he gets crazier every day.

Go over, Arab, Professor Kooba says. Ask him what kind of homage. Or what *is* homage ask him.

Swiftly as the lowliest chickadee doth soarest in free flight through the blue, leaning and beating of a fury into the typhoonic winds so that he may arrive upon a locus wherein he might pick up a few crumblies, so do I fly upon this errand, the Arab says.

Ah, come on, Cheech says. That's got to be Eddy Ellsworth.

Maybe it's Eddy the tire man, Red Miller says. He figures he'll slash a couple tires with that sword and drum up a little trade.

He doesn't know how to slash a tire, Kooba says. Neither of them.

Ah, Magician, the Arab says. May I enter the park to partake of its blissful bowers of floras?

Homage to me first, kind sirrah, the Magician says. Then we shall see about your amusingly base and serf-like request.

Yes, of course. What sort of homage stands in your eye as a just one? Lucre?

Money? Not *money.* I don't know. Ask Ticineti. He's schooled in such things. So they tell me.

But Ticineti is, at the moment, peering and peeking into Constance D'Amato's window with the aid of a Tom Mix telescope he purloined many moons ago from Willie Wepner. The Arab shakes his head.

That is one lowlife bastard, Irish Billy says.

One could hang one's head in shame for the blot he has placed on the neighborhood, Professor Kooba says. But rest assured—he'll be set down—with *justice*—in the "Americana Freakiana" section of "The Curse," under a different name but wholly recognizable.

Like a roman clef? the Drummer says.

A what? Kooba asks.

A roman clef. When you disguise your characters like with other names but you know who they are—like the Magician? Who we all know but who's supposed to be a king? Like if this was a novel, the Magician would be part of a roman clef technique.

Drummer, Kooba says, have a three-cent chocolate—on me. Roman clef. He shakes his head and walks into the park, past the Magician and his warnings.

What magician? Curtin says. I don't see the Magician.

In the park, Red Miller says. He's all dressed up like a king and wants you to pay him homage.

Me? Curtin says. Why me? Render unto Caesar, buddy.

No—I don't mean *you* you. Anybody who goes into the park—except Kooba just walked in and didn't pay him nothing.

O mighty sovereign! the Arab says. I cannot, as you know, broach out this question to Ticineti. The varlet is now utterly plunged and embroiled into an endeavor to catch an unholy glimpse of that lady's toilet. He would not know of homages anyway, I trust.

I *need* homage, the Magician says. And tomorrow, mark my words, I'm going to have a word with Kooba.

Professor Kooba, the Arab says, has been occupied up to the elbows with much diligence on a massive tome of a volume that works like a roman clef—so his cranium is lost to mortal cares among a crush of stars, up in the clouds, if your grace will perceive my drift-like conversation.

How the hell does he know about what I'm doing? Kooba says. At the moment he is on a ferry halfway to Staten Island. Cheech stands at the rail next to him. I love that salty spray, Professor, he says.

The night is falling, the Magician says, and, as of now, no one has paid me homage.

Hey! Eddy Ellsworth says. Where did that fruit in the park get my sword?

See? Cheech says.

See what? Kooba says.

I am the Magician King, the Magician says. This is not your sword, young man. But if you will pay me homage I'll grant any wish you make. Or as close to it as I can anyway.

O.K., Eddy Ellsworth says. What kind of homage? Money? I'm broke.

Not money! the Magician says. For Christ sake, ask Ticineti!

Who? Eddy Ellsworth says.

Ticineti, Ticineti! God almighty.

Eddy's got no clue who Ticineti is, Irish Billy says.

I think I may permanently settle in Staten Island, Kooba says, stepping off the ferry on the Brooklyn side. "By the light of the moon . . . " he says.

What moon? Red Miller says. It's dark as hell.

You could with nary a doubt complete your roman clef opus there in peace and tranquil bouts of calm, the Arab says. I myself have often entertained a cogitation on removal to the hilly bosks of the Borough of Richmond in order to labor over some scattered clutches of entomologic notes, and et cetera sorts of materials.

"By the light of the moon," Kooba says again. O.K.

There is a sudden silence, broken only by the sound of wheat fields rustling in the October wind.

Wheat fields? Irish Billy says. *Wheat* fields?

"By the light of the moon," Kooba says, "Arthur Warlock, robed in kingly raiment, with Ellis Edwardson's saber on his shoulder—and God only knows how he got ahold of it—sits at the entrance to the park, devoid of all homage. His ugly face is bathed in tears."

He's going to pay me for the sword! Eddy Ellsworth says. You can bet your fucking ass on that. The fruit.

This young maniac needs a trip to, say, Wilmington, Delaware, to get his head screwed on straight, Professor Kooba says.

Wilmington, Delaware? the Arab says. What in the name of heavenly stars and their planetous neighbors is Wilmington, Delaware to do with this all?

Don't worry, Kooba says. Don't worry. It's all going straight in here, he says, pointing at his manuscript.

52 Grey Cloud

Irma Huckle sits directly behind her apartment door at the end of the long corridor—she calls it a foyer—on a kitchen chair. In her hand she holds, bolt upright, something that looks as if it might well be a rolling pin.

She is, so to speak, mad as hell, Fat Frankie says.

Correct! the Arab says. Take note well of the massed grey clouds splotched about on the horizon. They are what is called "boiling." "Boiling clouds." What a wonderous infernious image!

Wherefore! the Drummer says. I mean to say, why is she sitting behind the door with a rolling pin? Why is she so mad?

Experience, than which there breathes no more greater puissant mentor, the Arab says, has taught her, in the school of hot knocks, that when both her hubby *and* Georgie are both late for supper upon a Friday night, they have discarded all their wages on the ponies, those little four-footed darlings.

Irma Huckle raises her left hand in a gesture of halfhearted anger—or perhaps a gesture of futility—and then lets it drop. She rocks the rolling pin back and forth slightly in her other hand.

I don't think I like the rolling-pin business, Fat Frankie says. Too perfect. Too careful. Almost like Irma is Mamie Mullins waiting for Willie and Moon to come home.

What I don't get is the clouds on the horizon, Irish Billy says. What horizon?

Not just "on" the horizon, the Arab says. "Boiling" on the horizon.

I don't like that Mamie Mullins business, Fat Frankie says. Literary bullshit.

Shure, Irma Huckle says, in a remarkably inept and phony Irish brogue, shure, an' wan dem pair o' spalpeens an' ne'er-do-wells do be gittin' home it'll be their good fortune t'avoid the lashins an' blastins o' dis rollin' pin. Shure, an' it'll be a touch o' the black an' blue they'll be gittin' soon as they set their brogans in th' door. Ah, Jayzus. A rollin' pin is yer only man!

Jesus, what an embarrassment, Irish Billy says.

I'm beginning to think that this isn't happening at all, Fat Frankie says.

Of course it's *happening,* the Drummer says. For God's sake, look at her. She's even wearing her Sunday hat, that silly thing sitting up there on top of her permanent. Why she's wearing it I don't know, but all you have to do is look to know it's happening. I mean, there it is.

Why? the Arab says. It seems of a clarity of perfect limpidness. The chapeau lends to Irma authority as the potentous and matriarchical figure of the entire family shebang that she is making believe that she wishes to be.

At this moment, Mr. Huckle and Georgie are walking, very slowly, toward home. They have, indeed, lost all their pay on the horses. Georgie had a tip. One might say that he had a number of tips, all touting the same horse.

And the horse's name? the Arab asks. It is much too much good to be true. It is even more incredulous than the rolling pin aclutch in Irma's big mitt. Venture on a guess.

Irma's Revenge? Fat Frankie says. Homburg? Shuffle Along? Hot Tip? Sure Thing?

No, no, although they smack of some worthiness. But the true name, the name on which Huckle *père* and Huckle *fils* laid upon all their lucre was—Grey Cloud!

I don't know what the big deal is, Irish Billy says. There are no clouds anywhere anyway. That's not an oddball name for a horse. I once hit a double that paid $105.90 and one nag's name was Cloudy Sky. So what?

You lack and sorely want the analogical framework of mentality, Billy, the Arab says. Grey Cloud. It is of absolute gorgeousness. It is of poetry. Don't ask any questions!

Anyway, Fat Frankie says, I agree with Billy. I don't see any clouds either. And who the hell says that Mamie Mullins has an Irish brogue?

Who indeed? the Drummer says. Nobody here suggested anything of the kind as far as I know.

Irma talked with that terrible fake brogue the minute somebody mentioned Mamie Mullins, Irish Billy says.

What is your implication? the Arab says. How, I impute with interrogation, could Irma Huckle even hear us discuss about Mamie Mullins? She is three blocks away and inside her residence. Do you think that she gazes down from the rooftops toward us? With gigantesque ears to boots? Dear, dear.

I don't know what—Fat Frankie begins. If we know what's going on with Irma, how come she don't know what's going on with us?

It doesn't work that way, the Drummer says.

I wish I knew what was going on with your mother, Mr. Huckle says to Georgie. I have a hunch she's waiting for us with that goddam rolling pin.

I have the same hunch, Pop. The idea of Mama waiting for us with a rolling pin sounds like *Moon Mullins*— but she probably is.

See? the Arab says. The analogyness of that imagistic symbol is too powerful to be desecrated and busted up. Aha!

Irma's dress has taken on the exact shade of the grey clouds boiling on the horizon. Mr. Huckle and Georgie cut down a street so as to add at least fifteen minutes to their journey home.

53 Temporary Insanity

We have been flitting like so many ephemeropteras from subject to subject, the Arab says. From topic to topic. A heliport
where the tennis court used to be. How to make millions in the
greeting-card business. The possibility of inventing a reusable
cundrum, like rubber gloves. What maniac designed the seats
in the Stanley moving-picture theater. And so forth. Is this the
sort of discussion that the creamy cream of the neighborhood
should partake in?

It's a sort of quiet day, the Drummer says. It's relaxing to
jump from one topic to another.

After my labors on my manuscript, Professor Kooba says,
such badinage is like a draft of icy mountain water.

Yet and yet, the Arab says, such jittery dilatoriness is the
sign, in some, of what may be named insanity. The crackerjack
factory is bursting at its brim with citizens who cannot keep
their mind on one thing for more than a moment. Are we to
consider ourselves loonies because of this behavioristic trend
of ours? Or—no *better* than loonies?

Speaking of loonies, the Drummer says, did you hear about
what Eddy Ellsworth did last winter when he suddenly disappeared and was found later to be a sailor in the Great Lakes
Training Center?

Ellsworth a gob? Kooba says. How could the moron ever tie
that funny scarf they wear? He can hardly tie his shoes.

Sneakers, the Arab says.

He's out now, they gave him a discharge, the Drummer says.
The story goes that he puked up all the food after every meal
and wasted away to a human skeleton.

This does not shock me overmuch with surprise, the Arab says. After a lifetime of sustenance on a diet of Pepsi and Yankee Doodles cupcakes, even a soft-boiled egg would be a trauma to his stomach. But—excuse me, Drummer—what is it that happened last winter?

Strictly hearsay this is. I heard it from Red Miller who heard it from Richie. Where Richie heard it I don't know.

Tell, Kooba says.

Picture Eddy, the Drummer says, at home, alone. His father is raising or lowering a bridge or installing a pipe or driving a subway or whatever the hell he does. His mother is at the movies watching Clark Gable and chomping her gums on a roll of Neccos. His sister—the one who's not at the funny farm—is in school failing Spanish or Home Economics. Eddy is alone. Suddenly, according to Richie, he's grabbed by the short hairs by what they call "remorse."

"Nameless remorse" is the accepted phrase among the literati, Professor Kooba says.

Fine—nameless remorse, the Drummer says.

A nice touch, Professor, the Arab says. *Now* we are having a discussion of worth of its name.

He goes to his room, the Drummer continues, and gets out that goddam cavalry sword he's had for years. Some crummy souvenir from one of the great and glorious wars of the past—you know the thing I mean.

I understand, Kooba says, that one of Eddy Ellsworth's long-lost and forgotten ancestors ran *down* San Juan Hill under that great heart, Old Rough Rider Teddy. An act of cowardice coupled with wisdom unmatched in that great adventure.

Really? the Drummer says. Maybe that's where the sword came from? Anyway, he gets the sword, he puts some kind of a helmet on his head—

Helmet? the Arab says. Where did he get a helmet? His father, and I crave pardons all around for the imputation of crudeness I am about to launch, shoveled shit in New Jersey throughout the length and breadth of the Great War, unless someone has been pulling upon my legs.

Not a real helmet, the Drummer says. Some goddam pot from the kitchen to look like a helmet.

This is too good, too pat, to be true, Kooba says. Like a scene from some banal novel of childhood that makes your stomach turn with nausea. A pot for a helmet! Not even Booth Tarkington would try to get away with that.

Who? the Arab says. Booth who?

Never mind, Kooba says. A writer of childhood tales and such, strictly for the chewing-gum clientele. A millionaire shyster and faker. There is no way in the world that he could conceive, in a million years, of an epic like my ongoing opus. In Chapter One Hundred and Four, I have—

Yes! Yes! Of course! the Arab says. I recall with dazzling clearness you mentioning it. How dullish of me to permit it to sidle out of my mind. Drummer?

O.K. He's got the sword and the pot is on his head.

Or else, Professor Kooba says, the pot on his head routine is like a phony fake picture you see on the cover of the *Saturday Evening Post* by that sugary bastard lowlife who thinks he knows and understands America. I'm afraid to glance at a magazine rack in case I should see by mistake a new cover of his and be stricken with instant diabetes.

Professor Kooba! the Arab says. These digressions of hostility, while certainly based on, even profoundly rooted down deep in justice, are turning this story into a kind of quintessence of ordure, I'm sure you'll agree. *Let us hear the story.*

He's got the sword, the Drummer says. He's got the pot on his head. This is what I heard like I said. He starts to ride through the house like he's on a white charger, like a knight. And he starts to slash and hack at everything, like this! Then he starts to yell and shout . . . That for you! You Polack cunt of a cocksucker! He cuts a lampshade in two. Can't go to the goddam dance because you have a blister on your foot! Aha! Avaunt! And you! You potbellied old fart! Here's a present for you, dear old dad, to put in your disgusting sandwich with the greasy peppers and eggs! And Eddy slices one of the pillows on the sofa open. You don't think it's nice for me to put my hand on your tit? How about if I put my pecker up your nose? And he thrusts through the radio speaker. No more Mr. District Attorney and Duffy's fucking Tavern! No more, no more, no more. You think I ought to give you more money for the house from my tycoon's job at the plastic factory? How about this instead of money? And Eddy smashes to smithereens all the windows in the whole house. And he keeps this up all afternoon until when his father gets home from the job there's not a goddam thing in the house that's not broken or smashed or cut to bits.

I relish the touch about the greasy peppers and eggs, the Arab says. It has a touch of the poet, a *soupçon* of elegantia.

His old man looks around, the Drummer continues. He reaches in his pocket and gives Eddy ten bucks. Join the Navy, kid, he says. Or the Army. Or get lost. Whatever, I don't want to see your pimply mug sucking up any more meals in this house. If there's anything you didn't break or rip and you want it— except for that fucking pot on your head—take it. And then get your ass out of here. Eddy takes the pot off his head and puts it on the floor, then he pisses in it and pours it over what's left of the radio. That's in case, he says, Mr. First Nighter, the homo bastard, gets thirsty. Very nice, his father says. Very nice. You really got a lot of class—like a cockaroach. Now—out! And Eddy leaves and joins the goddam Navy.

A wonderous tale, the Arab says. I would be sorely tempted to dub it not a mere slice of life, but an entire reeking and steaming slab of same. What do you, Professor, as a literary man, make of this episode? I admit posthaste that the materials are rough and raw, the point seems bluntful if not altogether in absentia, and there is a certain roughness of language that the omnivorent reader does not encounter in your basic master-pieces. But? And?

Yes, Kooba says, yes, there is a certain something to it. On page nine hundred and forty-seven of my own saga of the human fiasco, I begin the tale, in detail, of a young man who likewise went crazy for a short time. This was in Latvia and he killed a number of sheep and goats as well as savaging his par-ents' humble sod hut. Would you like to hear the section?

The Arab and the Drummer look wildly about them, but there is nothing that they can think of to put Kooba off. He is riffling the pages of his manuscript.

Did I tell you, Professor, the Arab says, hurriedly, that I per-ceived in a recent journal about a new publishing venture that is asedulously seeking out long saga-like epic fictional nonfic-tion treatments of life in Eastern Europe at the turning point of the century—as it was *really* lived?

No, Professor Kooba says. No, you didn't. Where? What's the name? Really? He places the manuscript back on the soda cooler.

54 Cantus Planus

"Voices for Victory" (to the tune of "K-K-K-Katy")
Lyrics by: Edward Beshary and Albert Pedersen
Research: Prof. Janos Kooba

V-V-V-Vogler!
Avuncular Vogler!
Yours the Prime Delight,
Platonic Form of "store"!
Not a m-moot point
If you should stymie,
For the hoi pollois do
S-s-sully sore!

Ph-Ph-Ph-Philip!
Fabulous Philip!
You thrust joie de vivre
To Odic heights of yore!
Are you f-fey, sir,
In your De Luxe bents?
No! Dear puissant comrade,
G-g-guard the door!

B-b-b-blade bared,
Gleamingly sharp bared,
You Leonidas!
Clark Gable plus Lamour!
Gird your l-loins, knight,

Saber in manus!
For the Huns are coming—
Wh-wh-wh-what a bore!

Yes, the Huns are raving—
Wh!—Wh!—Wh!—What! a bore!

55 Eddy Ellsworth's Fantasy

Eddy Ellsworth stands in the bitter cold. There is nobody on the street.

They saw me coming and all ran away, the bastards! Eddy says. He picks his nose nervously and swivels around to look down the block in the other direction.

They all went up somebody's house. They're on the roof watching me and laughing, the rats. He looks up at the roofs.

The sky over the bay toward Staten Island is a deep inky black. One slender horizontal bar of bright yellow is fixed just above the horizon. The wind blows in from the ocean, freezing. Gulls high above the gas tanks.

How I hate the bastards! I hate *all* you son of a bitches! Only the wind, as they say, replies.

I don't blame him a hell of a lot, Richie says. Christ, he's been humiliated for years by everybody—even Willie Wepner insults him.

There's always one, Professor Kooba says. The barbaric tribe must have a scapegoat to heap indignities on.

Make fun of this, make fun of that, Eddy says. Make believe they have to go up the house and sneak out later and meet somewhere. Laugh in my face. The lousy bastards. He cuts the air viciously with an imagined sword. Swish! Swish! Touché! You varlet son of a bitch rotten bastard!

All the people—and they are many—

They are what might be called "legion," Richie says.

All the many people who have humiliated Eddy combine in his mind into a single figure. It lies prone and helpless on a shore next to a sickly blue bay, or lake. The sky above is a deep inky black. One slender horizontal bar of bright yellow is fixed just above the horizon. The wind blows in from the ocean, freezing. Gulls high above the mountains.

For you, Sailor, for saying my new tie at Christmas looked like somebody puked on it—a thrust to the thigh! And a sword appears in that spot on the helpless victim's body. For Irish Billy, who always says my feet smell like a subway toilet—in the ass! The prone figure can be heard to groan. For Fat Frankie, who crosses his eyes and sticks out his tongue and drools and limps around with one arm twisted up behind his back making fun of my sister, a sharp blade in the base of the spine. To the Drummer, who should know better because he's supposed to be so goddam intelligent, for making fun of my aunt in Wilmington, Delaware, just because she happens to *live* in Wilmington, Delaware—a deep stab in the small of the back right through a kidney.

God *damn*, Richie says. Now that one hurt! You see the poor bastard twitch?

And Richie, that two-faced bastard— Eddy begins.

Oh oh, Richie says.

—who made fun of Irene, the only goddam girl who ever liked me enough to go out with me and who he called a stupid Polack cow, I'll give *him* a fucking stupid Polack cow right down straight into his shitty liver, uhh!

Jesus Christ! Richie says.

You thought he didn't mind? Kooba says. See? He minds.

The rotten shitty remarks about my new overcoat two winters ago, like horse blanket and moth food and dish rag that that guinea greaseball dago rat fuck Santo Tuccio made, for those cracks, Santo, and a lot of others I can't think of right now, eight inches of cold steel into the middle of your pimply back.

The figure lies still. Blood soaks the ground around it.

This is not too funny anymore, Richie says.

Who said it ever was? Kooba says.

And *you*, Big Duck, the king of acne, the champion and emperor of black filthy fingernails, you remember the time you ruined the record I made on 42nd Street in a penny arcade of me singing "All or Nothing at All"? Your payment for this rotten thing you done is a vicious shove of this sword in your back just under your shoulder.

My God! Richie says. Even I could feel that one.

Horrible to watch the man's mind clicking along that way, Kooba says.

And Pepper! Eddy says. Ah, Pepper, I can't forget good old Pepper, the drunk son of a bitching sot, who likes to make fun that I only drink Coke at the bar . . . that's a real *man's* drink, ha, ha, you say you bastard, grow up why don't you you lame-brain creep? Ah, dear Pepper. For your kind advice a generous hunk of razor-sharp blade directly into the heart. The sword quivers and hums with the force of the blow.

The sky seems—fittingly—to be growing blacker.

Curtin, the Catholic philosopher, the good Catholic who knows all about God and all the saints and why the Pope is so goddam holy—who also once laughed himself silly when he saw my mother didn't have any teeth—for you, you pile of religious shit, right in your holy neck!

Forgive me, Professor Kooba says, if I suggest that this particular thrust might be considered a just one.

Richie stares at the huge quantities of blood oozing out of the corpse.

And I'm sorry, Little Mickey, nice as you are most of the time and I feel bad also for you because of your drunk whore of a mother with that dago bastard getting in her pants all the time, but you were the one laughed a long time ago and told everyone the day I was playing Ringaleevio with the little kids and slipped in some dog shit and ripped my pants in half at the crotch and I didn't have no underwear on. I'm sorry, Little Mickey, but I'll have to smash your brains to smithereens by sticking this sword right in your ear.

Crunch! Richie says. That's enough. Let's go.

Wait, Kooba says, I think he's finished. Look how nice and calm his face looks.

Where's he going?

Looks like he's going into Pat's—for a Coke, Kooba laughs.

Pat's? O.K. Let's go the other way then.

The sky is now completely black. It begins to sleet.

A Coke, Eddy says to the bartender. Do you *mind?*

What? What's eating *you?*

Never mind, Eddy says.

56 Flowers Again

The Magician, in the guise of Professor Kooba, leans against the soda cooler, in a rumpled and sweat-stained seersucker suit and a crushed Panama hat.

I see a woman sitting up in bed, tense, and a mere fraction, a millimeter away from despair. The room is dark and the only sounds audible are those from the jukebox in the saloon on the corner. "Frenesi" is the tune that is being played.

The Arab is not pleased with this reference to what he considers popular culture. But he says nothing to the man he thinks is Kooba. He is somewhat startled at his interest in this woman.

I know what is making her life so miserable, the Magician says. That's my business. To know.

Dolores enters and orders two vanilla Mell-O-Rolls, gets herself a bottle of Mission cream soda, pays, and leaves.

Beneath those prim and pristinious and boxy-cut fashions of the archetypous parochial school uniform, I detect a beautifully blossoming frame, the Arab says.

Yet she too will be locked into misery soon enough, the Magician says. Soon enough. I see the woman still. She feels that she is behind bars and that her life has come to nothing. Tomorrow she will rise and go to her job behind the steam table at Bickford's. What, my profound Arabian compatriot, do you think she needs? Remember, the night is dark, she is alone, she is no longer young, and the loud beery voices of the men in the corner saloon frighten her.

Anomie? the Arab says.

What? Anomie? the Magician says.

Is this what they enterm anomie that has clutched and embraced her close in the dead witching hours of the night? is what I hint upon.

Call it what you will, the Magician says. He is uncomfortable because he has no idea of the meaning of the word.

I know what she needs, the Drummer says.

On this particular night, the Magician says, slightly overdoing Professor Kooba's rather heavy Eastern European accent, I have it at my beck and call—a felicitous phrase, is it not?

Pinnacle-ish, the Arab says.

In spades, the Drummer agrees. He goes to the door to watch Dolores cross the street, praying for a sudden gust of wind to lift her pleated navy-blue skirt.

I have then, at my beck and call, and to hand, the Magician says, a number of prizes, gifts, let us say, to give to this woman. They are: a quick bang from a lathe operator at the moment half-sprawled across the bar in Fritz's Tavern; a choice of feature films at the Albee, the Fabian Fox, or the Brooklyn Paramount; a ride to Lake Hopatcong in a Lincoln Zephyr—only one way, I'm sorry to say; a couple of silver fox tails and a little black hat with a veil; and six lessons from Madame Lazonga, if you will forgive me this weak joke. Will these help?

They won't hurt, will they? the Drummer asks.

Meaningless fripperlies and folderols, the Arab says. And by the by, *Professor Kooba,* you are being strangely and startledly unlike your usual and wontful self. Can that be because—may I venture a humbled opinion?—you are *not* Professor Kooba, but the Magician?

Ah, the Magician says. Oh well.

Allow it to pass impotently and sans harm over our heads, the Arab says. But as long as you are aquery, no. No, these guerdons and et ceteras that you clutch to your possession, ready to shower this lonely distaff member with, are indeed but trashful junk. She would be much better served with the small award of a free course in radio repairs or stenographic skills, if I may so give utterance.

I know that she'll know that these things are but temporary

distractions and anodynes—nice word?—for the misery that afflicts her, the Magician says, but—but, but, but, I have my tasks to perform.

Tomorrow she will scan perusingly the yellow journalism of Walter Winchell and find out how the fortunes of the stellars of the cincma, stage, and broadcasting world as well as the world of international politicians are getting along, the Arab says, plunged deep to the core with their endless and troubled tragedies as they are. She does not know, I gather up, as to which to impute her miserable life.

Right! the Drummer says. She can't use these things you have. She's like the Russians in Vladivostok which when we gave them bars of soap they ate them.

There must be something more you can rummage up to give the wench, the Arab says. Some magician! who dares to nominate and bruit around as such and who cannot reach into his sack of legerdemainical tricks for the precision thing.

I have only certain powers and those only at certain times, the Magician says. Oh yes, changing myself into anybody I like . . . But I will lessen the burden and horror of the imagined blue-grey bars that seem to lock her into her dark room by decorating her shabby and faded quilt with beautifully embroidered roses.

Oh Lord! the Arab says. Flowers? Again?

They'll at least be a nice surprise when she wakes up to the sun coming through her grimy windowpane, the Magician says. He is not very happy about the way that things have turned out.

Let me, the Arab says, evict this pale imitation of supreme magical feats—and I mean *pallidly* pale—by purchasing a *Green Sheet* and tracking the trail of thoroughbred possibilities at today's ovals.

I wonder if their underwear is a uniform too, those sweet Catholic schoolgirls, the Drummer says. Probably nice plain tight white things.

57 Pieces of Spectacle

I am Justice! Thelma Krulicewicz says from the auditorium stage of P.S. 170. She is in a long red robe, bound and blindfolded, and fenced in by a large sheet of oaktag on which Miss Flynn's sixth-grade art class has painted silver swords.

. . . and my sinews—last but not least—are the hopes and aspirations of—the People! Ha! Ha! And yet *they* think—as do *all* Tyrants . . .

Give me a root beer barrel! Irish Billy whispers to the boy next to him.

. . . even so inspired, the sinews that are the strength of the People and the irresistible force of the muscles that are Freedom and respect for God . . .

Even then, by Jesus, Thelma—Tania—had a nice body. You see how those phony ropes across her chest . . . ? Fat Frankie says. And *you* ask for a root beer barrel. What a jerk!

What? Irish Billy says. That's not me!

Pray tell what are you gentlemen ensconced in doing? the Arab says. Root beer barrels?

We're looking into the past, Fat Frankie says. See? See Tania up there?

That slip of a creature is Tania? the Arab says. Remarkable child. Quite well, uh, quite nicely constructed on the body side.

You see, Fat Frankie says, you see how those phony ropes . . . ?

. . . these Tyrants' moods and wishes are expressed in their mighty swords! Ha! Doth not the Tyrant know? that Freedom and its mighty yearning words! are greater! than *all* the swords of Kings, all their pomp and . . .

What is the maiden doing? the Arab asks.

With that blindfold on you could sneak up behind her . . . Fat Frankie says.

Damn it! Five lousy root beer barrels and you *need* them? Irish Billy says. All *five* of them?

It's the sixth-grade play, Irish Billy says. Pageant. *The Body of Justice.* Spectacle.

She's utterly darling, the Drummer says. Is *that* the body of Justice? Hmm.

He's drooling on his goddam tie, Fat Frankie says.

Anything would improve that lightning-bolt design, Irish Billy says.

. . . and with one swift movement of my arms, which are the speeches and free-spoken words of Free Men . . .

There you go, Billy, see? Fat Frankie says. There's this luscious dish up there and you're still trying to grub a root beer barrel.

Is that boy Billy? the Arab says. There is, now that I peer hawkishly, a subtle resembalance.

Bullshit, Billy says. That's not me! I don't even *like* root beer barrels. Never did. Why would I be trying to . . . ? And besides, Christ, she wasn't *that* terrific.

Look! Look at her when she opens up her arms, the Drummer says. Sweet suffering Christ.

. . . and *free!* Free at last, as Justice must *always* be free! Yet . . .

Look, she knocked the goddam cardboard down, Fat Frankie says. Oh the poor kid, she screwed up the whole—

She's supposed to knock it down, Irish Billy says. That's the idea of defeating kings and tyrants and dictators in the pageant. The swords are—

I get it, I *get* it, Fat Frankie says.

It is a paucity of wonder, the Arab says, when I gaze at this lovely budding creature of, what? twelve or thirteen years? that she grew up to shake off the dust of the neighborhood from off of her shoes.

My God almighty, the Drummer says. Look at her.

Where the hell are you now, Billy? Fat Frankie says. I don't see you there with the root beer barrel kid.

I told you. I'm not there, Billy says.

. . . thus, free of limits and bonds in order to exercise the wishes of a free People of a free Country, I, Justice, take again my rightful place in the midst of my countrymen—of my fellow Americans! And . . .

Is she supposed to walk all over the cardboard swords, Billy? Fat Frankie asks.

Sure. It was only one time they needed the damn thing.

. . . dark behind this blindfold which cruel and unheeding Despots placed upon my eyes. But they recked not that Justice *should* be blind, so that She may mete out proper decisions. And so Justice and Freedom again turn the tricks and deceits of desperate Dictators against them by . . .

You're not getting one goddam trade out of me in baseball cards or War cards either, Irish Billy says.

Oho! *There* you are, Fat Frankie says. Still not one glance at Thelma. What a weirdo kid you were, Billy.

That's. Not. Me.

I can see with gimletish clarity how she went from this humbled and puerilous stage to the name of Tania Crosse and out into the arms of the great and sophisticated world, the Arab says. A wonderously fetching damsel.

Jesus Christ, the Drummer says. Look when she takes a bow how the robe gets tight against her. Sweet, *sweet* little Tania.

A quite shockingly stunning young wench of a woman to be, the Arab says.

Hey, the Drummer says. How the hell did we manage to see all this? Hey! Maybe Billy knows? Billy?

But Billy has quietly left.

58 Country Gardens

Don't tell *me* about carnival life, Cookie LaNord says. The thrill of trouping. The romance of the open road. The enthusiastic audiences. That's all Hollywood stuff. Fantasies. Dreams.

Thou breakest my poor and gullible Irish heart, Irish Billy says. Say it ain't so, Cookie. Tell us gorgeous lies, invent gossamer bullshit wrought from moonbeams over Ohio and the wings of crickets. Spin out, O Cookie, tall tales of the carny for our jaded and stale urban ears. Right, Big Duck?

Right. Whatever you said.

Sing, O bringer of culture and good clean entertainment to the bucolic masses, weary as they are of shoveling sheepshit. Tell of the ecstasy and truth and hidden reality of America to be found asleep behind the barn. Tell us of *space*. Yes, space! S-P-A-C-E. That magical word that is the true key to us as plain folks who happen to go shit-ass crazy every couple of years or so. For here, in the polluted and filthy rotten cities, what can we know from reading newspapers and listening to the radio of the glory of a wheelbarrow full of rocks? Cut off as we are from corn, cowflop, highways leading to the bowling alley, floods, tornadoes, and billboards, what can we know of the outback, the true deep heart of—America?

Don't tell *me*, Cookie says. Rubes, hicks, appleknockers, fake cowboys, weedpullers, rednecks, and yokels. Thieves in red hats.

What? Irish Billy says.

You heard me. In red hats. That's how you can always tell them. We had one in some burg outside Chillicothe—you can imagine this dump if Chillicothe was the big attraction—who stole Ramón's swords. The same swords he swallowed for the Princess of Rumania or one of those noble broads. Gone.

Can it be, Irish Billy says, that you're going to tell us a tale that will be detrimental to the great pastoral masses who breathe free—as well as yearn? What do you think of this turn of events, Big Duck?

The country is nice for a weekend, Big Duck says. It's like the park only without fountains or toilets. Billy, how come you're talking like this? I mean so fancy?

Tut, tut, Billy says. And, no offense, Duck, but that last was spoken like the urban lout you are. The country is like nothing else. Nothing at all. It is not the park without fountains. One must *experience* those thick, those extra-thick shakes, those shit-encrusted rest rooms, those rugged faces 'neath Caterpillar caps, to know why Sherwood Anderson left home. Why he left home and stayed left. But I interrupt. Cookie? Go on, I beg you.

Why is Billy talking this way? Red Miller says.

Why ask me? Big Mickey replies. It's like a movie like with some guy in some fruit hat with a plume. Relax and enjoy it.

Ramón had seven swords, Cookie says. One for each day of the week. They were engraved like that too—Monday, Tuesday, Wednesday, and so on. Beautiful swords, made of what he called Saracen steel.

Glittering blades that almost kept all Europe Moorish! Billy says. Shining metal whose essence may still be found in the haunting tones of the flamenco song, and so on and et cetera.

They have really big thunder and lightning storms there too, Big Duck says.

Christ, Red Miller says. Duck is the dumbest son of a bitch I ever saw.

He's an Einstein with his head under a car hood, Big Mickey says. But in real life, he's about, oh, fifteen–twenty per cent, tops.

So we're outside Chillicothe, Cookie says, set up with our special holiday tents, it must have been a Labor Day matinee, you know, stripes and plaids and prints with pennants flying from the mainpole of each tent. And just before the show begins, Ramón sticks his swords in the ground outside the big top like he always does, all seven in a row. He says the sun gives them beauty and the ground gives them strength. He always does this except when it's raining or cloudy except sometimes even when it's cloudy but he forgets then about the sun giving them beauty part.

A poet! Irish Billy says. A bard with his ear to the wheat and the chomping jaws of the boll weevil, like the beloved Sandburg! With his bosom bared to the lonely birch, like the saintly Frost! With his face stuffed up to the ears in the crystal creek, pronounced crick, like the idiotic Kilmer!

If I didn't know this is Irish Billy, Red Miller says, I'd give you eight to five he's not.

I got to admit you're right, Red, Big Mickey says. What a line of crap. Who are all these guys he's talking about? You know any of them?

Not me, Red says.

So, Cookie says, some halfwit rube in a red hat, the Caterpillar kind like you mentioned, comes sneaking up in his cowshit boots and quick as hell snatches up Monday to Friday and runs away toward the woods. We all see him, but when Ramón starts after him he steps in a post hole or a pot hole or some kind of goddam hole they got out in the sticks and falls down. And when he gets up this yokel is long gone. And Ramón has just two damn swords left. He cried like a baby and wouldn't do his act for a week.

They get a lot of hailstones too, you know, Big Duck says. I saw in "Believe It Or Not" that one was as big as a basketball. And it's too damn lonely with all those funny animals and bugs. He shudders.

In other words, Cookie, Irish Billy says, you are attempting to imply that all is not peaches cream and roses in the bosky glens, the leafy glades, the sleepy villages, the vast and brooding heartland? What will literature say? What of the red clay roads baking in the midsummer sun? Huh?

Billy, I don't know what in the hell you been talking about, Cookie says. I'm saying that the carnival on the road stinks, at best. And when these hayseeds in their goddam red hats steal too . . . Well . . .

My God! Had Willa Cather lived! Billy says, and hides his eyes with his hand.

I still can't really believe that's Irish Billy! Red Miller says.

Damn right, Big Mickey agrees.

And they get a lot of typhoons too, Big Duck says.

Make that about ten–fifteen per cent, Big Mickey says. And that's generous.

59 Aesthetics

Doc Friday sees a picture which wakes a long-dead memory of youth. Weeks later, in Carroll's Tavern, just before closing time, he speaks of this, but carefully, carefully—and obliquely—to Curtin.

It's odd how a picture can make you remember things, the Doc says. I don't mean remember things that are in the picture, but things that the picture suggests—things that are more or less sort of just outside the picture.

Train of associations, Curtin says. Putting two and two together. Stream of consciousness, if you want to be disgustingly academic about it. Is this adverb necessary?

Curtin has been drinking boilermakers for three hours and is sailing under the weather, or as the Sailor might say, he is not exactly schooner-rigged at the moment.

No, no, I don't mean that, the Doc says. I don't mean that the picture, as is, brings up a memory because of something that's in it, but that the memory comes because of some figure or image in the picture, and this memory comes up even though it's outside what the picture is all about . . . and what the picture is all about has nothing to do with the memory that comes to you.

Oh my God, Curtin says. You are coming at me like the entire goddam Philosophy Seminar at Brooklyn College. What the hell are you talking about? You want to talk philosophy, give me a little Kant, a little Schopenhauer, a pinch of Heidegger, a touch of Marx, Groucho. What picture?

I mean, I mean that . . . let's say you look at a picture of three people in a room and somehow this picture makes you suddenly realize that behind the door in the back of the room in the picture there's another person—and *that* person is the one that makes you remember things.

I don't like pictures of rooms with people in them and doors.

The bartender starts turning out the lights. Curtin and Doc Friday leave and go their separate ways home.

What Doc Friday is getting at is this, Richie says, as far as I can see, anyway. The picture he saw—that he was talking about so carefully—was a color photograph on a travel folder he found on a seat on the West End Express. It shows a scene in Greece. A man is poling a little boat along, in the boat sit a woman and a child as passengers. The boat also contains a number of fence posts or fishing poles—the Doc can't remember which. The three people have their backs to us. The boat is in the middle of a lake or river, and is heading toward a distant shore which exists as a bluish landscape in the background. On that shore, some fifty yards inland, Doc Friday sits on a log with a girl. She is about sixteen and he is about eighteen. They are embracing and kissing and a soft wind off the water cools their flushed faces. The entire air seems perfumed because of their young love. Doc Friday can smell this perfume and also the perfume the girl wears. He can feel the texture of the sweater stretched over her back and shoulders and taste the sweetness of her tongue. He pulls his head back slightly and looks at her eyes as they open in the gauzy twilight. She says, I love you, Sam.

Doc Friday stands under a streetlamp suddenly feeling the whiskey he has drunk. He tries and tries to remember her name but keeps coming up with the name of his ex-wife, the slut.

60 Proem to "The Curse"

This story of a man who fights like heck for what is right
Your humble Author, one Kooba, has wrote for your delight.
And if you do not like it you can read another Book
I do not care what Book it is, such things are your bad luck.
You'll find here in this big fat Toam, the forrests of Europe
The Ocean called the Atlantic, the City called New York.
And always is this humble Fool (the Hero) of The Curse
A Gent who from a big pig's ear can make a silken perse.
His Enemys he beats to pulp and sends them packing quick
He takes away there mighty Swords and laughs until he's sick.
Look at the Sky! (He seems to shout) He seems to shout
    quite loud
In fact his voice is loud enough to knock down flat a Crowd.
But. What is this? The reader scoffs. Another Book of Thrills?
The last thing that I need, he spitts. Cheap Adventure and Chills!
But soft! And soft! And softer yet! So Kooba exhortes you.
I wouldn't bore you right to tears. There's plenty here to chew!
When I say Swords and Pulp and things I don't mean the Items.
I talk analogossly, see? In other words my Friends
These things are all just symbolous for deep and profound
    thought
Just like a man might say Harry when what he means is Mort.
The Mysterys and Tragedys of Life in these pages
Are shown with great understanding not just vulgar rages.
Though my Hero grins in winning he knows a lot of grief
The Evil men who weep and wail might *still* end up the Chief!
So do not be afraid Reader. But pick this up and brows
There's lots of meat here that I grant. Not cud for stupid cows.
Although I never learned to play on the Flute or Tuba
I've done my best with little words. The Curse, Janos Kooba.

61 Fireworks

The Magician lies supine on what appears to be a marble table and folds his hands together as if in prayer. He closes his eyes and instantly he too seems to take on the coldness and rigidity of marble. On the side of the table is drawn a rather awkward cross, parallel to the Magician's body and with its horizontal arm strangely small in terms of the length of its vertical one. On the wall, above the Magician, three more crosses, identical with the first, are drawn, parallel to each other and with their vertical arms pointed toward the Magician's body. A stained glass window admits thin, pale winter light. The Magician is in a trance, surrounded by these curious crosses, in order that he may see into the neighborhood's past. Certain facets anyway.

What's the point of raking up the past? Curtin says. Besides, I don't believe in magicians or in magic either. Especially *this* one.

How about the mass? Richie asks.

This guy's no Catholic, Curtin replies. And why the hell is he always barging in and out of the neighborhood? How come? What do you mean, the mass?

Forget it, Richie says. Let's go to the movies.

The Magician sees the rooftop of an apartment building called The Lucille. People sit in what he likes to call "the gloaming." The breeze is cool and the humidity seems to be dropping. The people are on straight chairs brought up from their kitchens and they gossip about neighborhood events.

It is almost dark now. Far away in the sky beyond the gas tanks of the Kings County Lighting Company, a Roman candle bursts in green and gold against the deep blue over Coney Island.

Ohhh! Irma Huckle says. I like the ones where the fireworks come out of fireworks. There's one! A burst of red, a burst of white, and, a moment later, a soft spray of blue float into nothingness.

Gene Phillips comes onto the roof carrying two pitchers of beer. Mr. Huckle follows him with two large pizzas.

Where's Curtin and Richie? Irish Billy says.

They wended their bored and ennui-stricken way to the Electra, the Arab says, not looking up from a magazine article on a paraplegic ice-hockey team in Flint.

Billy, he says, where is the location of Flint?

Ohio, Billy says. What's playing at the Electra?

I don't know. Ohio? What an odd and bizarrely freak-like environings that must be, he muses, as he reads: " 'Cornbread' Wallowicz executing a neat slap shot from his motorized 'wheelskate' against the Dearborn Otters."

Burst of pink. Splash of orange. Triple explosion of blues and whites.

As usual, not enough damn cheese, Gene Phillips says. We ought to start going to Lento's.

They cut off the crusts there, Dorothy Phillips says.

Is that a kite? Irma Huckle asks. Over there?

It is a kite, flying high over the bay. At the other end of the string is the Drummer, beside himself with delight that his experiment is working so well. What the experiment may be, no one can say—except perhaps the Magician.

A final razzmatazz display of skyrockets and Roman candles splatters across the sky, now pitch black. All the faces are turned toward Coney Island. The breeze is almost chilly.

All right, I'll get your sweater, Gene Phillips says to Dorothy. You might remember once in a while it gets cool up here at night this time of year.

Mr. Huckle leaves the roof with Mr. Phillips and continues on to Flynn's for two more pitchers of beer.

Everything disappears as the Magician comes out of his

trance. He is not what one might call disappointed, but he is now, finally, resigned to the fact that nothing ever really happened in the neighborhood.

In the Electra, Curtin and Richie are chuckling at a scene in the movie they are watching. Just as the romantic leads kiss passionately, a bedroom hazy in the background, there is a cut to fireworks exploding in the sky above a carnival—in Buenos Aires, of course.

Oh God, the Magician says, and slaps his forehead. That is just too much. Too, too much.

It's what's known as "resolving" the tension—or "symbolizing" certain events that we cannot see because they are filthy dirty, Irish Billy says.

What? I do not grasp with any tenaciousness what you are imputing, the Arab says.

Forget it, nothing. You feel like going up Sal's and shoot a little straight pool? I'll show you some *real* fireworks.

62 Big Duck's Valentine

My heart would croon in the sunbeams of your smiles,
Instead it's stuck, with three big swords.
Don't you know for you I'd walk a thousand miles?
Oh, my heart! It's in the stormy clouds.

One sword is misery, another loneliness and the last
   one, grief.
Oh! The grey rain is sizzling on my burning heart!
For you I'd be a beggar or a thief,
Or, anything at all, my love, Thou art!

Pluck out from this ruby organ this bad pain!
And give me a Hello! Or just a grin.
Let me be, the tracks, you be, the train.
Oh! Let me kiss and kiss your eyes ears nose, and chin.

That blinking light you see, up in the sky,
Is not a light, but is, my thumping core!
Ow! What a pain, you don't care! If I live or die.
While all I do is dream about you more, and more.

Dearest Dolores please, spare a date for me,
Or else, I'll go completely crazy, like a coot.
I know you're smart and soft and very pretty.
But be nice although I'm just a dumb galoot.

63 V for Vacuous

Tania Crosse is sitting on a huge leather couch dressed in a golden silk negligee. The luxuriously appointed room in which she sits is in the luxurious penthouse of a luxurious co-op. The huge windows overlook Lake Michigan which, at the moment, is glittering in brilliant sunshine. But Tania is crying. Anyway, that's the way it looks, Richie concludes.

Makes no sense, Irish Billy says. Slice of life, no more, no less. We need a *point*. We need a *moral*. We need something interpretative.

She's been looking, Richie suddenly begins again, she's been looking at some slick, expensive magazine and sees, let's say she sees a V in it somewhere, somehow.

The point! The moral! Billy says.

Well, Richie says, years ago, when she was still Thelma, she was in a school play in P.S. 170 . . . she was in lots of plays, as a matter of fact, in grammar school.

Lexington! It's you we hon-or! Hail one sev-en-ty! Santo Tuccio sings.

Keep moving, Irish Billy says. Get it going, flow, flow.

She was in this particular school play, Richie says, and she played . . . something . . . let's say Victory. She sat on a bench, in a long gown, blindfolded, with two swords crossed in front of her resting on either shoulder, in a V. You get it? A V?

For—our fond-est hopes and wish-es! Twi-ine themselves round theee! Santo sings.

O.K., O.K., I get it, Billy says. She sees the V in—hey! In *Vogue!* Get it? V-V-V-*Vogue*. That's what Tania would be reading anyway. And she remembers her innocent childhood and now she's in this big penthouse with a different name, filled with remorse and bitter, bitter nostalgia.

218

All right, Richie says. Let's say something like that. She's just a high-class whore, and—

Wait a minute, Billy says.

All right, she's a kept woman, Richie says. She was really swell when she was a girl, wasn't she, by the way? I remember how her dresses and hair ribbons and socks always matched.

A credit to her race, Fat Frankie says. And to P.S. 170. How come you remember all this so well, Richie?

She's weeping, Irish Billy says. She's weeping in the soft glow of the lamp! I can hear the whispering rustle of pongee. What about glamour now? What about luxury now? The brittle and sterile crowd of sophisticated people won't help her now. She's alone.

I say she's no kept woman, Fat Frankie says. As a matter of fact, I happen to know she's married to an officer in the Army.

Big Mickey said he saw her in Chicago, Big Duck says. Right, Mickey?

Well—more or less, Big Mickey says.

When were you in Chicago? Fat Frankie says.

I was more or less in Chicago once, Big Mickey says.

This is degenerating into the ridiculous, Irish Billy says. I say she's miserable and she's crying because she's alone. I don't care whether she's married or not married. Besides, maybe she's the one with the money and is supporting her husband, if she's got a husband. She was always smart. She could have plenty of money from a good job.

That's like a movie I saw, Santo Tuccio says. Bette Davis is this really rich broad and she marries this poor genius musician, Paul Henreid. And she has this terrific luxury penthouse apartment where she makes him live.

Oh for Christ sake, Irish Billy says. Tania's supposed to be married to an officer, if you believe Frankie, which I don't, not a goddam musician. And Bette Davis can't even hold Tania's coat, for Christ sake. And I *saw* that picture, Santo. You've got the wrong picture. You're thinking of the Bette Davis picture where George Brent is the army officer and he doesn't fit in with her set after her husband dies because he doesn't take love seriously, or marriage, or anything else. And they don't get married. There's some kids and some bitchy old broad who's the dead husband's mother. That's the picture.

How about the fucking penthouse then? Santo says. Hah? How about that?

I always remember Thelma when she wore yellow, Richie says. That's when she really looked great because her hair was so black.

And now look at her, for Christ sake, Irish Billy says. Trying to please that crowd she runs around with by bleaching her hair peroxide blond. Probably just fools around now. What do they call that?

A *puttana?* Santo Tuccio says.

Oh fuck you, Santo, Billy says. A playgirl is what I mean.

Yet in the somber lamplight her tears twinkle and shine, Fat Frankie says. Her sobs chime and tinkle among the cut glass decanters and glasses and the sterling silver. Her bosom heaves amid its French lace. Remorse! Remorse has seized her.

Tania may be crying because of a long-lost love, some handsome dog who went down in flames over Germany in his Mustang, Richie says.

No, Irish Billy says. Tania never loved anyone. We don't need any more ideas. We had *something*—maybe even a pretty good story there for a minute. Maybe we can talk about her miserable and unhappy married life for a while? What the hell, let's say she is married, or was. Nothing personal. Nothing spicy or dirty.

I say she's not married, Richie says. It's Frankie says she's married to some damn soldier. What the hell does he know about Chicago?

I was more or less in Chicago once, Big Mickey says.

Neither of them knows a goddam thing about Chicago, Santo says.

I say she's married, Fat Frankie says. I say she's married to an

Army officer who maybe is Major Gentry's and Sergeant Gentry's older brother. A colonel, maybe. Colonel Bruce Gentry. Bruce Lionel Gentry.

Maybe it could be possible, Richie says.

All right, Irish Billy says. Whatever she is, let's say something about her, let's go on. Richie?

There's nothing I can think of, Richie says. It's just an anecdote. About how meaningless is the life of bon-bons and champagne, caviar and spectacular views of Lake Michigan. More or less like this: No matter how fantastic Tania's life may seem to mere slobs and deadbeats, look, she is weeping bitterly.

A little touch of the old sudden insight into the empty world and the sterile lives of those who no longer live in the world of sweat and callouses and White Castle hamburgers? Fat Frankie says. Something like that?

Let's say yes, more or less, Richie says.

I think the whole goddam thing stinks, Santo Tuccio says. I thought maybe at least she'd get undressed and take a bath or something and we could get a look at her bare-ass.

You're a filthy lowlife son of a bitch, Santo, Irish Billy says. I don't like to hear that kind of talk about Tania—about women.

Billy, do you still—? Richie begins, and then stops.

There is a sudden shuffling of feet. Clearing of throats. Billy spins one of the stools at the fountain, blushing.

In the meantime, Tania Crosse has stopped crying and as the setting sun smears rich orange on Lake Michigan, she begins to nibble delicately on a bon-bon . . .

A bon-bon? Oh my God. Delicately?

She pours a glass of sparkling champagne . . .

Stop!

She spreads a triangle of toast with caviar and squeezes a wedge of lemon . . .

No!

Her heavy lace-cupped breasts move slightly as—

64 New Titles

My dear Professor Kooba, the Arab says, over the years—and only the good Lord in his infinitude of sapience and omniscientistic wisdom knows how many—over these years you have worked like a loony and foamy-jawed canine inflicted with the hydrophobia on your masterpiece, "The Curse." Is this not the absolute fact and the case?

Arab, Kooba says, don't start in on me. Please.

Au contrary, *au* contrary, my good Professor. What I with batches of shyness approach is, that over the past week or fortnight, I have constructed a small list of new titles for your opus.

Arab, I don't tell you how to do your entomologic word research, do I? *You* don't tell me about my book. It has been "The Curse." It is "The Curse." And it will be "The Curse" on the day it is published.

As you wish. As you desire deeply. But surely. However. This list contains certain items that seem to match in a perfectitude certain tonal values and spirits the snatches—if you will forgive such an expression—the orts and shards of the manuscript it has been my pleasure to audit over the years. Surely, a man of your scholiastic bents would not allow this research of mine to loll about and lay around fallowly like Onan's seeds without a fair airing? Who knows? You might glean up a fabulous gem from this humble rundown. Perhaps a utilintarian suggestion for a section heading? A chapter title? They may be thus interred within it. I beg you.

All right. Go ahead. I don't promise you anything.

Your fairness and good sportsmanship are imminent. Listen with a sensitive ear, I grovelly beg you. No hooligans are about to chip in with dullardly kibitzing.

Go ahead. As long as we're alone.

Varied suggestions for Professor Janos Kooba's opus as to title. The Arab clears his throat. "The Clutching Fist," "White Mitt," "An Upright Blade," "Clouds Over Mountains," "Purple and Blue and You," "Shaking Flames," "Floating Fire," "Grey Whipped Cream," "Diadem With Rubies," "Coronet With Garnets," "A Crown of Carbuncles," "Strange Weeds," "Red Berries," "The Ghostly Hand," "His Sword, His Word," "Shiny Manicure," "Weird Balloon," "Blue Phallic Symbol," "It Looks Like Rain," "A Fey Epée," "No Head," "Cool Hills," "Yellow Blobs," "Blue Steel," "Right in the Hole," "Vegetation," "Seaweed and Spinach," "No Body," "King Hat," "Soaring Knife," "Misty Arm," "Naughty Suggestion," and "Am I Dreaming?"

This is the list, Arab? New titles? This? These?

Yes. Of course, it's a little roughly shaped and bended, I admit, but you could transmute and metamorph here and there, for instance, uh, "Weird Hills." Or "Cool Balloon." "Blue Phallic Blob," let us hint. "King Manicure"? Well, at any rates, you see what I am driving on and entertaining. I mean, there is no rule that is hardened fast, no necessitous usage herein involved.

Arab, no. No good, Arab. They're no good for my book. It's "The Curse" and nothing but "The Curse."

"The Clutching Hole"?

No, Arab! "The Curse"!

"Right in the Vegetation"?

No, no, no! "The Curse"!

Mayhaps for a section heading? Perhaps the title of a chapter? A small and unobtruding chapter?

I don't think so. No, I don't think so.

But—perhaps? Not a firm and irrepressible negation, is it? Perhaps a picayune and runty chapter? "Naughty Mitt"? Not an absolute and irrevocal nay?

Kooba takes the list and silently puts it in his pocket.

Excellent! Excellent! the Arab says. "Diadem With Shaking Epée." *That* has a certain elegantishly turned *éclat*, no?

65 *Space and Time*

Let's assume that years pass, Richie says. Or that years have passed. One of the people around here has reached middle age—maybe Cheech, maybe Big Duck. I don't care who. Let's say he's become a highly successful businessman, despite what I have to call his "humble origins." Nothing strange about that. It's a fact of life in America, so they tell me.

Let's say it's Big Duck—the more unlikely the better. But now, with his greasy hair, acne, and black broken fingernails all forgotten and long behind him, he is Donald Halvorsen to everybody always. He owns a number of plants that have something to do with the manufacture of parts for oil burners. At this moment, our moment, he is on vacation in the country. He sits on a patio in the sun, bemused. In one hand he holds an empty plate that recently contained cold lobster, mayonnaise, potato salad with parsley and chives, and sliced tomatoes garnished with basil. In his other hand he has a fresh peach ice-cream cone. He is clad in an après-swim robe given him by his mistress, a patient woman who cheerfully puts up with his boring recitals of guilt over his marital infidelity. Although I have no idea what sort of woman she is, his robe has a motif of clusters of red grapes and green leaves against a black field and is made of heavy silk. While this may tell *you* something of the woman's character, it tells me nothing. Halvorsen, eating and having eaten, and engulfed, so to speak, in a garment that depicts both food and drink, has fallen into a reverie, beautiful word. He is flooded by memories of foods, the goodies he loved as a child.

Are we going to get a list now? Doc Friday says.

Perhaps you'd do better with just a few, a very few, symbols? the Drummer says.

Mayhaps a touch of condensation would amelorate things? the Arab says. Please?

Halvorsen, as I say, Richie goes on, is flooded with memories of these goodies, and sits, entranced, as they return to him in regiments of varied shape, color, odor, and taste. Scores of grainy root beer barrels, infinitely lengthy tapes of pink and white candy buttons, tangy apricot shoeleather, monstrous all-day suckers, chunks, hunks, and gobbets of bubble gum both pink and greyish-brown, oceans of Tropical Punch, Royal Punch, Dixie Shake, Frank's Orange Nectar, sarsaparilla, birch beer, vanilla egg creams, lime rickeys, and black and whites, puckery lemon drops, vermillion wax lips and snowy wax teeth all slick with sugar sweetness, vile sugar syrup in colors never seen in nature in crumbly wax bottles, stale marshmallow twists in thin layers of bitter chocolate, candy ropes the size of hawsers, red and black and brown for cherry, licorice, and chocolate ecstasy, thick quids of chewing tobacco made of densest licorice and licorice calabashes, white sugar-candy cigarettes tipped with pink sugar fires and hollow chocolate cigars, mansions and palaces of Hooton bars, with and without nuts, sourballs the size of Jupiter, crunchy sponge and heavy nougat, fake ice-cream cones of papery marshmallow, Mexican hats and Skippy sundaes, glaciers of crystal ice flecked with splinters from the ice-truck bed, winy fragments of stale mince cakes and buttery Scotch shortbread in greasy cardboard boats as big as the Queen Mary, Italian creams to stun the tongue, slick and shining red-hot dollars, rock-hard licorice buttons, an avalanche of cinnamon bee-bees, exotic greengrocers filled with exotic mounds of marzipan fruits, nigger babies mysterious as Mayan artifacts, Turkish-taffy pops of cherry, chocolate, vanilla, and banana to pull the fillings from the teeth, salt-water taffy in multicolored cardboard Gladstone bags, opaque candy balls with secret cores of pepper that magically change taste and color as they diminish, chewy twigs of anise wood, pink and white and yellow sugar-candy pies in tin plates with sharp tin spoons to cut the tongue and lips, chow mein sandwiches and bar-b-q hot and sloppy for a dime, lemon Epco, pink and white popcorn by the truck full, Jack o' Lantern lollipops, Cracker Jacks, cherry Santa Clauses—

That's enough, Doc Friday says. It's all crap and garbage anyway. Why all this fake nostalgia? For crap?

The nutritionalness of these foods leaves sore much to be desired, the Arab says.

Nary a vitamin, the Drummer says. These were the good old days?

I'm talking about *Donald Halvorsen's* memories, Richie says.

I just saw Big Duck, the Drummer says. What memories? He's right over in the Cities Service station with his nose up a carburetor. He's right here.

We're all *here,* Richie says. Jesus. I'm assuming assumptions, I'm imagining images, I'm making believe a future where Big Duck—*for instance,* Big Duck—is a successful businessman. I thought this was all clear.

Big Duck? Doc Friday says. Don't, please, I implore you, don't send me into hysterics with any successful businessman stuff. The son of a bitch can't get the grease out of his toenails even. Even the whites of his eyes are turning grey with grease. You might as well say Cheech, for Christ sake.

I said you could say Cheech if you wanted, Richie says. Or anybody. It's all just making believe. I thought this was clear.

All so you could try out this goddam list on us of junk that's all here anyway if anybody wants it . . . a *longueur!* Doc Friday says.

Longueur! the Arab says. *Magnifique! Magnifique, Docteur!*

Well, maybe they won't be here when Duck becomes, if he

becomes, a businessman, Richie says. Or even grows up. I thought maybe historically that—

Big Duck? A successful businessman? Don't make me laugh, Doc Friday says. You might as well say Cheech!

Indeed he might, the Arab says. *Longueur!* Beauteous.

Who? Cheech? the Drummer says. Cheech? Don't make me laugh.

Donald Halvorsen, adrift in the imagined future, muses, muses, lost in bittersweet memory.

Big Duck enters the store eating a chow mein sandwich and pulls a bottle of Dixie Shake from the soda cooler.

See? Richie says. See?

As if it proves anything, Doc Friday says. What do you say, President Duck? How's it going with Amalgamated Oil Burners?

66 An Anniversary

I'm sitting here, as anyone can see, on this chair on the lawn, under the grape arbor, just to get away from the house. The children are in there. And my husband is in his den—that's a good one—with his friends, watching the football game. Game?

A domestic scene, the usual? Complete with boredom? And so on and so on and so on. This old red rag of a robe I'm wearing is the "morning coat" my husband gave me two years ago. The chair is from the basement rumpus room—makes you sick, right?—of the neighbors we used to have and play cards with. Things got sticky with them because my husband said that the guy used to be too free with his hands with me. Always watching out for me, God bless him. You see the usual parched grass, the usual bug-infested roses all dying, the boring view that raised the price of this cracker box. I could cry. My God. Better than Brooklyn though. Right?

And you can also see and if you can't see you can imagine a cutesy-wutesy cuddly funny little bunny rabbit hippity-hopping past on his way to eat the last leaf of lettuce in the garden. Garden? He'd eat the strawberries too if I ever put them in which I did not and will not.

My sun hat is no bargain either. An anniversary present from my Lothario a couple of years back, everything is a couple of years back, except Brooklyn which is a couple of centuries back. Dirty old rotten Brooklyn. Yes, yes. I think that's a river behind me but I never look at it and I don't know and I don't care either. Maybe it's a pond with cutesy-wutesy fishies in it.

I can hear what the crummy novels I read call gruff male laughter coming from the goddamned den. Hubby, and his friend Ralph, the one with the bleeding madras sport coats, the brilliant accountant, oh yeah? And Charlie the life-insurance salesman who shakes your hand like he's taking your pulse, he should have been a doctor, and Ed, I don't want to forget Ed. The high-school gym teacher who likes to wear cowboy hats on the weekend and who is the world's leading closet queen. Oh, he is really gay. What a word for Ed. I could get sick right here.

By the way, I'm sorry, you probably can't guess who I am by looking at me, I'm Berta. Time, as they say, hasn't been too kind to my face. Once I was the runner-up in the Lake Hiawatha Labor Day beauty contest—about three thousand years ago—my friend Margie won because her chest was bigger. God only knows what happened to her. Probably married some dental surgeon who reads *The New Yorker* then puts it in the waiting room. What do I care if I'm talking to myself? Who else?

It's hard to believe that I had a B+ average at Smith and a straight A in my major. An attractive young woman. Now a faithful wife. My husband dries the dishes, puts in new light bulbs, and washes the car, and tells everybody we share the housework. I'm going to get a drink soon, it's almost five, some nice gin. Two. One for me and one for you, dear friend.

This thing on my lap is, yes, it *is* exactly what you think it is. A basketball. That's—I swear it—this year's anniversary present to me. He figures he can practice one-on-one with me—it's about the only one-on-one he can manage anymore. He's like the wife in those dumb jokes in the wonderful world of showbiz, not tonight, I've got a headache. He's the one with the headache. Pretty typical, if what I hear is true. How about you?

A basketball. For me. Berta. A basketball for Berta.

So I married this nice young guy of the same religion. I could have had almost any boy I wanted back then. That boy I went to the prom with. But my mother with her weak little smile. My father with his stern handshake. Now they're both dead and here I am. He's probably an accountant in Teaneck anyway.

So here I am with this one with the football games and the

anniversary presents. And this year, along with the shore dinner we have every goddamned year, I've got, instead of a sun
hat, so I can "work in the garden," I've got a real basketball, official, all my own. I'm so ashamed I could die. So he can practice one-on-one and impress Ed the homo, that they don't call
them anymore, and what was that other word? Fruit! Right,
fruit. Yes, so he can impress him that he's a real city kid and
grew up playing basketball with all the tough kids. My God, Big
Mickey would have had him for breakfast. Why can't he just
say he plugged away at Stuyvesant with all the other little assistant account executives and dentists and psychological social workers? What does he want? Impress Ed the homo. A
blow job? Excuse me—a young mother and good wife shouldn't
say blow job. Fellatio is the word. They use it in the *Times* and
every other damn place now that cocksucking has become respectable, a respectable skill. When I was in high school, we
used to think— who cares what we used to think? The way he
lies there though with his legs twitching and gasping I feel like
cracking him across the face. I'm too old for all that silliness.

And there's the little bunny rabbit again. I hope to God he ate
some of the trees this time, these sacred trees. God, how I hate
all these dumb trees! When the kids were small I used to hope
they'd kill them climbing on them and maybe we could go back
to Brooklyn. See those old streets, look for . . . look for, ghosts
now, I guess. I bet nobody lives there anymore. Why would you
live there, when you can move and have some *trees?* Maybe I'll
go back myself soon, the kids are just about big enough. Yes,
children, I'm leaving your father because he's a boring kid who
went to Stuyvesant and he laughs at Ed the homo's jokes and I
can't stand these trees and I think fellatio is cocksucking.

I don't know why I should be surprised. I'm really not surprised. I'd be surprised if I got this if he were somebody else. I'm
surprised he didn't give me some boxing gloves so he could
knock the hell out of me once a week, man to man. Next year
probably. Unless I pack a bag and run away and live over a store

somewhere where he'll never find me. I'm not surprised. Did I say the kids are just about big enough? My God, they're in college for a year already one of them and the other starting. You see, I want to be young. I think I'm losing my mind, no such luck.

How can I be surprised, I ask you, when I really think about this man? A man who wears boxer shorts that say HELLO, I'M DAVE; takes a course in "The Erogenous Zones" in some adult-education mill; scoffs at take-out hamburgers when I don't want to cook and likes ketchup sandwiches; thinks the newspapers are educational; swears that air conditioning gives him colds because his mother, that blue-haired bitch, told him so; tries, without fail, to bugger me when he's had too much to drink; can't get it hard enough when I want him to bugger me, not for a long time now; thinks that athletes are "our" true intellectuals; says "Marcel Prowst"; can't mix a decent martini or even a lousy martini; wants novels, the one and a half he reads every year, to be more real; considers Jack Benny to be a comic genius, likewise Jerry Lewis, my God; likes what he calls Alger Hiss's strong face; gets weepy over any damn rotten flower; sucks in his stomach at the beach; thinks he can still do a great Lindy, but he never could do even a decent Lindy; wears a ragged sweatshirt that says UPSALA COLLEGE on it, filthy rag; saves piles of *The New Yorker* so he can get to all the terrific fiction he calls it some day; asks me, or used to, about once a year to see if I can buy a real, old-fashioned corset; buys cheesecake magazines and reads them in the garage; likes peanut butter and cucumber sandwiches; is convinced that all Sicilian names end in "i" even though I tell him about Cheech and Rocky Giuffredo; always says that the girl with the biggest boobs or the tightest skirt at a party was really interesting and can't wait to screw me when we get home; loves that old faker, Chagall; wishes he'd studied public speaking; breaks every fountain pen and mechanical pencil he touches and then asks who broke them; wears chinos that are too short; admires badminton and every summer swears he'll learn how to play; hates ale and drinks it to impress me—*me*; says "look at that pompadour of mine" when he goes through our wedding pictures; wears socks with holes in the heels on Saturdays; thinks that movies are a great art form, plain old lousy movies; admires the way Lou Gehrig died though he died like everybody else as far as I can tell; hates cats because they don't, he says, do things; says "you even had on all white underwear" when he goes through our wedding pictures; looks for any excuse not to take the goddam dog out; knows the corny Indian name of that goddamned river or creek back there; can't play softball to save himself but plays two or three games every spring and then, without fail, says "am I out of shape"; always, always, and for twenty-one years asks me why I bother to wear a slip in the summer until I could strangle him; buys Southern Comfort once every two or three years and then wonders why he bought the crap and decides he bought it for me; wants me to buy those panties without any crotch; thinks Ed's wife is great because she keeps score at baseball games; says he loves venison but never ate it in his life; still won't believe me and gets mad when I tell him that pornographic pictures make me laugh; wants us to play nurse and patient after he goes through our wedding pictures; won't even *try* raw oysters; buys every goddamned stupid boring *Peanuts* book the minute it's published; puts a whoopee cushion on my chair when the kids are home from school and have friends over; asks me to try it, try it he says, with a candle in my backside; refers to the boy who took me to the high school prom as "that guinea kid"; says pantyhose was invented by a fag, hm, probably Ed the homo; sings the words of "Autumn in New York" to the tune of "Moonlight in Vermont"; thinks the Chinese have some pretty good ideas but can't remember what; talks in the movies; gets annoyed when I tell him that canned ravioli makes me sick just thinking of it; spends hundreds of dollars on fishing equipment and can't cast; buys me black mesh opera stockings every Christmas and then wonders what I did with them; talks about the Brooklyn Dodgers and Ebbets Field but never cared at all about baseball; gets excited if I wear a girdle; drinks Vermouth Cassis whenever we go to an expensive restaurant about once every four hundred years; talks about the lore of pipes and says, I swear it, "the lore of pipes"; asks me to try it on *him* with a candle; cries at the end of *Gunga Din* and then says "they don't make movies like *that* anymore"; begins every year but never finishes *USA*; has sexual fantasies about Gloria Swanson—Gloria *Swanson!*; wants to read my college diaries; can't poach eggs; couldn't find my clitoris for eight years; sharpens pencils with his teeth; never finishes a crossword puzzle; loves instant coffee and hates whole wheat bread but says the opposite; washes his little bit of hair every goddamned day and asks me why I'm always washing my hair; loves those rotten old Laurel and Hardy movies; reads recipes out of the newspapers to me and says "maybe we should try this out?"—*we*; thinks it would be fun, he calls it, to learn to ski; says sanitary napkins are a real luxury and then says something about "real women"; and, *and*, he calls me Bert.

So. So you see. Or I see. We see. This gorgeous and beautiful anniversary present is appropriate.

Now I'll go in and make a nice drink or two and not talk to the children who are probably still arguing over the car for tonight. We didn't have a car in Brooklyn. Nobody ever had a car in Brooklyn. And I will ignore him if he asks me if I'd like to have a brew—a brew!—and watch the last quarter with the guys. I'll make some nice big drinks and come out with them and sit right here under these sacred trees with my back to the pond over there. Sometimes I don't really believe any of this ever happened, that it's a dream like some corny movie.

Talking about happened, I wonder what ever happened to Isabel? I wonder what ever happened to everybody? All ghosts. Including me.

Well, what do you think? the Magician says. He stands slumped, sweat pouring from his face, exhausted.

All upon all and taken as an exemplum of whole cloth, the

Arab says, it must stand proud as an incredulously cogentious performance of wizardry. Huzzahs for you!

I've got to admit it was a bitch, Doc Friday says. The voice—the voice is what got me. Jesus, gave me a chill. It's like Berta, I mean just like Berta grown into a woman. Jesus.

Why Berta? Richie says. He is pale.

Yeah, Irish Billy says. How come you picked Berta? Billy is, if possible, paler than Richie.

A magician has certain tasks, certain things he must do, must accept. Sometimes he performs well, other times . . . To tell you the truth, I thought that this would be amusing. I didn't know that it would be—that it would be, well . . .

It was too sad, Richie says. I'm sorry I listened. I thought, I didn't think it would be so goddamned sad.

And spooky, the Doc says.

I too admit upon being harrowed up and enchilled, the Arab says.

None of you better say a goddam word to Berta, Irish Billy says. Not a word.

Pray lucidify my thoughts, Magician, the Arab says. For an instance or two, what is the *Peanuts* book and what is this pantyhose?

I don't know. When I do this I don't know what will come out. It just comes out. It's hard enough to just *be* somebody. I don't even know if this will be true or even half-true. I just don't know. Maybe it's all just fiction. I just don't know.

It is of an engrossment, the Arab says.

Jesus, Richie says, and shivers.

I'm telling you guys, Irish Billy says. None of you say a word to Berta. Fiction or not. Not one word.

67 The Perils of Advertising

Is that the fruit man? Irish Billy says.

Who else? Fat Frankie replies.

But what the *hell* is that on his horse? Billy runs out to the corner to get a better look. Jesus, it's that guy off the boat who helps him out. What's his name?

Salvatore, Cheech says. From Bari.

What's he doing up on the horse? Billy asks. And what's in his hand?

In his hand, Salvatore holds an acorn squash.

A-corna squasha! Salvatore yells. A-corna squasha! Today spesh! Spesh! Today! Spesh acorn-a squasha!

It's advertising, Santo Tuccio says. The fruit man is—what do you say?—at breast with the times.

What do you mean, advertising? Cheech says. Who the hell knows what Salvatore is saying? Listen to him. What's this "spesh"?

Special, special he means, Richie says. Go ahead, Cheech, ask Salvatore what he's doing.

He don't know English, Santo says.

Talk in Italian. Ticineti—you talk to him in Italian, Richie says.

O.K. We'll *all* talk to him in Italian. Hey, Salvatore! Ticineti yells. Cosi di Salvatore, hah? Che s' dice the acorn-a squasha? Tutti squasha? Che s' dice "spesh"?

Oh Jesus, Cheech says. That's some Italian.

Salvatore looks at Ticineti and holds the squash a little higher, smiling.

Salvatore! Fat Frankie yells. Guaglio! Basta the squasha! Uh . . . como no sella the zucchinis?

Mussolini! Cheech shouts.

Hey! Spesh! Spesh! Salvatore yells.

Faccia di bruto! the fruit man yells at Cheech. Tutti pazz'!

Marconi! Santo yells. Lavagetto!

DiMaggio! DiMaggio calamari e sopresatta! Fat Frankie hollers, shaking his fist at the fruit man.

U'cazz'! the fruit man yells back. Puttan'! Puttan a la madonn'!

Si, signore, Ticineti yells. Basta, basta. You gotta the melanzan'? Nice-a spesh on a nice-a peacha?

Dante Alighieri! Richie shouts and starts to dance up and down.

Camilli rizzuto an' cul'! Santo bellows. Fra diavolo di Presidenta Street! And-a Baltic Street!

The fruit man makes a circular movement with his index finger pointing at his temple. Pazz', he says sadly, shaking his head. Tutti pazz'.

Pazz' your ass! Cheech yells. Pasta! you mean. Pasta cicc'! Pasta fagiol'! Galento graziano la motta di pair o' balls-a!

Hey! Spesh! Spesh! Salvatore cries. A-corna squasha! Pair o' balls-a!

Basta, animal'! the fruit man says, and pulls Salvatore off the horse.

Signore, Ticineti yells, as the wagon turns the corner and starts down the block. You like-a spesh? A nice-a Swissa cheese? Hah? You like-a nice-a cazz' an' cul'?

Enrico Caruso cabuzzell'! Sfogliatelle! Richie yells.

Is a nice-a spesh! A-corna squasha you colleones! Ticineti hollers after the wagon.

Ravioli! Cheech shouts, waving good-by.

And a spinaci macaroni too, Santo screams, fluttering his handkerchief. Impellitteri garibaldi! Louis Prima!

Nice-a a-corna squasha! the fruit man cries. On a spesh today! On a spesh! He stops dead and knocks Salvatore's hat off, then reaches down and picks it up. Looking up at the sky, he gathers in from it three handfuls of air, with each calling, in turn, Gesù! Maria! e Giuseppe! He throws each name into Salvatore's hat, hurls the hat to the street, and stamps up and down on it.

Take it easy! Richie yells, fruit-a man! Your ass-a will wind uppa in the inferno!

68 Christmas News

The Arab, in a new overcoat, under which he wears an equally new bright green lounge jacket over brown tweed slacks, holds aloft a sheaf of typewritten pages on the cover sheet of which he has drawn a five-pointed star.

The Bay Ridge–South Brooklyn–Bath Beach–Bensonhurst *Star,* he says.

Should be the Arabian *Star,* Pepper says. Don't we get enough news—all the goddam news we need—just standing around on the corner?

Ah, but this is a redolence of *society* news, the Arab smiles. Whom is engaged in performing what, where, and how—and with who! I admit brusquely that perhaps a fact or trey is slightly hyperboled for the sake of piquancy of flavor and effluvia.

And you'll read it, right? Pepper says. No matter what.

But *oui oui.* It is a holiday, a Yuletides tradition.

What tradition? You never did this before, ever.

Read, worthy scribe, read, the Drummer says.

A tradition I have decided to initialate *this* festive season, the Arab says. The spiceful information and luscious gossip in this journal has been gleaned up and garnered together via the most painful research and with a fig for expense. As for the valuable time consumed withal—I say naught. Nor do I breathe or impute one syllable as to who acted as investigating reporters for all this factual datas, neither as to who in yeomanish mode assisted to write and edit same to elegantish and stern professionism.

Hear! Hear! the Drummer says.

For Christ sake, then, read it, Pepper says.

The Arab removes his overcoat and hands it to the Drummer. He clears his throat.

Irish Billy enters the store, stamping snow from his shoes.

Ah, Billy, Pepper says. Just in time for the society news from the hobo wrongo's Walter Winchell.

Irish Billy grasps the situation and walks out into the snowstorm to head for the Royal and another cup of coffee.

Philistine, the Drummer says.

The Arab clears his throat again, turns the top sheet over, and begins.

Constance Maria LaNord, Cookie to her confidantes, the cordé bag and busted-rubber heiress and patroness and past engagée of the performing arts, was quietly married several weeks ago in Bensonhurst to ex-Marine John McGlynn, an attractive vet who has resided for some years in the psychiatric wing of the V.A. hospital . . . The svelte ceremony took place at the new bride's spanking-new apartment on Fifteenth Avenue. She also maintains a *pied-à-terre* on Fifth Avenue over Fritz's Tavern, the latest spot for the glitter-and-guzzle crowd, and a beautiful teeny-tiny room in her mother's house on Fort Hamilton Parkway . . . The deliriously twinkly couple are spending the Christmas holidays there because of its proximitness to the sylvan delights of McKinley Park. Who else would tell you these things?

Princess Scupari, the delightfully dynamic cousin of slick stickball champ Artie Salvato, has been shopping around madly for a place of her own. (The dear has decided to spend her life in Brooklyn.) A little pigeon has cooed in my ear that she, at last report, had almost settled for a three-room stunner on 68th Street, just across the street from the *intime* cellar abode of Black Tom Murphy, a very, and we mean *very*, chic caretaker. And how many of you know that Tommy is passionately fond of the humble potato? . . . One's not a broth of a lad for nothing, is one? . . . Speaking of houses, and why shouldn't we, the unacknowledged goodwill ambassador to Red Hook, that *interesting* neighborhood, Tommy Azzolini, reportedly just plunked down a whopping $5000 for a lovenest for himself and his clever spouse, Linda, out in bosky Levittown. Tommy, you automotive buffs will remember, has the coveted Kings Highway–Saratoga Avenue bus run for his very own, and it looks like it's for life, dears. Goody-goody. Linda's daddy is, of course, Patsy Collucci, the policy biggie. Oh dear, are we allowed to *breathe* that?

Jimmy "The Earl" Early, and Jamie to his chums (of which he has a *barrel*), will marry Joanne "The Nose" Cassiliano, Frankie Cassiliano's kid sis, in Sheepshead Bay on March 8, with a gala reception, we're told, at the Flo-Ral Club on mellow old New Utrecht Avenue. The twenty-four-year-old Jamie, an oiler for the Waterman Line, has been one of the most ubiquitously carefree bachelors in South Brooklyn . . . He's a cousin of the Dobbins brothers, those gaddy-gaddy gadabouts, and, rumor has it, Mission Bell's very best darlingest customers . . . "The Earl" spends his time "on the beach"—we're as nautical as the next one!—between bustling Finn Hall and Irishtown in the salty Rockaways. (Where *do* you think he got those cracked front teeth, darlings?) Educated at Alexander Hamilton High and Automotive Trades, "The Earl's" motto is "Back Up This Shot." Wise innkeepers usually do . . . As for the future bride, the bubbly Joanne, twenty, is the product of one of the oldest families on Bay Ridge Avenue, 69th Street to you aliens. "The Nose's" family crest reads "Tutti Pazzo In Il Capo," which, roughly translated means, "Heart Not Head." How swell for the lovely Joanne that she has both aplenty. By the by, should we whisper that "The Nose's" pet name is "Chesty"?

In the peaceful and sereneful setting of St. Rocco's near that city within a city, Bush Terminal, tiny pink-and-white and red-cheeked Yolanda Maria Anna Flom was christened last week, surrounded by the very young and very old members of the infant's father's venerable and charmingly raucous Scandinavian family . . . Teeny pink-and-white Yolanda wore the twenty-year-old imitation lace baptismal gown her proud mommy, the former Anna Mangini, has been saving since she wore it as a wee tot on DeGraw Street. And you say dreams don't come true?

The church altar was flanked by great urns filled with traditional holly and poinsettias by the oodles! And to symbolize the alliance between these two proud and pleased-as-punch families of different backgrounds, with fresh basil and scads of colorful lingonberries too.

The baby's papa, Georgie Flom, a Private First Class on leave from the famed Second Armored Division, old Hell on Wheels, in Fort Hood, Texas, never *looked* more puffed up . . . Also absolutely gross with pride were pink-and-white Yolanda's godmothers, Sylvia Metz, the wife of Buddy "Ashcan" Metz of Senator Street, and Anne O'Neill, a Carmelite nun (aren't they the dears who can't speak?) and also the sister of Joseph O'Neill, the world-renowned Missal collector . . . Sylvia and Anne are dear dear childhood chums of the baby's mommy from the old days in Coney Island. Georgette Marshall stood by, a dream in lime-green organdy, as a kind of sweet unofficial godmother. She's the granddaughter of the ex-middleweight battler, Kid Mulloon, and for those of you with too too lazy memories, she was maid of honor, and a stunner too, at Anna's wedding. Okay?

Baby Yo's godpapas were Kenneth Thompson, daddy's brother-in-law and the best man at the wedding (yes, there *was* talk about him and Georgette), and Ivar Rydstrom, the son of electrical-union shop steward Ole Rydstrom and his unilingual mate, Marte . . . The old folks trained in for the fete from a holiday in Asbury Park. Ivar's mother is a Hultmann, and everyone knows that the Hultmanns are the Nathan's Famous of the Jersey shore, doesn't everyone? . . . George Berlund stood tall as a special friend. He's been living in a deliciously *soign*ée furnished room above Lento's Bar and Grill and is the nephew of Mrs. Ingrid Johannesen Flom, the tot's grandma. I wonder how they *ever* got him away from Bingo, that darling toy bull he just adores?

Among the very very *distingué* members of the family and friends who were present were Joanie Holsten, the baby's dad's sister, whose husband is Otto Holsten of the ice-cream parlor clan, the "Tyrants of Tutti-Fruitti"; "Countess" Connie D'Amato Glynn, another of Anna's pals from the *ancien régime*, who's also the ex of Jack Glynn, who was recently named most handsome ex-altar boy at Our Lady of Angels but who hasn't been in these parts lately; Sal Barbieri and his knockout wife, Helen (she's the former Helen Mahoney, the four-time Lindy queen); Vincent and Rocco Giuffredo—Cheech and Rocky's Custom Pants of course; Frank Toto; Whitey the Greek; Sallie Magrino; John "Black Mac" McGoldrick; Plato and Iris Arvenites, who zoomed in for the fun from a holiday junket to Ozone Park at the home of Augusta "Gussie" Maklaros, the cigar-store heiress who's been seen gallivanting all up and down Flatbush Avenue with Joseph Keene, one of the season's most sought-after guests . . . must be his really infectious laugh and *bundles* of funny anecdotes; John Anderson, of boating fame, enough said for you *au courant* folks; Jack Gannon and his quiet brother, Benito; George Burkhardt (who turned the town on its ear last spring with his witty essay, "History of Belches"), and his devoted publisher, Patrick McGlade, of whom it's said he's bought his own personal stool at Gallagher's Subway Inn; Jack Cullen, Jakie to those who love him, the chemical something-or-other mogul; and others of that stripe . . . As stripes go, you'll admit it's not half bad.

Joan Dolores Militi, Mimi to you if you please, had a few bosom buddies, boys and girls, in for a Christmas cocktail at her efficiency flat on Ovington Avenue. Mimi was super-Yuleish in Henri Marsh's holly-green and berry-red extra-heavy crepe to the floor, lined in ice-blue silk and cut, if that's the word! top and bottom to you know where ... Wowee! ... Pushing in, milling about, and elbowing out of the snug retreat were Carmine DeFeo and his cousin Richie Gallo from Carroll Street; Donato Gramegna, the young whiz with a finger or five in the Maxwell House coffee biz; Tony DelRosa; Corporal "Red" Ziccarrilli, who's nail-biting a pending BCD (that's Bad Conduct Discharge to you civilians) from the Leathernecks—naughty, naughty, Red!; Danny DeMonda and Bubbsy Brown, who, despite all the talk, make a swellegant pair; Joseph Delaney of Ridge Boulevard, "Kicky" still to his longtime pals; plump and pert Aram Kurkjian, whose pop provided the olives 'n' stuff for the soirée from his specialty shoppe on 69th Street; Edward Bromo; Bobby Drumm and his brother, "Lord" Finn Drumm, still a wee pale from a sojourn in Coxsackie; Georgene Marshall (yep! she's Georgette's younger sis) in an emerald-green chemise so-o fitting since her pater is a mucky-muck in the Emerald Society, isn't that cute?; darling Nettie Euphemia with an eye-popping coif from Mr. Pasquale; Michael Crane and cousin John McNamee, the Big and Little Mickeys who've cornered the market in crabs; Mario Pucci, a real scream in rubbers and a cab-driver's cap and his newest flame, hubba-hubba, Joyce Lunde, who when we saw her was putting her head together with Ed Ellsworth's on what a little birdie tells me is a new line of colored *femme* undies that'll be called "Wilming-tones"—made, girls, out of cellophane! Crackle, crackle; Maxim and "Pet" Stoope; Alfredo "Fritzi" Hernandez; "Cubby" Hubert and his sidekick from the Red Hook Writing Consultants Seminars up in Westchester, Norman Perlmutter (Cub calls him "Benjy"—goodness knows why!); Dr. Nils Astrup; Dr. Charles Taylor; Angus MacGinnis; Liz Bochnik; George Whittle in a hilarious postman's suit; Philomena

Rourke, whose oldest friends still call her "Big Cockeye"; Edith Mertis, svelte and slender after a stay in the Bronx; Arthur Shaerenbach, sticking to ice water on the rocks—attaboy, Art!; Candace "Chicky" Klein in Loeser's black-and-white-and-blue sheath that had some of the boys all atrance; and a gaggle more just like them.

And a Happy Yule to you! Jingle jingle!

69 An Epistolary Novel

Dear Dolores,

I hope you can forgive me for writing this note to you but I have to write you this note to tell you what is bothering me a lot. You're probably laughing right now, unless, you're so mad allready that you crinkled up this paper and thrown it in the garbage.

I didn't mean to insult you the other night when I mentioned come joke about your nationality. It was very dum of me and I'm writing this letter to you to appologize from the botom of my heart. It allmost killed me later on that night in bed when I realized that the rotten joke I told was not only a terrible thing to say about peoples nationality but, allso it was a joke about the size of a persons' nose. I wouldn't blame you if you never talked to me again or even, looked at me. Especialy me, who, have troubles of my own like you know. Such as, pimples, acne, black heads, ect. plus my hands that are allways black and grimey under the finger nails no matter how much I wash with a nailbrush and allso my callusses.

I wanted a lot to kiss you in your hallway, and instead, got so nervous that I made that rotten joke about a persons' nationality plus the part allso about peoples noses instead. I knew that you were mad even though, you are too sweet and fine a girl ever to say a word about such rude things even spoke right in your face. God. How dum I am some times. I could kick myself for mentioning these things especially, stupid things that belong in the school yard at grammer school.

But that dream, that I have allways of I and you together, is true even though you probably hate and dispise me, more than any human being in the world, except maybe, Santo, who said that dirty thing to you that time we went to Steeplechase. I told you, that I allways imagine us together out in the country in front of our big country house. With trees all around it. And we are standing talking, to each other under some really teriffic stone arch way like the kind you walk under in the park when you are going down to the ferry only, of course not a tunnel but sort of like an entrance way, to our Estate. My vishion is all ways the same, there we are standing, in the same place allmost touching and your face is shining with happyness just like a beautiful actresses like Merl Oberron's. The sky is blue and all around us, there are big glowing stars that shine brightly and gold.

Maybe you remember me telling you this wonderful dream I have of us two together in some Paradise, allthough I wouldn't blame you if you laughed and felt like spitting allover the dream and allso allover my face, except I know, that you would never spitt. Although I don't remember if I told you, about the stars part which seemed to come later when I had this vishion dream, at first, it was just us together peacefuly together in the country, outside a beautiful country house, and grounds like you said you fell in love with in the Philadelphia Storey when we saw it some time back in the Albee. You remember that rainy Friday night when you wore your blue velvet dress.

Any way, believe me, my *dear* friend Dolores, that no matter how bad my manners are in the rude behavior of my dum crack about nationalities and the nose remark I still, have that vishion because, I really Love You so much that I think I am going crazy. As a matter of fact the other day, I was doing a ring job on a 47 Chevy and, in the middle of the job I forgot for a minute how to do a ring job. Me who can do ring jobs in my sleep allmost. It is true.

I don't want to call for you til I know your feelings about all this, and, about me. But I really want to see you again and thought that, if you are not mad enough to kill me or give me the cold shoulder that I could call for you, on Friday night and we could go out for a walk or may be see the movies at the Dyker and have a soda, or some coffee after. Whatever you like.

I can't seem to think of any thing but you Dolores, Dolores, Dolores and I am so sorry about all this that I even cryed last night. Yes I really cryed like a baby after I went to bed thinking, of how I put my foot in my mouth about what I said and which about a persons' nose I didn't mean a bit. I swear to God.

Very truely yours,
Donald

Dear Donald,

Thank you for your nice letter which I received today. I am very happy that you would go to the trouble of writing me to apologize for your remarks the other night. You are right that you think that you hurt my feelings. It is not very gentlemanly to tell a girl a joke that not only makes fun of her descent but also of a certain physical part of her body that she cannot help.

But what really hurt my feelings was the following. I have told you and told you that I have caused unhappiness in my family, and I have had arguments with my Aunt who has really been a mother to me all these years, ever since I was a little girl, about my dating you so much because of the difference in our national descent and our religion and because they do not think that you are going to get anywhere as a garage mechanic. Then, to hear you say, something about my descent was really an awful blow to me, because it made me think that maybe my family and my Aunt are right about everything they say about you. The part about the girl's nose was another thing that made me say to myself, "maybe they are right." It was also a joke that boys do not usually tell young ladies. When I went in I went straight to bed without even doing my Math and cried myself to sleep, I was so upset and nervous.

I thought the next day that maybe you thought I was mad at you because I went in so fast, because of what you were trying to do in the Alpine. You know, Donald, that I am not that kind of girl and that the Alpine is not that dark, so that even though we were sitting in the last row, somebody who knows my Aunt could see us and mention it to her and I don't know what I could say to her after all these years that she has raised me to be a clean girl, and sent me to Catholic Schools too, so that I can learn how to grow up to be a good wife to her husband. I like you very much, Donald, I really mean it, but I don't think that gives you the right to take advantage of me and use your hands like that, even though we are almost going steady. Why do you think when we had that argument six months ago and stopped seeing each other I would never go out with Richie, even though he is a Catholic and also of the same descent as I? But I was not mad at you about that although I thought it would be a good idea to mention it as long as we are putting our cards on the table.

Of course I remember your dream, in fact it was so beautiful in my thoughts that I could see it just as if it was my own dream. And also, I saw in my dream when I thought about yours, not only us together but a cute little boy about two or three, our darling son, hanging on to my skirt as we are talking, and just outside the entranceway my oldest Uncle, who sits there, looking at us understandingly and with two dogs at his feet. My oldest Uncle, Uncle Frank, does not think too much of us seeing each other too often. He is very old fashioned and he has even said to my Aunt that he wonders what it is you want, going out with me all the time. So, this dream of mine, with my Uncle Frank being so kind and giving us his blessing may be a sign of Good Luck. Or maybe, it's just wishful thinking.

I am sorry that you have been sad because of this incident, and please believe me when I say that I have been sad also. You mention having trouble with a mechanical job. What would you say if I told you that yesterday in Latin when Sister Beatrice called on me to conjugate audire in the future passive I couldn't get it right, and she said in front of the whole class "Dolores must be in love." Because you know I always get the highest marks in the class in Latin. I got as red as a beet.

I would very much like to see you and take a walk with you on Friday night if you'd like to call for me at seven. I'll tell my Aunt that we're going to the O.L.P.H. dance and that will probably avoid an argument because she'll think it's allright since it's a Catholic dance. Be sure to wear your Sunday suit, that nice dark blue one with the stripe, and a white shirt, so that we'll look like we're going to a dance.

Your friend,
Dolores

P.S. It was very sweet of you to remember that I wore my blue velvet dress that time.

70 The Bad Joke

Tania Crosse stands in her garden. It may not be her garden. As a matter of fact, let's make it clear that it is not. She's a weekend guest of the manor house, Richie says.

The manor house? Professor Kooba says.

Yes. The manor house. She's surrounded by vines heavy with great bunches of purple grapes. The very fact that she stands in this garden speaks volumes.

Speaks what? Kooba says.

Speaks volumes, I say. Volumes. A figure of speech, a manner of speaking, an expression, a trope, which means—

I get you, Kooba says. I didn't hear you the first time. For some reason I thought you said "cartons."

I was about to say, that the very fact that Tania is in this garden at all speaks volumes on the all-pervasive quality of democracy. Miss America, her well-known work-worn mother, who, to borrow a colorful phrase, busted her chops all her life, would probably not believe that this modish young woman is the daughter born to her in Sister Elizabeth's Lying-In Hospital.

One is fraught and racked with amaze how such ameloration may come about to pass in a single generation, the Arab says.

Tania is gazing abstractedly at a strange-looking bird perched on her gauntleted left hand, Richie says.

As well she might, Kooba says.

Has someone in the manor played a cruel trick on Tania? Richie says. Has someone asked her here for a sophisticated and genteel weekend in a petty spirit of mockery in order to humiliate her? In order to throw in her face her humble Polish-American background? In order to cause her—in front of all the other guests, perhaps around the coin-shaped pool— embarrassment upon being called "Miss Krulicewicz"?

Who gives a goddam shit? the Sailor says. She was always a snooty broad anyway. I'm tired of hearing about her.

Must we hear from the vulgar likes and types of the Sailor? the Arab says. His sallies and forayings into opinionating sully the waters of discourse.

Take a walk, you Arab creep, the Sailor says.

But Richie, Professor Kooba says. What about this bird? Does it have anything to do with the cruel trick somebody maybe played on Tania?

Maybe. Closer inspection of this scene shows a slightly pained expression on Tania's face, probably the same sort of expression she wore, years ago, when her brother, Pete, would leave the apartment of an evening for his third pitcher of beer.

In those days, some old-timers still called it a growler of beer, Professor Kooba says.

Imagine that scene, Richie says. Peter, mumbling drunkenly as he rummages for change in an old Ann Page mayonnaise jar, Miss America, stunned into silence by the "Lux Radio Theatre," and Tania—Thelma—trying to lose herself in the never-never land of Viña Delmar.

A typical sensitive young woman of her time, Kooba says. Itching and dying to get away from such sordidness.

In any event, the pained expression is the same, Richie says. In this case, though, it is caused by the fact that the "bird" that perches on her hand is not a bird at all, but merely a bit of cotton, feathers, wire, and glue. And to add insult to injury, the "bird's" head is nothing more than an overripe tomato.

A what? the Arab says. An overripe . . . ?

An overripe tomato, Richie says. A "gift" from the owner of the manor, this "bird." Suddenly, her true fate is clear to Tania.

She will never be free of those smells of frying sausage and boiled cabbage. At this moment, she is gently singing a gentle ditty of self-mockery and wretchedness. Listen.

O Bird, thou art but scraps and tatters,
And artificial as an elevator.
  But that which my heart busts and shatters
  Is that your sconce is made of—
A tomater!

A nice voice emits from her lovely throat, the Arab says. Sconce? Hmm. He is laughing in spite of himself. It does smack a jot of the absurd, he says.

Perhaps it is some kind of fertility symbol, Professor Kooba says. And if so—what does *that* portend?

What a bunch of shit, the Sailor says. Fuck the broad!

Anyway, whatever is transpiring, Kooba says, they are a bunch of bastards up there in the manor house. I've described such cavalier and arrogant treatment by such oppressors in "The Curse," as you all know.

The world is oft a grim and grime-choked place, ethnically speaking, to be emplaced upon, the Arab says.

A shadow begins to cross Tania's face, Richie says. Or is it a growing flush of embarrassment? She imagines she can hear the nasty, petty laughter from the manor house far away on the hill. She may be the beautiful and brilliant Tania Crosse, and yet . . . and yet . . .

One never outgrows one's vulnerability to humiliation, Professor Kooba says. It's one way we can tell if we're human.

Tania doesn't, however, Richie says, as you can see, throw the ugly construction away from her in horror and shame, but continues her walk through the garden, her eyes stinging with tears, her ears burning with the laughter from the manor house, smiling and cooing at the doll, and singing her ditty over and over.

It does not in any way partake any longer of the facetious, the Arab says. Not at all.

Here you're feeling sorry for the broad, the Sailor says. Don't make me laugh! You have a porterhouse for supper last night? I'll carry that fucking phony bird around all day long for that bitch's breaks.

71 Stars! Stars! Stars!

This is the racket, the Sailor says, shaking a magazine at the others in the store. Here's a picture of some goddam artist who makes nothing but stars out of metal and sells them for about five grand each. See?

A color photograph in a magazine to go along with a story shows an artist in his studio, with tools in hand, making a star out of some kind of yellow metal. Around him are seven other stars, all identical to the one he is working on.

Five grand it says, sure as hell, Doc Friday says. The Sailor's right. He makes these, it says, out of bronze . . . it says last year he made them out of aluminum. Same stars though.

And people buy this? the Drummer asks. For five grand?

Loathsome and toadyish followers of chicness, the Arab says. Panders to novelty items. Cretinish boors.

That's the life for me, Cheech says. The hell with Civil Service.

You're better off being a character actor, Santo Tuccio says. Lots of loot, lots of prestige, lots of broads. Hollywood!

Next they'll make some bronze shit and sell it to some sap, Irish Billy says.

They do already! Fat Frankie says. Some guy makes bronze shit—and silver shit, too. He's a big-time artist out in California.

How about silver piss? Cheech says.

You may jest and josh in levitous good humor, the Arab says, but I have read of an oaf who spends his days creating mounds of maggot-encrusted garbage out of plastical material.

All crap, Santo says. What's the matter with being like Edward S. Brophy, hah? Edgar Dearing, Edward Gargan, Paul Hurst. How about Frank Sully, hah? That's bad?

Some guy framed a fucking *Daily News* and wrote "PAPER" across it and put it in a goddam museum, Fat Frankie says. I read it in *Coronet.*

Matt McHugh! Santo says. These are good actors. Miles Mander and Halliwell Hobbes. Ernst Cossart.

Some retrogradely inert imbecile stood on a pedestal-like structure of a podium in a large metropolitan art gallery with his buttocks empainted blue and cerise, the Arab says.

Ah, come on, the Drummer says. His *ass* painted blue?

Blue *and* cerise, the Arab says. The clod-like amoeba sold *himself* as an artistic opus. This is upright truth.

Did he sell his whole body or did you have to cut his ass off him? the Sailor says.

You can't knock the women either, no matter what you damn fools say, Santo says.

Who is knocking persons, Santo? the Arab says. Who mouthed a jot about the thespian profession? We are not discussing actors.

Character actors, Santo says. Character actors! These ain't dumb stars who stand around with square jaws and big tits. These are actors. Actors! You know Margaret Wycherly? Beryl Mercer? You ever see Aline McMahon? I'm not talking about tits and asses and muscles! These are real goddam actors. Jesus!

The sun has got Santo, the Drummer says. Santo, we're talking about *art.*

How about the guy I read about in the *Reader's Digest* sold a box of chalk? Irish Billy says. Yeah, to some natives or something in Australia. A goddam penny box of chalk. Well, three cents now, but just a box of chalk.

Let the customer beware, the Arab says. *Caveor emptat* as the ancient Latins were wont to enounce. I read of what Irish Billy speaks. How veracious it may be I cannot vouchsafe. But! I believe one hundred and fifty per cent correct an article I saw in the Lebanese press at my cousin's abode about a young whip-snapper dauber who placed the word "RED" in red paints upon a red background. Why do I accept this gruesome report as veridical? Because, it fits like hands in gloves with the shabby era in which we attempt to survive.

Don't give me this red shit, Santo says. It's all crapola. Alan Baxter, hah? How about him? You think he gives a fuck about red? There's an actor! Harold Huber? What about terrific talents such as John Hoyt and Rondo Hatton? You think a stellar player like Paul Cavanaugh would stand still for this bullshit art? Or Abner Biberman and Ivan MacDonald? Ha!

There's also a sculptor from Paris who dipped his balls in melted chocolate, Irish Billy says. I saw it in the *Tablet*. Yeah, he's listed as "Restricted." You can't even look at the guy or you commit a mortal sin.

Oh well, the Drummer says. *Paris.*

I fling it open to suggestion, the Arab says, that Billy bends the truth just a tittle, the merest jot. However, I comprehend his drifting point. And there was, I seem to recall, a Parisian, in truths, a grub of a hack who sold his telephone number cut from some old oilcloth.

Jack Lambert! Santo says, and bangs the soda cooler. Oilcloth my ass. Jack LaRue! Sara Allgood and Mary Boyd and the great Una O'Connor. Now there are people who don't know shit from Shinola about goddam fucking oilcloth and don't *have* to know!

Some chooch took a picture of his pecker and painted it pink, Cheech says. I swear. I read it in *Sexology.*

That, my dear Cheech, the Arab says, cannot by any stretched imagination be called art. One must term such an aberranation.

He sold it, it said, whatever you call it, Cheech says.

Oh, come on, Fat Frankie says. Next you'll tell me he painted his hat, some guy, and sold that.

An entrepreneur of a schemer painted a hat he claimed was worn by Clark Gable in some movie with honeysuckle leaves or some such foliage and sold *that,* the Drummer says. For infantile paralysis or something.

Clark Gable? Santo says. I told you I'm not talking about handsome-handsome or curvy legs. I'm talking Ruth Donnelly, Kathleen Freeman, Rosalind Ivan, Mary Wicker. I suggest to you guys Charles Arnt, Irving Bacon, Robert Emmett Keane, Gus Schilling. *Charles Lane!*

Some son of a bitch made the Eiffel Tower out of toothpicks, the Sailor says. Yeah, with a flag on top made out of a Kotex. Twenty grand.

Ah God, enough! Irish Billy says. You never read that anywhere, Sailor.

Yeah, I did. I saw it in something at the barber.

Billy Halop? Santo says. Charles Smith? Yagoda Momo! Constantine Anus? Folderol McFuck? What the hell do you guys *want?*

Who wants anything? the Drummer says.

Me, I want something, the Sailor says. I want to make a couple quick grand like these guys. Hey Drummer, pull your pants down and I'll tie a yo-yo around your dick and ship you over to New York to the museum.

Very funny, the Drummer says. Hilarious.

Pay no heeds to the churlish brute, the Arab says. He would not know art if it came smashing and crashing through his grimed-up window.

Elgar Peepee! Santo says, and leaves the store, muttering.

What the hell picture was he in? Cheech says. I don't think there's really an Edgar Peepee. Is there?

72 A Paradise

I shall grow a garden, the Arab says, to enableate me to be liberated from the economical and financious stricturations and exigents of the capitalistic system. In the eyes of my mind, those eyes that are now not neither so lucent or so limpid as betimes they were in youthful salady years, I perceive with clearness myself—leaning on a hoe or rake or some other genre or specie of sod-busting device-like implement favored in time-honored fashion by Okies and dirty farmers for aeons past. I gaze, in splendored raptness, upon a bush or shrub heavily laden and weighted down with golden honeydews or casabas, perhaps glittering cantaloupes spanking freshly in the sun. Around me sprout and writhe in glorious confused profusionness and richness vegetables, legumes, fruits, leafies, berries, all in riots of color and terraneous earthy goodness. Though I gaze with fervent bents upon the auriferous melons, I have the type of leanly tanned visage that bespeaks with stentorous tones love and affection as well as profound deep understanding of all the glories that Mother Nature offers from her goodly bowels. Tender and veiny okras by the score, blushing tomatoes nodding lazily upon their verdurous stems, huge blooming trees crammed with strawberries, blackberries, huckleberries, blueberries, gooseberries, and lingonberries, a few shady arbors of a repletion of avocados and nectarines. And grapes of course, of all dusky and sunnish hues, not excluding those juice-jammed type that possess a skin kind of chartreuse-ish in tint and tone. Boston lettuces, Simpson lettuces, and plain old Brooklyn lettuces will friendly vie for their spots from out under the bushel in the light of old Sal with escarole and Swiss chard as well as sandyish, grit-filled, deep-dark green spinach. You are partial to and experience craving yens about carrots and radishes and beets and other crunchy growths that are packed full of vitamins and crabohydrates down there in the cool and moisty earth? I'll plant a hundred vines of them! Watermelons will hurl their cool and crepusculant shadiness over the little flagstone path that wends its way to the potato patch. Because of their shyly violetish nature, which they cannot help since that is their nature, a small clump or two of raspberries will edge, with their famed and wonted desultoriness, a vast bed of snap beans, wax beans, butter beans, lima beans, string beans, Italian beans, and red beans. Boston beans, because of their cheery brownish-red hues, will be planted next to pinto beans and navy beans, and huddled close in rioting frenzy, I'll sow baby peas and black-eyed peas, whose little black-eyed-Susan flowers will grace many a precious heirloom vase at the breakfast nook on those mornings when I'll feast hearty on my fresh corns, wheat, timothy, and baked groats. Not to forget the snow peas either, of which there will be a sufficious handful. Beyond—but just beyond the groats plot—there will be exploding pods of bell peppers, red, green, yellow, and God knows what else all colors, to compliment my plum shrubs and my miniature peach and orange vines. All these things will rush and trample through my brains as I gaze with fondly good affection on the ripe and oozing melons that will make up my humble sup of a farc that evening. They are not only good by themselves, raw and crinkly, but they are olympiac rolled in some flour and eggs and fried. They are also amberosial with rhubarbs, plucked fresh, along with celery and limes and lemons, all of which exotica will crowd insanely together in planty happiness in a shady corner, since their scrumptious and delicately engineered beings are such that they are most replete with joy out of the strong rays of the afternoon sunbeams.

Do you urban classes entertain for split seconds the idea that I require these sterile streets in order to hold close to my heart happiness? I shall have onion tarts and leek casseroles! Scallions with a garnishee of tender rye stalks! Squash purees and soups with lashings of garlic buds to pass the wintry evenings with a good book in the other hand! All these glorious things are what I espy when I see myself as the brooding agriculturist. They are etched into my rapt face.

I don't even deign to breathe about such things as herbs and spices, but they shall spring up with a loud flourish too. And of course there will be a small mango patch, with a few rows of plantains, rice, and papayas.

By God, looking at myself in my imagination, my face is almost handsome and a brace of lustras younger. And, believe my pronouncement, the doings of the horses and the tracks will be far, far away from my desires and greeny reflections. Even the oat bushes that I plant to make my own home-made nerve-building porridge will not bring to me a pang for the loss of whinny, neigh, or swell double!

And I may impart to you the idea, held secretly by me up to this very moment, that I have placed my eye upon a small lot out in far Canarsie. Tomorrow I shall employ myself in the library and therein commence my agriculture research and boning upon.

73 Box Office

Any foolish person can make millions and billions of dollars of the realm with some modicums of talents and hard labors plus and also including a small pinch and dash of luck, the Arab says. I asserted it strongly in the past and I further and more pointingly assert it now. I myself have had the most recurrent idea for a brilliant cinema for a clutch of years now and perhaps the time is nigh for an all-out and full-scale assault upon this idea by myself and some other soul who can write this idea into glowing life.

Like Professor Kooba, the Drummer says, turning around to point at the Professor, who is riffling through *Beauty Parade*.

I don't like to exhaust my strength on vulgar and commercial enterprise, Arab, Kooba says. My God! Look at this one in the black corset! It is positively indecent.

His old hands tremble with barely repressed excitement.

He stares in amazed lust at the photograph of the partially clad beauty.

Vulgar and commercial enterprise? the Arab says. You tender me insults chock and block, Professor. Had I wished to sell myself for a mass of porridge I would have done so long ago—I have as much ability to whore and huckster myself for the almighty lucre as the next man. But I have oft and with concrete-like firmness declined—waiting to become a wealthy Midas in my own terms!

What's the idea for the movie? the Drummer asks. He is sucking a gumball.

Are you sucking upon a gumball? the Arab says.

Uh-huh.

A grossly and crassly crude act for one who is in the line to be the assistant scenario scribe, the Arab says.

Jesus. Thanks! But what's the idea? How can I assist if I don't know what the . . . *germ* is?

If the excellent and Solomonish Professor Kooba will for the nonce stop and desist his ogling of those deshabille sluts in that vulgar booklet and attend me, I'll take a shot, as they say in argot, at the attempt to sketch and lie out the broad outlines of the idea.

Kooba puts the *Beauty Parade* back in the rack. O.K., he says. Let's hear it. I am not agreeing to help because even if I like the idea I have before me a third revision of Part Nine of "The Curse" to take care of for the purposes of final polishing. But rest assured I am all ears.

You realize, the Arab says, that this is merely the skeletonish outline of what *can* become a vast panorama of sweep and profoundness. I envisionate a gigantesque and mammoth canvas of the American Way—a saga of its glories, tears, and all-around triumphings over base and tyrant-like foreign modes—and yet, buried within these victories and heart-throbbing wonderous things, are many small heartaches as well as large and garbage-like tragicness.

Tragedy? Kooba says.

Exactly! the Arab says. This will be the story of a mogul, a rich and fabled tycoon with hogsheads and fifty-gallon oil drums filled with money like olden time sultans and emirs and sheiks that we can read about even yet today in legends and sagas of yore.

Exactly what is a mogul? the Drummer asks. The phrase "hogsheads and fifty-gallon oil drums filled with money" has caused him to doff his fedora.

I see, Drummer, that you have whipped your fedora off at the merest mention of money, Kooba says. I have a character like that in "The Curse." He comes, and I don't mind telling you, to a bad end.

I'm in "The Curse"? Me?

You are *not* in "The Curse." I said only that there is a character—

Gentlemen! the Arab says. You requested, if I do not fall into errors, a celeritous outline of this mogul's saga and now I am peeping, or so it seems, correct me if I am wrong, the seeds and sprouts of digressiveness. Shall I go on?

Go on, Kooba says. My apologies.

The mogul has, the Arab says, by dint of Herculesish labors in work, risen upon the pinnacle of the rat race and has become an eccentric who strolls through the streets of all the slums and rotten boroughs of American cities, giving away doubloons and golden eagles and such forth to the wretched and stinking slobs, bums, tramps, hobos, skells, winos, geeks, and other assortments of low lifes of the earth. He garbs himself in raiments and costumes that make him appear to the naked eyes to be somebody else. The press, in its wontish way, goes wild. I envisionate here Jimmy Gleason as a hard-boiled egg of a city editor for this cinema and maybe Frank McHugh as a bumblish reporter looking for a scoop with his hat brim pushed up in the front.

Hey! That's not bad, Professor Kooba says. You can get much mileage out of craziness—maybe the mogul can be Eugene Pallette.

I was thinking of Edward Arnold maybe, the Drummer says.

Let us go one tiny toe at a time, the Arab says. Let us not become too incisive about casting this cinema until we have to hands the completed scenario. You will allow me however to bend my knee in thanks for your scintillating ideas, I trust and pray.

We got carried away, the Drummer says. Sorry.

Anyway, the Arab says. The results of this is that we are given a deep-seated view of this mogul. He is led along almost by the nose by guilt over his hoards of gold and mounds of dollars and such to give it away as if he is absolutely crazy insane.

And I suggest that mayhaps the moral of the story is that he actually begins to creep up upon the state of being bughouse crackers as the cinema progresses along.

Preston Sturges would eat this up with his fingers! Professor Kooba says. Lord! Give me a scene outline and I think I can rough-hew it out with absolute perfection. Maybe even tonight—after, of course, I do my regular work on "The Curse."

All right, the Arab says. Excellent! Let me give you one small dramatic scene for your creative grist. I have always imaged forth *this* as the last scene, he goes on, drawing a rough rectangle in the air with his hands. The tycoon-mogul, by this time what our Mexican-speaking friends would enterm totally loco, is dispersing alms in the shapes of golden coins to two miserable hobos on the outskirts of Wisconsin or Nebraska or some other small town out in Ohio. It is late in the evening, almost completely dark, but not thoroughly pitchy.

The stars shine down! the Drummer says. I can see the whole damn thing.

Shh, Kooba says.

The mogul is so incorrigiblely loony and loco that he's got a pair of scales so that he is perceptive of how many gold coins and doubloons to drop into the greedy palms that grasp and clutch. These two filthy and putridous hobos are on their knees in a genuflex with their hands stuck forth for the lucre. I am entranced by this scene as being in utter silence. I mean no chattering or gabbling of any kind. Not an iota of a decibel.

And the stars shining down! the Drummer says. Wow! Wow-wow!

The scene, the Arab continues, is one of bone-freezing and tooth-shattering poignance *because*—because the audience knows by this time—although our praecoxian mogul does not—that one of the hobo beggars is the illegitimate bastard half-brother of the mogul who got penniless trying to find in his laboratory back around the beginning of the cinema a cure for the dreadful disease that inflicted the mogul's first wife and that wrecked and devastated her fetching muliebrity, so that the mogul deserted her for some young chippy and thusly ground and pulverized her heart to a talcumish powdery residue.

Go on, go on, Professor Kooba says.

And the stars! Blinking up there! the Drummer says. Yahoo!

The other greedy lumpish clod of a hobo beggar is not really a man at all but is the mogul's first wife, disgustingly inflicted, whose head is as bald as a cueball except for some dwarfy tufts of hair like ancient duffers possess. The first wife had wedded the bastard half-brother because even though she has no feelings of amour for him she is soaked through with an impetus of thanks that the poor stumbly bum crushed his vitalness and lost all his finances as well as thwarted and dynamited his career trying to find the cure for the nauseous and sickly disease that has ravaged her tresses and made her a shambles of a catastrophe. And by now, this last scene, the poor scientist half-brother has also contractuated the disease too.

I must admit, Kooba says, that that is box office!

Millions, millions! The Drummer says. I'm spending the money already.

Can you assist and support me in the outline of scenes leading up to this debacle of a smash ending? the Arab asks.

Can I? the Drummer says. Let's go get some coffee and start work right now.

And I'll go home and work this finale out, Professor Kooba says. It's got to be really subtle, Arab, subtle and beautiful and without any cheap laughs like perhaps one might expect from a bald-headed woman.

No laughs! the Arab says. Not even a titter must be heard from the entire audience. I wish for deadly serious and somber business herein.

I'm thinking of maybe a Charlie Chaplin *City Lights* look on the loony mogul's face? Kooba says. A small suggestion of recognition of his bastard of a brother and long-suffering wife? A touch of hearts and flowers?

It might suffice to work, the Arab says. You, sir, when it comes to scribal duties, are the doctor.

And don't forget the stars, the Drummer says. How they twinkle and blink in their remote aloofness—how far away they are from mortal woes in this tragic vale of sadness.

I'll take care of everything, Kooba says. Stars, the bald head, disease, the crazed millionaire—and a touch of the beloved tramp's magic as well.

Gentlemen, the Arab says, to work!

Arab, the Drummer says, just exactly what is a mogul? I think I know but just exactly.

74 Many-Colored Glass, Snow, Fire, Etc.

An audience is thunderously applauding a poet *soi disant*, who has just finished reading a poem about his sexual impotence and his wife's subsequent frigidity, Richie says. Nothing has helped. Bondage, a mite of sado-masochism, underwear adornment, high-heel fetishism, nothing. The more he has outlined his misery, the more has his audience been enraptured.

Wrong, Curtin says, taking another swallow of his beer. He speaks rather loudly because he must raise his voice to be heard above the barroom jukebox from which comes "Tennessee Waltz."

Wrong? Richie says. This is *my* poet *soi disant*.

Still and all, wrong. The poem, I should think, is about his wife's frigidity and his subsequent sexual problems. This syndrome—pardon the word—is well goddam known in song and story and can be cured by long, intimate conversations, respect for one another, caresses, and carefully administered doses of great art.

All right. But by now our poet has launched out on another poem. This one has the image of two homeless people caught in a snowstorm while the warm lights of a huge townhouse fall upon them and the streets of white on which they stagger forward into what dim poetic future?

What one?

A manner of speaking. I don't know. The window beneath which they reel and stagger and shuffle and hobble, freezing—one is on crutches to strengthen the powerful misery of the image—is of stained glass—

Like Henry's? Like Henry's on Sunday afternoon when the

sun comes in those windows and the whole place is different colors?

That's right. Yeah, right.

Now *that's* getting drunk. That's getting drunk as a work of art.

Take it easy with the art . . . I'm talking about art right now . . . the colors of the stained-glass window, the dazzling whiteness of the snow, the—

You know "Adonais"?

Sure. I read it in school. Keats.

That's right. One of those guys. Platonism! Sheer Platonism. This many-colored glass. This pure white light. Trashy rubbish. Curtin drinks off his beer.

White *snow*, Richie says. Snow, not light.

Anyway. It reminded me of that crap.

It's not the same. You can't make allusions like that, it's what they call sophistry, I think. Somebody said.

Who said? Not Plato! He didn't know his ass from a hole in the ground about it. A more morose and gloomy son of a bitch never lived.

Kant maybe?

Serves him right a broad threw a pisspot on his head.

That was his wife. And Socrates.

The jukebox is now playing "On a Chinese Honeymoon."

Listen, Richie says. Is that art?

It is to many people. But who are they? And where are they?

The poet, anyway, the poet, Richie says. He goes on and on. It turns out, and you might have goddam well known it, that the two people in the snow are *not* a goddam image, but two characters in a long narrative poem about courage and married love. The basic problem with this poet is that he died about twenty years ago. Why then is the audience applauding him? There they go *again*.

A ridiculous question, Curtin says, ordering a Fleischmann's to go with his fresh beer. It is a miracle! They are applauding the fact that a dead man can not only stand there, but that he can speak, and speak what they wish to believe are poems. But why ask me?

The homeless wanderer on crutches, who is discovered to be a man, turns to his companion, a woman, of course, and disregarding the snow that flies into his mouth as he opens it, says: I weep for Adonais.

Oh Christ, she croaks. Take a powder.

In the meantime, the light is still pouring out in all its multicolored and lambent elegance upon the snow and the two figures who, it appears, have not got anywhere at all, despite their constant shuffling and reeling.

They're trapped in the poem, Richie says.

Somehow, all this proves that Berkeley had a point, Curtin says. These goddam stupid things and people are only around when God says so. Right?

What?

Hey Richie! Cheech yells in the door. Your goddam house is on fire! I swear to God!

Take a powder, Cheech! Richie says. Jesus!

I'm not kidding! Cheech says. Take a look.

It won't be there if you don't look, Curtin says.

There is thunderous applause as the poet ends his reading, Richie says. Most of the poems were taken from his new book, soon to be published, *Standing Around and Falling Down.* More thunderous applause as he leaves the stage.

I swear to God, Richie, Cheech says.

Jesus Christ! It *is* my house! Richie says, and begins to run down the block toward the flames. It is snowing quite heavily.

Another whiskey, Curtin says. It will be there because I wish it to be there, or something. He shakes a cigarette out of his pack and it falls into his beer.

Do you recall what George Washington is supposed to have said when he crossed the Delaware? the cripple says to his companion. For some strange reason, he said it in Italian.

They are still bathed in the light and haven't moved an inch, though they reel and shuffle through the snow.

Oh God! the woman says, and looks up to the snowy skies for succor.

Which is not forthcoming in *this* poem, Curtin says, knocking his beer over with his elbow.

75 Burning Desire

I want a girl! I want a girl! Somebody. Anybody. Georgie Huckle howls at the sky. The sky is silent and devoid of either hope or anything else.

A girl! A woman! Young or old. Skinny or fat. Pretty or ugly.

He is so distraught that his father's homburg is wobbling and sliding around on his head.

It's probably that goddam lid that makes the broads run the other way when they see him, Fat Frankie says.

Hat or not—Georgie is not what you would call your Romeo, Red Miller says. But who knows? Miracles happen.

A girl, a girl, Georgie says again. Am I the only son of a bitch in the whole neighborhood and in the whole United States that will never get laid? Please! Somebody.

As is often the case, the Magician says, suddenly appearing in a theatrical puff of blue smoke, I appear in situations like this one. Now, my son, he says to Georgie, what exactly seems to be the trouble?

Magician, I need a girl, Georgie says. I mean real bad.

The man is clearly an oafish dummy who has not got claim one to dignity, the Arab says. What you might jot down as a maladroit.

That's what the ponies will do to you, the Sailor says.

Perhaps I can assist you, the Magician says. Here. And with this, he hands Georgie four old plates, chipped and cracked, with a roughly drawn star in the center of each.

I want a broad, Georgie says. I don't want no lunch.

Ha, ha, the Magician says.

He says it sans mirth and warmthness, the Arab says. Let the record show thusly.

Record? the Sailor says. What record?

Despite your feeble attempt at a joke, the Magician says, I still feel it my duty—God knows why—to give you a helping hand. You shall take these discs. You shall ride to Canarsie with them and sit in one of the thousands of vacant lots out there. You shall face toward the Borough of Queens. You shall put one disc on your head, grasp another in both arms and hug it, and put the other two under your feet—one under each foot. Understand?

Ridiculous badinage and fiddlesticks! the Arab says.

What? Georgie says. And what will that do?

Note well and deep his wide-awake interest, the Arab says. Although any stupid with the brains to button up his fly can apperceive that the Magician is embarked upon the playing of a practical joke, Georgie is buying all this, hook, line, and floater.

What will it do? the Magician says. It will bring you the girl—or *girls*—that you wish for. On each star you shall wish for a different girl. Four stars, four girls. That's your limit.

That's called, Fat Frankie says, wishing on—

Do not emote this old saw, please, I beg you, the Arab says.

—a star, Frankie laughs.

You emoted after all, the Arab says. A chintzy-like pun on words. May I say a tawdry one?

Say tawdry, the Sailor says.

And this will work? Georgie says.

The moronic fish is panting and all aheave with lust, the Arab says. I don't think I wish to witness this.

Not only work, the Magician says—but work to perfection! But heed—oh heed! As you wish for these damsels you must enumerate those things about them that most appeal to your masculinity and virility. Only in this way will the potent magic of the secret discs effect the ends you desire.

A nice little patter the bastard's got, Fat Frankie says.

Observe how our loco amigo, the hopeless Huckle, jumps for

it like a jack-of-the-box, the Arab says. Is this the proper no-menclature?

Jack-*in*-the-box, Fat Frankie says.

My obeisance, the Arab says.

Georgie rushes to Canarsie, the magical discs under his arm.

The Magician begins to laugh. What a sap, he says. What a sucker.

Things must be slow in the magic racket, the Sailor says.

Silence, Sailor! the Magician roars. Or I'll turn you into something disgusting, I can't think exactly what at the moment.

Oh, magic stars! Georgie says. I'll wish upon you for some delightful thrills. I cannot dare wish for such nice broads as Dolores and Berta and Isabel. Or for babes who drive me nuts like Helen Walsh and Connie Glynn and Tania Crosse. I don't even think that magic can bring them here on their—oh my God!—lovely knees.

He is A-number-one correct in his assumptioning there, the Arab says.

But, Georgie says, placing one of the discs on the crown of his father's homburg, and arranging the others under his feet and in his arms, but! I can wish for easy girls. Easy, easy, easy girls. Girls who'll do things even without magic. So, my stars, my magic dishes, I now begin—bring me the following girls, or at least *one* of them.

Dishes, he says, the Magician says, and spits. This lump isn't even *worth* a joke.

Oh come to me, Georgie says, oh come, Cookie LaNord! With your rich and heavy and thick make-up, especially on your wet lips, with your permanent wave and chubby silver-fox jacket, your satin dresses above your knees, your black mesh stockings and ankle-strap high heels. God! The pearl chokers you wear, the cordé handbags you carry, the way you crack your Juicy Fruit gum and its odor from your big mouth. Your toilet water, oh! Your Pall Malls, your capped front tooth and mascara. Your plucked eyebrows and big pointy tits and heavy ass. Your rhinestone-studded harlequin glasses. Your reputation for humping anybody with pants in the park. Oh, come!

And you, Joycie Lunde! Come on, Joycie! I go crazy thinking about your plaid skirts and cardigans buttoned down the back. The clean white collars of your blouses outside your sweaters. Shined loafers! Thick white socks! Oh, Jesus! Those bright red lips and straight blond hair, that friendship ring around your neck on a silver chain. And the small gold cross also. The swirl of your pink slips at the hem of your skirts, the white slips, your transparent blue eyes and your dumb giggle. What else? The way you hold an armload of schoolbooks against your little bulging belly, and the dirty raincoat filled with India-ink names of all the guys who've got you down the cellar. Even your orange nail polish and the fat Bible you carry on Sunday morning with the purple and red tongues hanging out of it. *Tongues.* Oh my God! And your tight tweed suit and tan high heels and long and slender legs and sheer stockings that are held up by—oh Jesus! I can always see the bumps your garters make underneath. And the rumor that you give terrific, slow hand jobs in your hallway. Appear! Appear, Joycie Lunde!

Show yourself, Bony Ruth! Show me your flat chest and skinny ass, your acne scars and thin lips, give me a sexy smile with your cigarette-stained teeth, touch me with your yellowish-brown fingers with the nails bit down to the raw flesh so you bleed. I want to see you in your soiled skirt with the broken zipper and your slip showing with the torn lace hem! The filthy saddle shoes! Your fake sapphire birthstone ring! I am also thinking of your stringy oily hair under that dirty sailor cap you wear and your Army field jacket that says OH FRANKIE on the back. Let me watch you light up a clippie. Oh, Bony Ruth, they say you blow anybody anywhere until they fall down begging for mercy and a rest. Show yourself!

And last and maybe even least—come to this vacant lot, Lizzie Mulvaney! I'm going apeshit thinking of your red face and piano legs that can probably break a guy's back wrapped around him, those thick ankles, slobbery mouth, and big ears! I even like your Bishop MacDonald uniform because it's too small for your ass and hips. Those cute wiry curls in your frizzy red hair and your dopey-looking eyes behind your crummy smudgy glasses make me sweat. Big body and big bones. Big feet! Those rundown heels on your old Mary Janes, those shabby scapulars and also your greyish and frayed brassiere straps that show when you wear wide-necked blouses! Your freckles! Your fat neck with the dirt in the creases with the Infant Jesus of Prague hanging around a chain. It's all mine! Come on, come on, Lizzie. The guys say you can dry hump for hours without stopping. Let me see you smile with your greenish teeth right *here.*

The son of a bitch actually went through the whole routine, the Magician says. I almost feel bad about it now.

And so you should indeed, the Arab says. If you'll forgive, so to speak out, my editorial glossolalia.

I said almost, the Magician says. Anybody who would wear a hat like that deserves what happens to him. And he has no self-respect anyway. Begging for girls!

You think if I took a shot at it, Fat Frankie says, I could get Constance Glynn out to Canarsie for a little action?

Be careful Ticineti doesn't hear you, the Magician says. He has gone quite soft on Mrs. Glynn of late.

Nobody's here yet, Georgie says, and it's getting cold as hell. Maybe it's this goddam hat? Don't bring me no luck anyway. Maybe I should have got my suit pressed.

Innocent baby in the woods, the Arab says. One almost wishes that the magic worked so that—Oho! Ruth! Ruth! Say, Bony Ruth!

Yeah? Ruth says as she starts across the street. What?

Are you contemplating a trip to Canarsie today in any events sometime?

Canarsie? Go fuck yourself with Canarsie, you Arab fuck! Canarsie!

Maybe I should have got a shine, Georgie Huckle says.

76 White Port: A Drama of the Streets

Scene: The cellar of a small apartment house in which BURLY lives in his capacity as Superintendent.
Time: Midafternoon of a cold winter day.

BURLY (banging at the wall with a hammer): I could swear it was in here! (He continues battering the cement wall with great vigor.)

Enter SANTO TUCCIO *and* LITTLE MICKEY'S MOTHER

SANTO TUCCIO: What? What the hell?

LITTLE MICKEY'S MOTHER: Looks like Burly.

BURLY: Damn it! God *damn* it!

SANTO TUCCIO (approaching BURLY): Why you bashing the wall in with that hammer? Your sister will be mad as a bitch.

LITTLE MICKEY'S MOTHER: Santo, let's go have a drink. I could really go for a Carstairs and ginger about now.

BURLY (aside): She could go for anything, with or without ginger, any time. Fucking disgrace.

SANTO TUCCIO: Shh. Shut up. I think Burly said something we weren't supposed to hear. You say something, Burly?

BURLY: You weren't supposed to hear it, like you said. I said it to myself. (With enormous ferocity, he recommences battering at the wall—this time concentrating on a different spot.)

LITTLE MICKEY'S MOTHER: Or even a beer.

BURLY (aside): Or *even* a beer. Drunk disgraceful goddamned slut.

SANTO TUCCIO (sarcastically): Why don't you get up on that bench there, Burly? Then you can bash away at the part of the wall up by the ceiling.

BURLY (getting up on the bench): Say . . . thanks, Santo! What a good idea. You know, you're all right.

SANTO TUCCIO: Sure, get right up there. That's it, kid.

LITTLE MICKEY'S MOTHER: I'm getting a headache from all the noise and dust. Santo, what are we doing here? Why are we here?

SANTO TUCCIO: Where else should we be? Do you have a better place to be on a freezing day?

BURLY: Aha! I think I found the spot. (With a supreme effort, he smashes at a spot high on the wall, chips of plaster, paint, and cement flying. One hits LITTLE MICKEY'S MOTHER on the forehead.)

LITTLE MICKEY'S MOTHER: Ouch! One of those goddam pieces of brick hit me!

SANTO TUCCIO: That's cement, cement.

LITTLE MICKEY'S MOTHER: A better place to be? How about the Lion's Den—or Pat's?

SANTO TUCCIO: I got enough money to start you off in the afternoon? Jesus!

BURLY (reaching into a hollow in the wall exposed by his hammering): There's the son of a bitch, you'll excuse my French, there she is! (He removes a gallon jug of white port.)

LITTLE MICKEY'S MOTHER (brightening): There's nothing I like better than a nice glass of wine. Candlelight. Flowers. Santo, did you see the last *Liberty?*

SANTO TUCCIO: I got my movie work to keep up with. I can't even find the time to read *Modern Screen* and *Photoplay* and you tell me about *Liberty!*

LITTLE MICKEY'S MOTHER: Oh, Sant—you work so hard, I know. I think you work *too* hard. What do you think, Burly?

BURLY (getting down from the bench, jug in hand): I don't get paid to think. As a matter of goddam fact, my scumbag sister, excuse my French, hardly ever pays me anymore anyway. You think I sleep in a goddam coalbin because I like it?

SANTO TUCCIO: I been thinking of bringing you an old Boy

Scout sleeping bag, kid. You could spread it like on top of the coal and at least stay a little clean. Hmm. What kind of white port is that?

BURLY (peering at the label): The label just says "Wine." That's all. Say, what do you want down here? Who told you I was trying to find some wine I stashed so my bitch sister couldn't find it, excuse my French.

LITTLE MICKEY'S MOTHER: Burly! How could you think we came down here to—Well, I don't even like to think it, let alone say it out loud.

SANTO TUCCIO (sadly): It's a hell of a note when an old friend thinks we come down here because we heard you had some wine. (He shakes his head.)

BURLY: It looks pretty damn funny to me. Why else would you come down here to this filthy cellar? I don't see you go visiting Black Tom, do I? You don't go over to have a nice chat around the furnace with Miss America. Do you? How come you want to come down and talk things over with your old pal Burly? Good old Burly—with the *wine.*

SANTO TUCCIO: How do you know it ain't your sparkling wittiness?

LITTLE MICKEY'S MOTHER: I thought maybe we could discuss Viña Delmar.

BURLY: What? Who Mar?

LITTLE MICKEY'S MOTHER: Doc Friday, I think it was, said he thought you were a great fan. Especially *Bad Girl.*

BURLY: What? Doc Friday don't know shit about me.

SANTO TUCCIO: Let's go sit down on the coal pile.

BURLY: Why not sit on the bench? You can watch me drink this wine nice from there.

LITTLE MICKEY'S MOTHER (ignoring the final remark): You were just standing on the bench with your dirty shoes. Have some sense.

BURLY: Excuse me. I didn't notice you had a new coat on.

LITTLE MICKEY'S MOTHER: This old thing? (She laughs girl-ishly.)

SANTO TUCCIO: Old thing? Old my ass! I got the fucking coat for you in November right after Thanksgiving in Namm's.

LITTLE MICKEY'S MOTHER: "Old thing" is just an expression they use, Sant. You can read it in books all the time, such as Viña Delmar.

BURLY: What? Who is this?

SANTO TUCCIO (leading the others to the coal bin): Now we can at least be comfortable.

They all sit

LITTLE MICKEY'S MOTHER: I never *knew* that coal could be so comfortable!

BURLY: There's coal and there's coal. This coal is anthracite. The soft coal is lumpy and also filthy. Say—you were worrying about getting your new coat dirty from the bench and here you are sitting on the coal pile.

LITTLE MICKEY'S MOTHER: It *is* silly, isn't it?

SANTO TUCCIO: A cellar always for some reason gets you thirsty.

BURLY (winking at him): A little wine could clear the dust out of your throat, right, Santo?

SANTO TUCCIO: I didn't mean . . .

BURLY: Oh, what the hell. (He opens the jug.) Let's share the goddam poison. (He passes the jug to LITTLE MICKEY'S MOTHER.)

LITTLE MICKEY'S MOTHER (drinking): It has a really subtle flavor and bouquet. It would be just *perfect* for dessert with glazed pears or apple pie.

SANTO TUCCIO: Dessert? (He drinks.)

BURLY: Does this Vera Demar drink this stuff? (He drinks.) For dessert?

LITTLE MICKEY'S MOTHER: I wouldn't be surprised. She's really so famous though that I'm sure she adores French wine.

SANTO TUCCIO: This a French wine, Burly?

LITTLE MICKEY'S MOTHER: Oh, Santo, don't be silly.

BURLY: French wine? I didn't know they made wine in France! The doughboys must have give them the idea. (He takes another long swallow of the wine and lies back on the coal.) How's Mickey, by the way?

LITTLE MICKEY'S MOTHER: Oh, he's very good. We hear from him all the time.

SANTO TUCCIO: *You* hear from him. He wants to join the Navy. Can you imagine that squirt in the Navy? I remember when he didn't even know who it was went crazy in *Lost Patrol.*

BURLY: Victor McLaglen?

SANTO TUCCIO: No! Jesus Christ! Boris Karloff!

BURLY: Oh yeah.

LITTLE MICKEY'S MOTHER: I don't know whether I should sign the papers or not.

SANTO TUCCIO: Sign them! I thought it was all settled. Maybe the Navy will put some meat on his bones and teach him a little respect.

BURLY: That's right. Or the Army too.

LITTLE MICKEY'S MOTHER: Oh, not the Army! You get so dirty in the Army. The Navy is nice and clean, a nice clean life.

SANTO TUCCIO: That's right. I saw a movie short once showed sailors on a battleship. You should see the food! This time they showed them making french fries and big steaks, yeah! For the just regular sailors, steaks! Say, Burly. What made you put this jug in the wall and cement it over?

BURLY: I thought it was to hide it from my cunt sister, excuse my French, but now I don't know. I mean, I don't even think I *did* put it there. I just figured it was there. And, son of a bitch, it was.

SANTO TUCCIO: What?

LITTLE MICKEY'S MOTHER: Anyway, you're supposed to keep wine down in the cellar. That's how they keep it in France. They have cellars all over the place.

BURLY: Those goddam frogs! You got to hand it to them.

SANTO TUCCIO: Honey, really, don't forget to sign the papers, O.K.? Tonight, honey.

LITTLE MICKEY'S MOTHER (musing): Mickey always writes such nice letters.

SANTO TUCCIO: He'll write even nicer in the Navy.

BURLY (passing the jug again): What a good idea that was to stand up on the bench. I got to give you credit, Santo.

SANTO TUCCIO: You learn a lot of things when you study the movies like I do.

LITTLE MICKEY'S MOTHER: *Also* from reading, don't forget.

They continue to drink and talk. BURLY *lets the fire in the furnace go out. As the cellar becomes darker and colder, the outraged shouts and curses of the building's tenants may be heard*
Enter LITTLE MICKEY, *dressed as a sailor*

LITTLE MICKEY (gesturing toward the three figures supine on the coal pile): I'll carry all this shit around with me right to the grave. (Shaking his head:) What a bust. What a goddam bust.

Blackout

77 The Enigma

Ah! the Drummer says. Now this is what I call an extraordinary talent. More than a simple "act"—hateful word!—more than a gimmick, this is sheer art. He holds the newspaper out to show a photograph captioned "Italian Juggler Here."

Jesus Christ, another bullshit variety routine, Irish Billy says.

A juggler? Cheech says. I thought this was some big deal.

Ignorant clucks! the Drummer says. This is Gaetano Stella, probably the world's greatest juggler. What? You think he's one of those imbeciles throws a couple oranges and eggs up in the air, a few plates that he balances on his toe? God. Speak to them, Arab.

But the Arab is as ignorant of the fine, the subtle points of juggling as everyone else.

No, no, the Arab says. You explain, boonsome compadre.

All right, the Drummer says. In this picture, look, Stella is doing a difficult, a very fast and intricate dance, as he flips between his hands—*in* the pattern of a figure-eight, mind you—two burning and red-hot globes of fire. These are not your crummy oranges and pimpy little eggs—these are real globes of intensely hot and fiery fire! He don't stand there like a zombie either. He does a joyous and wild tarantella or something. He don't just fling these globes from hand to hand—he begins a definite, wondrous, and terrifically exciting pattern of a figure-eight and keeps to it as he builds up to mind-boggling speeds. And this is just *one* of his many routines. This is nothing but a teaser, a warmer-upper.

Let's see that, Irish Billy says. He looks at the picture and smiles. You know, I saw Burly do a dance like this a few years ago—same goddam dance.

Burly? the Drummer says. *Burly?* That drunken slob can hardly walk, let alone dance. Baloney!

I *saw* him, you phony. In Ebbets Field a couple of years back at a Sunday doubleheader.

You went with Burly to the ballgame? Cheech says. Wow.

He had some free ducats from his sister wanted to get him the hell out of the house. So we went.

I despise and abhorrate the baseball, the Arab says. And akinly, all sporting ventures. Save the racing ovals and their equine contests which oft are of a spectaculous beauty.

It's the bottom of the ninth of the first game, Billy says. The Cubs are ahead, 3-2, and we got two men on with two out and Reiser is up. Burly's just coming back from getting some hot dogs and beer and just as he gets to the seat Reiser doubles and wins the game. Old Burly goes into a dance just like this wop in the picture—hop-hop, hop-hop.

Wop! the Drummer says. You ignorant person! Gaetano Stella—a wop!

Yeah! Cheech says. What, wop?

Then, he don't know *what* he's doing, Billy goes on. He throws up his mitts yelling at the top of his lungs, "Pistol Pete! Pistol Pete!" and all the crap he's carrying goes flying in the air, the hot dogs with the beer and the goddam mustard all over, everything—down comes this shower of stuff!

A cloudburst of comestibles, the Arab says. A pouring-down of potables. A mass of mustard.

So? What's this got to do with Gaetano Stella? the Drummer says. Burly dancing like Gaetano Stella! Ha.

Everything comes down on this beautiful woman, Billy says. All over her clothes.

Oh, Jesus, Cheech laughs. Then?

And then, she gets up, by Christ, she gets up and she's smiling at fucking Burly. She's not only smiling, she's *laughing,* with the damn mustard all over her, the beer, all over her dress. Jesus! She's a *knockout.*

Go on, the Arab says. My interest waxes up and quickens along apace.

Gaetano Stella—the Drummer begins.

She takes the son of a bitch by the arm and walks out of the ballpark with him. She's chatting with him, she's laughing, she's for Christ sake rumpling his hair.

Mussing, the Arab says. She's mussing his hair.

And what happens? Cheech says. Does he come back? Do they come back?

Nope, Irish Billy says. That's it. But Burly won't ever tell me what happened.

Actually, Professor Kooba says, from the rear of the store where he's been standing for the past fifteen minutes in a phone booth for reasons best known to him, Actually, he hit this woman's *husband* with the foodstuffs.

Ah, Kooba, what do you know? Billy says. Were *you* there?

I? Professor Kooba says. I? I follow the New York Giants. Should I enrich the groaning coffers of the Brooklyn Baseball Club? Ha ha and ha. But I know that the bumbling sot of the neighborhood could only have hit her husband.

How come? Cheech says.

How come? Kooba replies. By logical deduction. By irresistible reasoning. Gentlemen, all the clues are present in the case. The Professor leaves the phone booth and walks to the front of the store.

You're crazy, Kooba, Irish Billy says. Burly didn't hit any husband of anybody.

Ah, you simple soul. You trusting naïf.

Damn it, he didn't hit any husband and he didn't hit any wife of anybody either. He didn't hit anybody. I made up the whole goddam story just to get on the Drummer's ass about this guinea here.

How cheap, the Drummer says. How mean-spirited.

No beauteous woman? the Arab says. And I have stood here agog with ears flung wide all this time? I could have been quaffing down a draft Ballantine or a brace of same in Gallagher's while peaceably checking divers results?

Ah, Billy, Professor Kooba says. Ingenuous youth. Innocent babe. You are indeed the baby in the taking-candy-from-a-baby metaphor.

Simile is the appellation of that syndrome, the Arab says.

I'm telling you, Kooba, Irish Billy says. It's just a story. No dance. No throwing up anything in the air. No beautiful woman. No husband. Nobody. *No body.* It was just to get the Drummer's goat. Jesus Christ.

If that's what you wish to think, fine, Professor Kooba says. It is all crystal clear to me, however.

Limpid? the Arab says.

Limpid, agrees the Professor. Exactly. A soothing word.

Reiser could hit but, Cheech says. Hah?

78 Red White and Blue

Let's imagine, Doc Friday says, or recall if you like, I don't give a shit, Isabel and Berta, as they used to be long ago, as lovely young girls, lost in tender smiles amid flowers and gently perfumed air, happy as only young girls, pure and chaste, can be happy, let's imagine or recall them unaffected by what is known as the ravages of time and so on and so forth, unmarried and young forever like the voice of your first love recollected in tranquillity far out on a darkling plain minus the usual mosquitoes dust and heat, let us try, try, and try again, try, mind you, to imagine once again their sweet and swell faces, their shining white teeth, their delicate noses and pellucid eyes ablaze with the excitement that only youth and innocence, luscious and lovely youth and innocence—Christ only knows where it's gone for all of us! as the poet says, melted like the snows of yesterday—that only it can bring, let us think back on their days of young womanhood, their first party dresses, their first high heels, their first nylon stockings, their first—

Doc, Fat Frankie says, Doc, I think you're a little drunk. You're going on and on here and I don't think you ever even really knew those girls. And I don't even know if any of us really knew them, it was so long ago.

And also, Doctor, the Arab says, your language smacks harshly of the fustianish, the purplish, the rhetoricish. I do not follow what you are attempting to enounce.

Fustianish, eh? Doc Friday says. The pot speaks. The man in the glass house opens his mouth and throws a rock or two.

What's the matter, Doc? Irish Billy says. *Something's* eating him.

Eating him? the Arab says. The remark tremors on the lips of

286

the obscene, as well as the grossly crass. It is almost what some
commenter on the human comedy called a *blague,* I think.

Oh God, Big Mickey says.

Obscene or gross, Doc Friday says, perhaps something *is* eating me, as Billy says. Something lost, something to hell and
gone. It has settled, I don't know how or why, on the images of
those two young girls, Isabel and Berta. Who I really did *not*
know, as Frankie says. But. But. And nevertheless. There it is.

Master Sergeant Jim Gentry passes by, Richie says, in a loud
aside. Perhaps, he says, he is on another boringly mysterious
mission. The good sarge is a lover of truth. How come nobody
likes him? And there goes the Magician!

Oh dear, the Arab says. In his red shirt. His brain emperco-
lates.

Nevertheless! Doc Friday says. Recall them. It's good for you.
I ask for nothing less than a miracle, certainly a small thing for
the Creator to perform. And it would do all our busted and broken hearts a world of good. I see a garden. A garden of red and
white flowers, red roses and white lilies, the lovely lovely flowers of summer. God's very own hand, a huge hand of love and
compassion and strength, caresses a great star that hangs in the
heavens above the garden.

Perhaps "skies" instead of "heavens"? the Arab says. It has
less of the banalsome a-cling to it.

A star in the heavens, Doc Friday says. A narrow path leads
through the garden to a verdant green hedge which has an
archway cut out of it, shaped. What do they call that when they
cut hedges and trees into odd shapes?

Aviary? Fat Frankie says.

Tropism, the Arab says. Tropiary.

Whatever they call it, Doc Friday says, there's an archway
leading out into the great world and far away lie mountains in a
blue haze.

Blue haze? the Drummer says. Blue haze and mountains? By
the way, Arab, I have one for you. What do they call a mountain

lake? Hah? He does a little jig, holding the brim of his fedora with both hands.

Sh! For a moment, Drummer. Go on, Doc.

I didn't notice the Magician was carrying a glass in his hand, Richie says in another loud aside.

It behooves that he is up to some shanigans, the Arab says. A score of pardons, Doctor. Please go on.

That's about all, the Doc says. All I want to get across is that God could do this if he wanted. Oh yes, I should say that outside the garden—this is the most important part and I almost forgot the goddam thing—just to the left or the right of the archway, Isabel and Berta could be put right there by Him, just as they were, as they were so beautifully so long long ago. Sitting on a blue blanket decorated with the same flowers as the garden, embroidered flowers, red roses and white lilies, eating cream cheese and strawberry jam, drinking Burgundy and Chablis. Unsullied by time.

I get it, Fat Frankie says. Not bad. But still something a little off, I mean lacking.

There is nothing alack in the imagery-like picture of red and white, the Arab says. As a matter of cold fact, Doctor, if I may inject a note of the most amical and constructive critique, your image-like picture is too pat-like. By which I imply that it borders heavily on the labored. The red, the white, the red, the white, and so on and so on. Painstakely constructed, I hazard.

Perhaps, Doc Friday says. But I was thinking more of the colors as being but parts of an overall comment on the *American* aspects of the loss of innocence and youth. What about that?

What? the Arab says. American aspects? I have missed this by a huge mile.

The red and the white. The flowers. And—*and* the unobtrusive mountains in the distance, Doc Friday says. You see?

The Magician is starting to gesture with his fucking glass, Richie says. I think he heard you guys.

Mountains? the Arab says.

Mountains? Fat Frankie says.

Mountains? Irish Billy says. You're right, Richie. There he goes with the glass. You think the son of a bitch could get himself a real wand.

A tarn! the Drummer says. A tarn, a tarn! Hurray! he shouts, and throws his hat in the air.

Yes, mountains! Doc Friday says. The red roses, the white lilies, and the *mountains.* You remember? Lost in a . . .

Exquisite! the Arab says. In a blue haze! Impeccably trig! Huzzah!

And in the haze, a tarn! the Drummer says.

What's he doing over there with the goddam glass? Richie says.

Making *something,* Irish Billy says.

Yes, yes, the whole thing turns out to be so subtlelishly and unerredly *American,* the Arab says. No small success, Doctor, I assure.

Thank you, thank you, Doc Friday says. Hooray! And you don't mind if I pat myself on the back for the *blue* blanket?

New York 1975–1976

DALKEY ARCHIVE PAPERBACKS

Visit our website: www.dalkeyarchive.com

DALKEY ARCHIVE PAPERBACKS